New York
5/11

PRIZE OF WAR

PRIZE OF WAR

Michael Cohn

Illustrated by
Erik Ronnberg

Library of Congress Control Number:		2010918838
ISBN:	Hardcover	978-1-4568-3487-6
	Softcover	978-1-4568-3486-9
	Ebook	978-1-4568-3488-3

This book was printed in the United States of America.

To order additional copies of this book, contact:
Xlibris Corporation
1-888-795-4274
www.Xlibris.com
Orders@Xlibris.com
88085

CONTENTS

Dedicated to

RUDYARD KIPLING

A writer about young people for young people

and those who are young at heart

with deep respect

Introduction And Acknowledgements

Revolutions uproot people. Political debates turn into to-the-death combat where families and bystanders get hurt. The uprooted survivors, both winners and losers, may, if they are lucky, find new homes where they can plant themselves. They always will bear the scars of their struggle and the patterns of the behavior of their upbringing. This is a tale of one such survivor.

I make no apology for what I have written of how refugees and occupying troops behaved. I have been a member of both refugees and occupying troops. This is how they behave, always have and always will.

Many thanks are due to the sailors of the reconstructed Revolutionary War sloop *Providence*, the crew of the USCG barque *Eagle* and the crews of the many other ships I have travelled on for the little I have absorbed of their skills. As so often, Erik Ronnberg tried to save me from the errors in ship construction and handling.

England will always be England. The county of Kent retains many portions of its beautiful landscape, its Georgian houses and country inns. Greater London too retains traces of its past. For those who wish to visit some of the sites of those days the *HMS Victory* is still afloat in Portsmouth harbor and the Tower of London stands on the banks of the Thames. The last executions at the Tower were carried out during the First World War though by shooting rather than the axe.

Besides reading the many memoirs, orderly books and studies of the period of the American Revolution I have made use of the results of the archeological digs on sites of the period in New York City where I have dug, the writings of the Bronte sisters, C.S. Forester and Rudyard Kipling. The Osprey series on military history have been most useful. The mistakes are my own.

Michael Cohn
New York City 2011

Expulsion From Carolina

Elizabeth Troyes was going to travel from her home in Carolina to Boston. That was a long trip and one not without risk in wartime. The British were fighting against the rebellious American colonies and the British had bases at Savannah, Charleston, Norfolk and New York. Fast moving mounted raiders from both sides in this war had cut the land routes between north and south. So Elizabeth would have to travel by sea. That wasn't really safe either but it was better than trying it by land.

There was no future for Elizabeth in Carolina. The family farm had been sold. Her uncle had put her up temporarily, but his wife and her two girls were living there. That had left little room for Elizabeth. So she was being sent to live with her uncle's cousins in Boston.

At least Boston is a big city, Elizabeth thought. I have never been in a big city. As a matter of fact she had never been further than twenty five miles from her home in her twelve and a half years. Now she was going down the muddy road with its dead end in her uncle's wagon. There was a ship waiting for her at the river's edge. She stared straight ahead over the horses ears, trying to grasp what was happening to her. She tried to think things out but her mind kept going blank. Too much had happened to her and she hadn't been able to do anything about it.

Her uncle's voice intruded into her thoughts. "I've done my best for you," he was saying. "You will probably improve yourself in Boston."

"But I don't want to be a nursemaid."

"We've talked about that times before. You're just as willful as your mother was. I told her time and again to get married again after your father was killed fighting against the King but she wouldn't. She was bound and determined to run the farm herself and bring you up proper.

She did it too, I'll admit, until she took the lung fever and died. That was a month ago or so. You take after her. You'll manage just like she did."

Elizabeth just nodded. Her mother's death was still too recent to talk about or even think about. Besides her uncle had made up his mind about what to do with her and there was no sense talking against it.

"You and my Anne didn't get along none either," her uncle continued. "She told me I couldn't keep you and her and the two girls. Not nohow. She wanted you bound out as a farm girl."

That wasn't all her step-aunt had wanted either. The mahogany sideboard from her mother's house already graced her uncle's parlor. So did the small tables and the side chairs. The fine china that her father had brought from England also was set out in her step-aunt's cabin. Elizabeth had overheard one of the arguments between her uncle and his wife. "We could use Liz's money to dress our two girls decent," her aunt had argued.

"Now Anne, it's against right and reason for Elizabeth to pay for the girl's clothing. They are no kin of hers."

"Neither are you kin if it comes to that. Elizabeth's mother was your first wife's sister and they are both dead now. But if that makes you kin you are entitled to their things, all of them I say. And the sooner that uppity girl goes to work for a decent farmer the better. She is just an orphan on the town with no real folks. She has no reason to give herself airs and cast my girls in the shade."

Elizabeth's folks had been gentry. Her uncle and his wife weren't and that rankled. Elizabeth hadn't wanted to be uppity but she was different. Both she and the two girls knew it. They talked differently. They acted differently. The two girls had resented her moving in from the first. They had been jealous that she could read, write and figure. They were jealous of her fine dresses and her other things as well. The Presbyterian minister was in charge of orphans for the town and he had declared her uncle to be her guardian and that was that. What he said went. Her uncle was a member of his congregation and her folks hadn't been. They were Anglicans.

"Now Anne you know what the Good Book says about taking care of orphans."

"The Good Book also has something to say about putting strangers above your own flesh and blood."

Her uncle had won that particular argument by pointing out that the two girls were not his flesh and blood but had been adopted after he married Anne, but a few days later he had written his cousins in Boston.

They had answered that they could use a girl around the house and to help bring up their three young children. So here was Elizabeth setting out for Boston. Her uncle thought that was the best solution for his and her problems.

"I've done my best for you," her uncle repeated. "I've put what's left of the hard money, the silver spoons and the other things in your chest. I think it's a fair share and perhaps a bit over. You be careful of it, you hear. There is plenty of sinful people in this world willing to rob a twelve year old girl. You know about that from helping to run the farm with your mother. Maybe you'll be better away from here with 'Bloody Tarleton' and his Tories rampaging about.

Elizabeth knew what money her uncle had received from the sale of the farm. He had paid the funeral expenses for her mother, the taxes and Elizabeth's keep out of it but maybe her ideas of a fair share differed from those of her uncle. The minister had appointed him her guardian and she had no right to complain and nobody to complain to. She knew about the dangers of the war too. The British had shattered the American army at Camden and now the Tory cavalry was free to ride all over. The Tories had fortified posts all over Georgia and Carolina and they were none too careful how people they considered rebels were treated. Patriot guerilla bands behaved no better and neutrals were simply targets for both groups.

Elizabeth cast her mind over the years since the colonists had risen against King George the Third, the Hanoverian King of England in 1774. Her father had been strong on the side of the Revolution. He had tried to get his neighbors to share his views with little success. He was Church of England and they were Scotch Presbyterians and that mattered. At first most of them had followed Flora MacDonald. She was as loyal to this king as she had been to the Stuart kings when she smuggled Bonnie Prince Charlie out of Scotland after the failed Rising of 1745. After that she had convinced many of her fellow Scots to settle in the Carolinas. She was loyal to the crown rather than the Continental Congress. She didn't believe in rebellion against any king even though she considered this one an upsurper. As far as she was concerned a king was the anointed of God and what he did was rightful.

Elizabeth's father had raised his voice against the rule or rather misrule of the king. The two sides had fought it out at the Battle of Moore's Bridge and the loyalist Highlanders had lost. Her father had been killed at that battle. The Loyalists, or Tories as they were now called, hadn't given up. They had formed militia regiments and guerilla bands to aid the British army.

Elizabeth was an ardent Patriot like her father. She believed that the Americans were fighting for their rights, rights the English already had in England. All the people around her called themselves Patriots. Anybody who held any other opinion had fled. Yet Elizabeth still retained her respect for Flora MacDonald. She admired her as much as she did her father. Elizabeth respected strength. She didn't talk about her respect for Flora MacDonald. She didn't want to be accused of being a "tory-lover". People were quick with accusations in wartime and accusations were often followed by barn burning, cattle maiming or worse.

Elizabeth's mother had been strong as well as good looking and had owned a good farm. She had refused all offers of marriage after the death of her husband and decided to run the farm herself. Elizabeth had helped as much as she could. She had learned to read, write and figure so she could keep the accounts. She had managed to do that in the last three years. Now she was going to be a nursemaid. It's not fair, she thought rebelliously, it's just not fair. She didn't want to cry in front of her uncle or anyone else for that matter. She was going to be strong just like her parents or Flora MacDonald. She wasn't a little girl. She was twelve years old, almost thirteen. She was almost a woman. The tears kept coming anyway. She wiped them away with her sleeve. Her uncle didn't seem to notice. She was going to miss her uncle despite everything. He wasn't strong willed but he had tried to be kind to her, as kind as he was to his two step-daughters. Perhaps he had really tried to do his best for her. And Boston was a big city where things happened. Elizabeth didn't mind going to a big city half as much as she minded being a nursemaid and a servant. But it was better to be a nursemaid in the north than to be bound out to a farmer here in Carolina. That was almost like being a slave. Elizabeth had learned the hard way to look at the bright side of things. That attitude had saved her when her father was killed and again when her mother took sick and died. Thinking about the past wouldn't change things. She was going to think about the things that were going on now, the ship she was going to be travelling on and the future.

Elizabeth looked at the landing down the hill. The single mast of the sloop showed slim and tall above the sheds. Elizabeth could see another wagon and a couple of people clustered around. She was glad that there weren't a lot of neighbors to see her being sent away. She felt like she was a girl who had done something wrong, stole or become pregnant. There weren't going to be any long good byes either, not if she could help it. She was going to act like a lady, like her mother would have or Flora MacDonald. She was going to try anyway, she decided. Good byes were hard. This was going to be a good bye to all the people she knew and all the places she had ever been in her twelve and a half years. *I haven't done anything wrong and I am only taking those things with me that are truly mine.* She held on to her resolution with all the strength she had. Throwing a tantrum or weeping wouldn't help her now or ever again.

Rolls of tobacco were being taken aboard the ship as well as bundles and boxes of other things. A broad shouldered and grizzled haired man came over and introduced himself as Captain Abner. Her uncle introduced her in turn as Miss Elizabeth Troyes. That sounded nice and adult. It helped Elizabeth steady herself. She noted that Captain Abner had brown eyes and a nice smile. Elizabeth thought that she was going to like him. The captain and her uncle lifted her chest out of the wagon and carried it down to the ship.

"Be a good girl, Liz." Her uncle gave her a tight hug.

"Good bye, uncle." Elizabeth didn't know what else to say. There was so much she wished had been straightened out between them but all she could do now was to hug him back. It was too late for anything else. They stood there without being able to say anything to each other. Elizabeth noted that her tears had started up again and saw that her uncle's eyes were wet too. Then suddenly he turned back to his wagon, climbed aboard and slapped the backs of the horses with his reins. The wagon vanished uphill quickly. She would never see her uncle again. Elizabeth was glad when Captain Abner came up to her. He had treated her just like an adult.

"That chest is pretty big," he told her. "It'll kind of clutter up your cabin. Why don't you just take out an extra dress, your cloak and the toilet things and we will strike the rest below. Put it in the bottom of the ship." he added when he saw that she didn't understand his nautical term.

Elizabeth did take out an extra dress. Not her best one but one that would do for shipboard. Then she took out her cloak, the toilet case, her sewing kit and carefully relocked the chest. She followed the captain into the back of the ship where there was a raised part with two staircases leading up and a door behind them. Through the door they went down a short hallway with a door opening into a largish room facing the rear of the ship. There were windows facing out. When the captain opened one of the doors off the hallway Elizabeth saw her cabin. It was awfully small. There was just room for a narrow cot, a shelf for a canvas wash basin and some pegs on the opposite wall to hang her clothing. The captain noted her dismay and smiled.

"My *Phoebe* is no East Indiaman with fancy cabins for passengers but she will do. You won't be spending much time in your cabin except for sleeping. You'll either be up on deck or in the wardroom." He indicated the room in the back with the windows. Her cabin didn't have any windows. "Ever been on a ship before?"

"Not one big enough to have staircases."

"Ladders, dear, ladders. There ain't no staircases aboard ship."

Elizabeth looked and was confused. They didn't look like any ladders at home. Obviously sailors used words that meant something entirely different than they meant on land. She would have to learn this language. The captain saw her confusion. "Don't worry. By the time this trip is over you will be spouting salty language with the best of them." Then he went back outside to supervise the loading of the cargo.

By the time Elizabeth had washed her face and hung up her clothing she heard the captain shouting orders. She went up on deck and saw the sailors untie the ropes that held the sloop to the dock. She now took time to examine the ship on which she would spend the next two weeks or so, the time it would take to get to Boston. She didn't look back to the shore of Carolina that they were leaving. That was the past and the past was gone.

The *Phoebe* was about sixty feet long with a single mast sticking straight up and another on her front set slant wise. It was only later she learned to call it the mainmast and bowsprit. The mainsail was large and took two men to raise it and the wooden boom to which it was attached. Smaller triangular sails connected the mainmast to the bowsprit, jibs she learned to call them. On each side of the deck stood two cannons. They didn't look very big to Elizabeth. Two even smaller guns were fastened to the rails near the big steering tiller. She asked the captain about the guns.

"I sail to the islands sometimes and them cannons do keep pirates in rowboats off but we are no warship. If we do meet a real warship we make like rabbits, we hide or run."

Elizabeth found that she liked being at sea. One of the sailors made her a hammock chair with pillows stuffed with oakum to sit on. She loved to sit on it and watch the waves and the ocean change color. Captain Abner also came over often to talk to her. She soon realized that he loved to talk and she was his favorite audience on this trip. But most of the time there was only the sound of the waves and the creaks of the wooden hull. She didn't have time to think of the past or worry about the future. She wasn't afraid of the ocean. Besides the captain never took the *Phoebe* out of sight of land. "Go out into the open sea and a Britisher will snap you up for sure," he told her.

The mate, Mr. Somers, was not as friendly and the cook wouldn't let her help in the galley. Elizabeth had offered to help. "You're a lady and a passenger. You got no business in my galley." Elizabeth was sorry. She not only wanted to be helpful but also thought the meals could be better prepared. In Carolina both she and her mother had helped in the kitchen, particularly in busy times like the harvest season. It was expected that all women helped in the kitchen with the cooking.

In the week that the *Phoebe* sailed northwards Elizabeth learned to box the compass and compare what she saw with the navigational guide book. Captain Abner didn't use a sextant but guided himself by the landmarks he saw on the shore. She was told about the steady traffic of small sloops and schooners that ran freight, passengers and mail north and south among the thirteen colonies even in wartime. Captain Abner had made the trip a number of times. This time his luck ran out.

Dawn found them with a British frigate two miles off their starboard bow. She was on an opposite course from the sloop. In the first light they saw her swing about and additional sails blossom on her masts. The frigate sailed much faster than the *Phoebe*, about two feet to her one. A string of flag signals told Captain Abner to heave to. He ignored them. The boom of a cannon reenforced the signal. Captain Abner answered by hoisting an English flag. He kept going as if that was the normal thing to do. A second shot and the splash of a cannon ball in front of the *Phoebe's* bowsprit showed that the frigate meant business. Captain Abner shrugged his shoulders, lowered the mainsail and hove to. He couldn't even run his sloop into shallow water where the frigate couldn't follow because here the sand banks extended too far out. *Phoebe* was truly caught. The Britisher was taking no chances. He surged to within a quarter mile with his guns run out. The boat he lowered was filled with armed men. Captain Abner turned to her. "You stay in your cabin, I'll call you when I need you and remember, you are a helpless girl. It might come in handy."

Waiting in the cabin was almost enough to reduce Elizabeth to the frightened little girl she was supposed to act like. She heard the frigate's boat bump alongside and the tramp of men on deck.

Prize Of War

On the British frigate *Amazon* Midshipman Jeffrey Kent was just coming off the midnight watch. The *Amazon* was on patrol south of New York looking for French or American privateers and intercepting Rebel coastal shipping. They had caught a few prizes on this patrol but nothing much ever happened at night. None of the prizes had shown fight either. The twenty eight guns of the frigate were fairly intimidating.

Jeffrey had spent his time on this dull watch thinking about the last two years. His idle thoughts had only been interrupted once when the *Amazon* had tacked. Like many younger sons of the British nobility Jeffrey had joined the navy at the age of twelve. He was fourteen now. Joining the navy seemed better to him than hanging around his father's estate in southern England. He didn't care to go to school at Eton and Oxford either. His uncle, the Earl of Severn, had used his influence to get Captain Hartman to give Jeffrey a warrant as midshipman on his ship. Jeffrey couldn't get a commission from the King until he was eighteen and had passed an examination but a midshipman rated as an officer. He had endured the hazing from the older boys in the crowded midshipmen's berth, the bad food and the very little shore leave he had gotten in New York where the *Amazon* was based. Captain Hartman was training him as a signal officer rather than placing him in command of a section of the guns. He was also learning the other duties of a sea-going officer with the help of the bosun, the carpenter, the sailmaker and the other petty officers. He needed that more than expertese in gunnery. The *Amazon's* guns had never been fired in anger in the entire two years of this commission. Jeffrey dreamed of distinguishing himself in some heroic action but there had been no opportunity for heroics so far. He was just preparing to go below at the end of the watch when he heard the lookout's yell from the masthead. "Sail Ho."

"What do you make?" Lieutenant Younge, officer of the deck, was alert.

"A small sloop about two miles off out starboard quarter. Can't make out any colors, sir."

"All hands, all hands on deck. Stand by to go about and make sail." The bosun's whistles reenforced the lieutenants shout. "Midshipman, inform the captain." Captain Hartman was already coming on deck so Jeffrey moved to his station at the signal halyards. The men who had been leaving the deck at the end of the watch raced back to their places. The officer of the deck touched his hat in salute to the captain. "Should I clear for action, sir?"

"Don't bother. Just tip the fires overboard and have the men stand by the guns. Run down to him and he'll surrender quietly." He turned to Jeffrey. "Signal him to heave to."

"Aye aye, sir." Jeffrey didn't have to consult the signal book. He knew this signal by heart. The signal flags rose on the halyard. He also noted that the British ensign had been hoisted on the gaff. After a minute he turned to Captain Hartman. "He doesn't answer, sir."

The captain was annoyed. "Mr. Smith, fire a blank shot from number one gun of the portside battery. Maybe that will wake him up. Those dog-bark sailors can't read signals anyway." The gun roared out.

"He's hoisted British colors, sir, but he hasn't hove to." Jeffrey was getting exited. This is what he had joined the navy for. If this was a prize there might be prize money too. It wouldn't be much for a midshipman but it might be something even for him to spend. New York wasn't London but it would do for Jeffrey.

"Mr. Smith, a shot with ball across his bow. Don't hit him though."

"Aye aye, sir." The twelve pounder roared out again. Jeffrey saw the ball throw up a fountain of water thirty yards in front of the sloop. That was good shooting. The sloop's captain must have thought so too. His sails came down on the run. The sloop hove to, bow to the wind.

"Mr. Kent, muster your boat crew, cutlasses and pistols. Take posession and send that damned captain and his crew to me. Keep four men and a bosun's mate aboard. If our signal comes down, set sail for New York. I hope I can trust your navigation that far and you will have the shore in sight to port."

"Captain, what if he is a Loyalist?" Lieutenant Younge was bold enough to question his superior.

"Then we will teach him to respect the Royal Navy and obey signals."

The crew of the cutter were already lifting the boat off its chocks. Jeffrey issued cutlasses and boarding pikes but only he and Mr. Guerney, the bosun's mate, took pistols. It was too easy to have an accident with firearms. Besides he didn't think there would be any resistance. The *Amazon* was standing just a quarter mile off and opening all its gun ports. There were twelve pounders being run out.

Jeffrey was very exited. He was going to be in command of a ship. Alright, it was only a small sloop but he was going to be her captain even if it was only for a few days. He blessed the dysentery that had kept the two senior midshipmen sick in New York. The other midshipman, Thomas Deveril, was junior to Jeffrey and weak in navigation besides. Jeffrey was going to be able to do something besides chipping, painting and polishing. He wouldn't have to listen to lessons either. The Reverend Albert Wistham wasn't an inspiring teacher or preacher for that matter.

The cutter had run alongside the sloop and Jeffrey mounted over the side with five men behind him. The others in the boat would reinforce them if it was needed. He didn't think it would be. He and his men had drawn their cutlasses and that should be enough.

The captain of the sloop was an elderly man and he had only five crew members. "Alright mister, get yourself and your crew into that boat. Captain Hartman wants to see you and your papers." The captain called something and a girl stepped out on deck, a girl about Jeffrey's age. This was no trollop or servant. This dark haired girl was a well bred miss. Jeffrey could see that at a glance.

Elizabeth walked out onto the deck and gave a look at the *Phoebe's* crew surrounded by British sailors waving weapons. Captain Abner motioned her over to face a young officer from the frigate in a worn uniform. A very young officer, Elizabeth realized. "This is Miss Elizabeth Troyes. I am taking her to her relatives." Captain Abner tactfully didn't mention where Elizabeth's relatives lived. Elizabeth found herself blushing. It was so adult to be formally introduced.

"Midshipman Jeffrey Kent of His Brittanic Majesty's ship *Amazon*, very much at your service," the officer answered and bowed stiffly. He was not really a young man, Elizabeth decided. He was a boy not much older than herself.

"She is travelling alone? In wartime?" Jeffrey was shocked. In his world young ladies did not travel alone. They at least had a maid with them.

"She is not travelling alone. She is under my protection, placed there by her guardian. Her parents died. That happens even in wartime, lieutenant. I'll be thankful now if you let us continue on our voyage. We will undoubtedly see you in New York." Elizabeth saw what Captain Abner was trying to do. He was hoping the midshipman would let them sail on. Then the *Phoebe* could duck into a near-by Rebel held port until the frigate had disappeared. If that was impossible they could sail on to New York and try to talk themselves out of trouble there. Captain Abner was also flattering the young man by calling him lieutenant instead of the lower rank of midshipman. The midshipman hesitated and then stiffened.

Jeffrey was not impressed. He knew his lowly rank all too well. "Sorry but I have my orders from Captain Hartman. You shift yourself and your men to the *Amazon* like I said."

"You'd expose a young girl to a hundred and fifty strange men, would you? I don't know where they taught you manners, young man, but I don't think much of them if this is a sample." Elizabeth didn't know whether Captain Abner really cared about her or if this was simply a ploy. It didn't matter which because it wasn't working.

Jeffrey was thinking hard. The American was right. A young and pretty girl on the *Amazon* would be a disturbance and no mistake. Jeffrey himself had been sexually attacked in his first year on the frigate. The girl would be even more at risk. Captain Hartman wouldn't thank him for bringing her aboard. He came up with an answer. "She can stay aboard this ship. I am making myself responsible for her and I am prize master. No harm will come to her. Now you get yourself and your men into that boat. Lively now. Captain Hartman isn't a patient man and we have wasted enough time."

Captain Abner opened his mouth for further argument but the midshipman had already turned away. Some of the British sailors were making emphatic motions with their weapons. Captain Abner shrugged his shoulders in surrender and climbed down into the boat. His men followed.

"Should I go with you?" Elizabeth called out.

"No," Captain Abner called back. "That Britisher is right. You had best stay where you are. I can't do anything for you as a prisoner aboard the frigate. You'll just have to trust that British sprig of nobility of the Royal Navy."

Elizabeth could see that the midshipman was getting angry at Captain Abner's words. Well, they weren't exactly flattering. She thought a smile might smoothe things over even though she didn't feel like smiling. "I guess I am your prisoner, Mr. Kent."

"Please miss. Don't take it so hard. The Royal Navy doesn't make war on young ladies."

Jeffrey's attention was already on other things than the girl. He turned to the sailors who had stayed aboard the *Phoebe* with him. "Mr. Guerney, let's get ready to get under way. That signal on the *Amazon* has come down. That means we are to proceed on our own. Get that mainsail hoisted and set a course for New York, north by northeast."

"North by northeast. Aye aye, sir."

Jeffrey watched the operation critically. "Can you handle this rig?"

"Yes sir. It's very much like handling the *Amazon* under jibs and staysails."

Elizabeth saw the frigate swing around on her old course southwards away from the *Phoebe*. Jeffrey felt the responsibility of command settle on his shoulders like a leaden cloak. Mr. Guerney's answer had reassured him about the handling of the sails but there was much else to think about. He headed for the captain's cabin. He was lucky. There was not only a map of the coast but a printed guide book detailing all the landmarks visible from the sea and all the harbor approaches. Since Jeffrey had left his sextant back on the *Amazon* those, his sea sense and the deep sea lead was all he had to guide him. Mr. Guerney might know more than he about sail handling but Jeffrey thought his own navigational skills were better. Then he went forward to check on food supplies and water. That inspection was also reassuring. Hams, onions, turnips and carrots were hanging from the deck beams. They wouldn't starve. Maynard, one of the crewmen, had served as gun room steward so Jeffrey appointed him as temporary cook. Appointing regular cooks was one of the valued perogatives of the Navy Board, not the Admiralty, so Jeffrey could not give him a real warrant. Mr. Guerney divided the small crew into watches. One would be under Jeffrey and the other commanded by the bosun but Jeffrey knew he would be called for any change of course or shortening of sail in bad weather. Well, he had learned to do with only short snatches of sleep before.

Elizabeth felt alone again, but then she had really been alone ever since she had left Carolina. She hadn't known Captain Abner long or well so she would have to trust this Midshipman Jeffrey Kent of the British navy.

"I am sorry about this, miss, but it is wartime." He had come back to stand beside her on the deck. "Being prizemaster like this is my first independent command. The *Amazon* already has one lieutenant gone as prize master on a brig and two of the midshipmen were left behind in New York with fever. Otherwise I would have never gotten this command."

"I understand but it is hard to be suddenly separated from every one you know. Would it really been dangerous to have been transferred to the *Amazon*?"

"Well, the *Amazon* is a warship and crowded. There are no accommodations for passengers, especially female ones. You couldn't be put among the prisoners either. Captain Hartman would have had to turn one of the lieutenants out of his cabin and station a marine in front of it to keep you safe. That wouldn't make the captain nor the lieutenant turned out of his cabin like you better. Nor like me who put them into that position. Midshipmen always get the blame for everything anyway whether it is their fault or not. No, I think it is better for both of us that you stayed here. Don't worry. I will see that nothing happens to you. You are my responsibility now."

In the three days it took them to get to New York their relationship was peculiar. Elizabeth tried to help Maynard in the galley. Neither really had any experience in cooking for a ship's crew but they did their best. Elizabeth and Jeffrey could talk about the weather, the sea and the ship. They couldn't talk about politics or the progress of the war because that would have led to arguments. They wanted to stay polite to each other. They didn't even talk much about their personal life or their families. That wouldn't have been polite either. By the time they arrived in New York Elizabeth had told him nothing except that her parents were dead and that she liked the sea. She knew nothing about Jeffrey except that his home was in southern England, that he was fourteen and had been a midshipman for two years. As they had drawn closer to New York Jeffrey talked less and less. His answers to Elizabeth became almost gruff. Obviously something about her was bothering him. She didn't know what she had done wrong.

She was correct in her guess. Jeffrey was bothered about her. He took his responsibilities seriously and he had said she would come to no harm.

Besides he had come to almost like this girl. When they got to New York he would have to drop her just like that. She wouldn't have any posessions either. All her posessions on the *Phoebe* would be forfeit to the navy under the laws of war. That American captain wouldn't be able to help her either, even when the *Amazon* came in. He would be a prisoner of war and since he was not an officer of the American armed forces he wouldn't be eligible for parole or exchange. Jeffrey was all British officer when they came into the harbor, stiff and paying attention only to his duties.

Elizabeth stood quietly on the deck and looked at her first city. There were many ships clustered off Staten Island. Jeffrey saluted the flagship of the fleet by dipping the British ensign that Captain Abner had hoisted. He saluted again when they passed the fort at the south end of Manhattan Island. She saw many church steeples and brick houses. As they drew near the docks she could smell the city. The odor was a mixture of garbage and smoke. It had none of the clean smell of the sea or the Carolina woods. Jeffrey was bringing the *Phoebe* alongside one of the docks. His orders rang out as clearly as had those of Captain Abner. "Lower the mainsail. Hard starboard. Douse the jib." The tide pushed the sloop against the dock and some men fastened the ropes to hold her. She stood with her bow facing the land. The voyage was over.

"May I please have someone to carry my chest ashore?" Elizabeth asked pleasantly.

That was the moment Jeffrey had been afraid of. "I'm sorry, I cannot let you have that chest." Jeffrey's face was set in hard lines. "That chest as well as the ship and cargo are prizes of war. They belong to the navy now."

"But that chest is mine. It has all I own."

Jeffrey just shook his head and said nothing.

"But what should I do? That chest has all my clothing, my money, everything!" Fear and panic were making Elizabeth's voice shrill even in her own ears. "I'm heading for my cousins in Boston. I don't even know anyone to stay with in New York."

Jeffrey adressed the bosun who was standing near by watching the scene. "Mr. Guerney, set an anchor watch. No one is to go ashore until I have reported to the admiral. The *Amazon* hasn't come in yet from its patrol south. She'll probably come in soon." He turned to the girl. "You can come with me and appeal to the admiral if you wish."

The girl slumped and then straightened. "Very well," she said in a strained voice. "The admiral will know how to act like an officer and gentleman instead of a little boy who uses his uniform to rob the helpless."

Jeffrey looked and felt like he had been slapped. "That chest like the ship and all the cargo will be sold and the money distributed among the officers and men of the *Amazon* according to navy regulations. If I allowed you to take it or so much as touched it myself I would be court-martialled and thrown out of the service. Now I am going ashore to report. You can come with me or go where you please." He jumped down to the dock and wordlessly reached up a hand to help Elizabeth to the pier. She didn't want him to touch her but she needed help to get down. Her legs weren't long enough to reach the dock and her skirt would get in the way if she tried to jump. She didn't want to fall flat on her face. Common sense triumphed over anger. She let Jeffrey help her. The two walked through wartime New York not speaking. They had nothing to say to each other. At the head of the dock they passed some hastily built shacks housing refugees. Their arrival had been noted by those who lived in those shacks.

"Anything to sell, Captain?" an ill dressed man asked. "Give you a good price for linens or silver." Jeffrey just shook his head.

"A servant, miss? I'm used to taking care of young ladies." The speaker was a gaunt woman of undeterminate age, Elizabeth noted. Her dress had been good once but it was dirty now and had crudely mended rips. Elizabeth walked on without speaking.

"Gimme a copper. I'm hungry." The speaker was a little boy, barefoot with his skin showing through the rents in his shirt. He was dirty as well. Elizabeth shuddered. So this was the big city. This was New York. These people could be her if she wasn't lucky and got her things back. This could happen to her because she was a rebel or a "Patriot" or at least her father had been one.

At the headquarters on Broadway the marine sentries who stood there saluted Jeffrey and stared at Elizabeth. The two of them went inside and Jeffrey saluted the captain sitting behind the desk. Elizabeth followed behind Jeffrey. "Midshipman Kent reporting the arrival of the sloop *Phoebe*, prize to the *HMS Amazon*, with a cargo of tobacco and the chest of Miss Elizabeth Troyes who wishes to protest the seizure of her personal baggage." He indicated Elizabeth with a wave of his hand. The captain swung around to face her.

"Mr. Kent told me that he had seized my chest as a prize of war," she burst out angrily.

"Quite correct," the captain answered calmly. "The sloop and everything on her belongs to the Royal Navy as a prize unless the prize court rules otherwise. If you have previously sworn an oath of loyalty to the King, the baggage might be returned to you if you can explain how you came to be on an armed Rebel ship. Bring the papers attesting to your oath with you to the hearing. That will probably be held in a month's time."

"But I have no papers. There wouldn't be anyone living in our section who could even issue such papers. Besides I am only twelve years old."

"Then have your father bring such papers as you have. The court will make a decision as to your loyalty to the crown." Elizabeth knew she couldn't say anything about her father. He had died in battle fighting against the crown. She couldn't say anything here that would matter at all. Not to this British officer she couldn't. The captain swung back to Jeffrey. "I will inform the admiral of your arrival. Meanwhile, mister, you better stay aboard her until the *Amazon* comes in or you get other orders." He turned to the secretary sitting behind him. "Have a crew sent to get her unloaded and the cargo into the warehouse. He turned to Jeffrey again. "She is docked down at the Fly Market?"

"Yes sir."

"Carry on then."

"Aye aye, sir."

Elizabeth numbly followed Jeffrey out of the building. A bit further up the street she saw a long line of refugees apparently getting rations. She visualized herself on that line. That was of course if the British would issue rations to a Rebel. If she swore loyalty to King George she could probably get rations. Her father had died fighting against King George. She didn't know what to do. She didn't think the British would allow her to go on to Boston or even back to Carolina. She didn't want to go back to the *Phoebe*.

Jeffrey touched her elbow. She turned away from him but saw his face anyway. He looked as pale and sick as she felt. This was a phase of war he had never seen before. There was nothing heroic about it. Jeffrey held out his hand. In it were five silver shillings. "That's all the money I have. I know it isn't much but that is all I have left of three month's pay. I'll see that you don't starve. Let's not be enemies."

Elizabeth almost had to smile despite her feelings of fear. This boy-officer who was responsible for all her troubles was now offering her five pieces of silver. She couldn't even be angry with him. "Thank you. That will last me all of three days if I am careful." Her anger grew stronger. "Then, I suppose, the royal navy will let me beg like those people we saw on the dock. But I will make out," she told him. "You don't have to worry. After all my grandmother made out when she landed with her sister as a penniless refugee from France at Teignmouth."

Jeffrey jumped as if he had been shot. "Where did you say?"

"Teignmouth. It's a small town in Devon. Not important. You wouldn't know about it."

"What do you mean I wouldn't know about it. All my mother's people came from there. Of course I know about it. Who was your grandmother anyway?"

"Her name was Margaret de Raython. She was a Huguenot."

"Than we are cousins," came Jeffries surprised reply. "Our grandmothers were sisters." Jeffrey's voice became more hesitant. "I guess I am really responsible for you now that you are family." He made a desperate attempt at a lighter tone. "I guess I am your oldest male relative around or your only one."

Elizabeth could no longer hold back her sobbing. This half-made officer, this Britisher who had made her lose all she had, now was going to claim he was her protector. Here she was in a strange city with no money, no home and nowhere to go and he said he was going to protect her. He was her kinsman, he said. She was crying unreservedly now.

Jeffrey was not feeling much better than she was. He was an officer and a gentleman and her older relative. That imposed certain obligations on him according to the code he had been brought up in but he hadn't the faintest idea of what to do. He had followed his duty and look where that left him now. Jeffrey slipped back into his role as a navy officer. That was his refuge from her tears. His voice became forceful again. "We are going back to the ship now. We will handle everything else later."

She let him guide her back to the *Phoebe* as if she was a little girl again. There was no fight left in her. She had been forced to be a big girl so long. When her father was killed, during the three week illness of her mother and when she had died, when her uncle told her he was sending her to Boston it had always been "You're a big girl now, Elizabeth." She didn't want to be a big girl anymore. She wanted someone to cling to, someone who would take care of her and tell her what to do. She clung to Jeffrey's arm. It was so much better than having no one.

They went back to the *Phoebe* but Jeffrey had no time for her there. He was the commanding officer of the ship and all the people with problems were waiting for him.

"The longshoremen will be here in the morning, sir" Mr. Guerney told him. "Should we strike the ballast while we have them?"

"There may be some fresh vegetables at the market, sir. Do I have your permission to buy them, sir?" Maynard asked.

Jeffrey made his decisions. "No, we haven't been placed on a separate allowance. Only Captain Hartman or the purser of the *Amazon* can authorize purchases except in emergencies. This isn't one." Then he turned to Mr. Guerney. "Leave the ballast. We don't want her capsizing when they remove the cargo. She'll be top heavy. And send a watering party to the tea pump. Only enough water for our stay in port. The regular watering place for the navy is on Staten Island."

Elizabeth watched in amazement. Jeffrey was acting like a real officer. However she was left all alone again. She went to her cabin and cried into her rough pillow. It was stuffed with oakum and could absorb a fair amount of tears. Jeffrey heard her sobs from his cabin and let her cry herself out. He did look into her cabin when all was quiet again and saw that she had fallen asleep. He figured that sleep was what she needed most and didn't bother her for supper or anything else.

Both Elizabeth and Jeffrey were up early the next morning. They met at the scuttlebutt, the big barrel of fresh water fixed to the deck. It was good to have fresh water to drink and even for washing. At sea everything was washed with salt water. Washing oneself in salt water meant that one felt sticky. The same was true of clothing washed in ocean water. The tea pump water also tasted good to have rather than the stale brown water from the barrels in the hold. The weather was warm and sunny too and they found that they could smile at one another. They had a quick breakfast of burgoo, the oatmeal of the navy, in the wardroom. It was nothing fancy but they both were hungry.

At seven in the morning. the longshoremen appeared to unload the cargo of the *Phoebe*. The longshoremen were prisoners watched by four marines with fixed bayonets and a hard faced sergeant. The sergeant made it clear to both Jeffrey and Mr. Guerney that he was in charge and they were not to interfere. Elizabeth watched with tight lips as her chest was carried off with the rest of the cargo to a navy storehouse. Officially the *Phoebe* was not a prize until the prize board said so but that was merely a formality.

"Those landsharks you got to watch them," one of the hands muttered. "Every finger is a fishook for stealing with them and the leathernecks are the same."

Jeffrey was watching that none of them went into the wardroom or the cabins. He didn't like having criminals aboard his ship. Often the marines were no better. It was common to offer convicted criminals a choice between jail, the marines or one of the marching regiments of the army. Sailors were obtained by inducement to volunteer for young men who couldn't get along in their villages or they were "pressed" under wartime powers from the streets, their house and taverns. If you were "pressed" you could still officially volunteer and at least get a small bonus. Marines or the army only offered the "King's shilling". The law said that only idle men were to be impressed but in fact armed gangs from the ships were very liberal in what they termed "idle". The fact that you were not in your workplace was sufficient. Naturally wealthy citizens or nobles who could identify themselves weren't taken.

"The *Amazon* has anchored up the bay, sir," Mr. Guerney suddenly told Jeffrey. "She must have cut short her patrol and sailed up from the south quicker than we did. Must have come in last night."

Jeffrey grabbed the telescope to make sure that it was the *Amazon* among all the ships in the harbor. Then his orders rang out clearly. "Man the jolly boat. Four men to the oars. Lively now." Elizabeth saw the lift of his shoulders. He looked relieved that he could drop all his troubles on someone else now. Then his face fell. "Belay that order. Two men to row will do." Elizabeth understood and appreciated his order. He still felt responsible for her and didn't want to leave her with just Mr. Guerney and the longshoremen aboard. The marines would be no protection from insult. She watched Jeffrey drop into the boat carrying his journals. Every midshipman was expected to record all he did. She felt alone again, despite the two sailors and Mr. Guerney. The feeling of wanting to cry came back again too. Here she was in New York with no friends and no money. No friends if she didn't count Jeffrey and she didn't want to count on Midshipman Jeffrey Kent. Not at all. He was only a boy and in the navy. He would drop her in a moment if that Captain Hartman told him to. Soon she might not even have the *Phoebe* to sleep on. Certainly that captain at headquarters wouldn't let her stay on the sloop if he heard about it. Not a single minute he wouldn't. He wouldn't help her get to her cousins in Boston either. He wouldn't even let her get back to Carolina. As far as he or any other British officer was concerned she was a "rebel" and rebels weren't entitled to anything. Besides if she got back to Carolina her uncle had no room for her. He had his other two girls to bring up. Those cousins of his might not want her anymore either, not when they heard she had a cousin who was a British officer. That wouldn't help her at all. She remembered how quick the people of Carolina had been with accusations of "tory-lover". And Boston was the hot bed of the Revolution. That left Jeffrey Kent and she wasn't sure of Jeffrey Kent. Her thoughts had travelled a full circle.

The bosun brought over the hammock chair for her. "This will be easier to sit on, miss."

"Thank you, Mr. Guerney." Elizabeth was sure this was the first time he had addressed her directly. She was glad she had remembered his name.

"Sorry about you losing your things. Hope everything will work out for you alright." The bosun seemed to be rubbing his hands in his trouser pocket. He stretched out his hand to her. She saw no reason to shake his hand but did it anyway. Girls didn't normally shake hands with men and besides she wasn't going anywhere. Then she realized that this was not an idle gesture. He was passing something to her. Something hard and round. "Got it from that lobsterback," he muttered.

Elizabeth opened her hand. In it lay the ivory miniature of her mother in its gold frame. It was a link with her past. It was pretty valuable too with its gold frame and back. Then the shock hit her. This had been in her locked chest. If somebody had gotten it they had probably also gotten at her money and the silver spoons as well as her few bits of jewelry. Everything of value would have been taken. It was gone now. Even if she got her chest back now there would be nothing in it except a few dresses and underwear. Everything not on her back or in her cabin was gone, irrevocably gone. Mentally she added up her posessions. Two shifts, two pettycoats, two dresses, a nightgown, her cloak and a few toilet things. There was also her sewing kit. That had a gold thimble in it. She hadn't trusted the lock of her cabin and so had taken nothing valuable out of the chest. Elizabeth didn't even go down to see if the things she had just counted were still there. She sat down hard on her hammock chair. Strangely enough she felt better. The decision had been made for her. Without money she would never get back to Carolina nor to Boston either. That could be ruled out. She could forget about them. Here in New York she was and here in New York she would have to make her way. A saying of her father's came into her mind. "The cards are on the table. Play them." She had no choice and would have to play the cards she held. They didn't look like very good cards but they were what she had been dealt. There would be no re-deal.

ON HIS MAJESTY'S SERVICE

Jeffrey stood at attention before Captain Hartman. "Your report is satisfactory, mister. The admiral is taking the sloop into the service. We need dispatch vessels now that our forces are spread out from Savannah to Halifax. Told me to furnish an experienced crew for her, an officer, two master's mates, ten men and a couple of boys. I'll give a warrant to Mr. Emmons. He is a cook and also has some training from the surgeon as loblolly man. I'm damned short of officers though. Collins and Howard haven't gotten over their flux yet either." He fixed Jeffrey with a hard stare. "I'm going to keep you in command of her, then. Better give you a warrant as acting lieutenant so there is no question of who is in command." Jeffrey's heart leaped. He was being given his own ship to command and a promotion. It was a small ship he would command, one of the smallest on the American station, but a ship none the less. The captain wasn't done yet. "Pass the word for Mr. Smith," he called out to the sentry outside his cabin. It didn't take long for the first lieutenant to appear. "Pick out ten men, a couple of boys, Mr. Emmons, Mr. McLeod and Mr. Lawton as a crew for the *Phoebe*. Good men, Mr. Smith, the admiral is personally interested in this. Mr. Kent will command her. Get the cutter ready to take them to the sloop while Mr. Kent gets his dunnage together and takes care of the paper work with the purser."

"Aye aye, sir." The first lieutenant looked dubious. He never had enough men for the crew of the *Amazon* but there was nothing else he could answer. He couldn't even use this opportunity to pass off his hard cases, not if the admiral was personally interested. "I will see to it, sir, at once."

Suddenly Jeffrey remembered Elizabeth. "There is a problem, sir."

"A problem, mister?"

"Yes sir. I reported the presence of a passenger aboard, sir. A young girl."

"I remember. You were wise to keep her on the sloop. There is no room on the *Amazon* for a female and a young female at that. We're in New York now, not at sea. Put her ashore."

"It turns out she is my cousin, sir. And we seized all her goods as prize of war. She has no one ashore here and I can't put her off like a sailor's doxy just like that. My uncle would have my hide. He is strong on kinship."

"A young relative?" The captain's fingers drummed on the desk. "Bring her to the admiral's supper tonight. They can always use a decent woman to make up the numbers. I'll send my barge for you after you have dropped down the bay. As for the rest, use your judgement, lieutenant, use your judgement. I want to hear no more about it. And send my regards to your uncle when you write him. You do, don't you?"

Jeffrey understood. Captain Hartman was backing him. Of course it was mainly for his uncle, but that didn't matter. If Jeffrey and Elizabeth appeared together at the admiral's supper that would smoothe things, too. And Lieutenant Smith was giving him a good crew for the *Phoebe*, his ship to command. It only took him an hour and a half to get a draft for purchases from the purser and thank Lieutenant Smith on deck. That way he could avoid trouble over his appointment in the midshipmen's berth. None of the lieutenants would be envious about so small a command and he was taking two master's mates. He liked Mr. McLeod. He had taught Jeffrey much about navigation and ship handling. He dropped into the jolly boat, checked that his warrant and orders were safe in his pocket and gave orders to shove off. The cutter would follow.

Elizabeth looked at the water of the East River with more interest. A scow-ferry was making its slow way to Brooklyn under sail. Just north of the dock there were close to three large ships swinging at anchor. One of them was hoisting loads of firewood up from a barge. To the south was a forest of masts where the British fleet was at anchor off Staten Island. Two boats were being rowed upstream near by.

"That's the *Amazon*'s cutter and our jolly boat." Mr. Guerney's voice was sharp. "Maybe we are getting a crew and going somewhere."

Elizabeth looked carefully. Jeffrey was in the jolly boat but there was no flash of gold braid from either boat. That meant no high officers like that bored captain from headquarters. That was good news.

Jeffrey climbed aboard the *Phoebe* to the sound of Mr. Guerney's silver pipe and the two members of the crew standing at attention. The two other sailors from the jolly boat came behind them and helped hoist the boat in. Elizabeth didn't know what to do but it became obvious that Jeffrey was not going to have time for her. "Mr. Guerney, cast loose." The men loosened the ropes that held *Phoebe* to the pier.

"Cutter there. Bring the bow around. Handsomely now." *Phoebe* swung around until her bow pointed into the middle of the river. "Take her off shore." The sailors put their backs into it and towed the sloop out. Elizabeth wondered whether they were already sailing somewhere. Then the order came to drop the anchor. The men from the cutter swarmed aboard and everyone gathered around the mast. Once the crew had formed up properly Jeffrey stood on the quarterdeck facing them. Then he took out some papers out of his breast pocket.

"Hats off," came the bellow of a heavy set man of the same type as Mr. Guerney. Jeffrey began reading in a loud voice.

"Orders from Thomas Arbuthnoth, Knight of the Honorable Order of the Bath, Vice-Admiral of the White, commanding His Majesty's ships and stations in North American waters under the authority of the Lords Commissioners of the Admiralty fulfilling the functions of the Lord High Admiral to Jeffrey Kent, master and acting lieutenant." Elizabeth realized that this was a formal occasion and stiffened into a kind of attention herself. "You are hereby directed and required to take charge of His Majesty's sloop *Phoebe*—." Elizabeth didn't understand all the rest of the orders but she understood the first part well enough. The ship was now part of the British navy and Jeffrey was in charge of it. What he would do with his charge remained to be seen and what he would do about Elizabeth remained to be seen. Jeffrey was now making a speech. Elizabeth heard all the stock phrases for this kind of thing. The king, the glory of the British navy and the need to do one's duty were all there. The words sounded a little pompous coming from the mouth of a fourteen year old boy but she saw that Jeffrey, at least, believed in them. Somehow they would apply to her. She realized that too. The crew gave a cheer. Then came the bellow, "Hats on. Dismiss." The crew picked up their hammocks and sea bags and trooped below.

Jeffrey's orders rang out again. "Mr. McLeod, take the cutter back to the *Amazon* with those men who don't belong to our crew. Return here as soon as you can. Mr. Guerney, take four hands and row to the boatyard. We have a requisition for bosun's stores, yardage and spare canvas. Mr. Lawton, you have the deck."

Jeffrey came down and went into the gangway and his cabin. After a moment Elizabeth followed him but he had shut his door. She went to her cabin. At least she hoped it was still her cabin. She sat and waited. After what seemed an eternity but was only an hour she opened her door. Jeffrey was sitting at the table of the wardroom with a mass of papers in front of him. He no longer looked like a bold navy officer. He looked like a school boy facing his homework. He saw her standing there. "I have to write all these papers out with two clean copies. There is no clerk aboard and none of the crew members can read and write. I don't like paper work. I never did. That's why I didn't want to go to Eton and Oxford."

"Can I help? I do know how to write and figure. I kept the accounts when mother ran the farm."

"Right." Jeffrey sounded relieved and he really was. "Start with this ration list. It needs two copies." He started passing papers to her.

"Aye aye, sir." Her nautical response brought a small smile to his lips.

"I guess we will have to rate you as acting clerk to the acting lieutenant. You do know that I was made acting lieutenant, don't you?"

"No, I don't know. Nobody tells me anything. You don't either. Is it important that you are acting lieutenant instead of midshipman?"

"Of course it's important. It's the most important thing there is. It's promotion. They can't give me a regular commission yet. I am too young and I have to pass an examination. Have to be eighteen to get a royal commission. I guess that I am the nephew of my uncle convinced Captain Hartman to give me a warrant."

"Your uncle?"

"Yes, my uncle. He is the Earl of Severn. Of course, that the two senior midshipmen are sick helped too."

"Your uncle is aboard the *Amazon*?"

"Of course not. He is in London. But even Captain Hartman pays attention to the nephew of an earl."

Elizabeth was puzzled. What had being the nephew of an earl to do with anything? For the next few minutes Jeffrey tried to explain the role of rank in the British social system. Elizabeth still didn't understand all this about birth. In the colonies there were few people with titles except the British officials. Titles weren't important in everyday life, not really.

However there was one important, overwhelmingly important question she had to ask. "Does that mean I can stay aboard the *Phoebe*?"

"Yes." Jeffrey's answer was firm. "Unofficially of course. There are plenty of captains and even some warrant officers who have women aboard, sometimes even at sea. It isn't supposed to happen. All women are supposed to be ashore when a ship sails. It doesn't always happen that way. Besides, I told Captain Hartman about you. I felt I had to. He invited us to supper tonight with Admiral Gambier at the "Royal Arms". Admiral Gambier is the port admiral of New York. He's under Arbuthnoth who is keeping station at Gardiner's Bay off Long Island so he can't be bottled up by a French fleet. I got told all this while I was aboard *Amazon*. Have to know it if I am in command of a ship."

Elizabeth wasn't interested in all this navy talk. She was concerned with her own role. "Won't there be talk? I mean with my staying here with you?"

"Not aboard this ship there won't be any talk. Any sailor who opens his mouth too wide will find himself at the gratings getting a dose of the cat."

"You'd have them whipped?"

"That is the way the navy keeps discipline. Guess there won't be much talk elsewhere, either. That's one of the reasons Captain Hartman invited both of us to the admiral's supper. After all you are a relative of an earl too."

"But—."

"Don't worry. Nobody will snub you. There aren't that many ladies of the quality around here in New York."

"But I haven't anything to wear. My best dress was in that chest of mine." Elizabeth stopped herself just in time before telling Jeffrey about her discovery of the robbing of her chest. He was capable of having everybody aboard at the time whipped. Just on the suspicion that they might have been involved. Perhaps even Mr. Guerney. She didn't want that and she didn't trust Jeffrey enough to tell him everything. Besides the chest was probably opened by one of those prisoner-longshoremen with the connivance of that sergeant of marines. Mr. Guerney must have known something about it though. Or how did he get her miniature back. There was a lot she was going to have to think about when she had the time. She wasn't going to get the time now. Jeffrey was shoving papers at her again. He had paid attention to her remark about dress.

"Admiral Gambier isn't going to be too fussy about what you have on. The captain just wants to make sure he doesn't think you are a loose woman. Gambier has the reputation for being pious. I haven't got a full dress uniform either. I will have to have a uniform for a lieutenant made but I don't have time for it now. I did draw a voucher from the purser for my pay and for purchases for the ship. Paper voucher of course. There isn't much hard money around here. Not unless someone captures a Spanish treasure galleon. They carry all the silver from Mexico and Peru back to Europe. Spanish pieces-of-eight are good all over the world." Jeffrey wanted to talk, but there were all these papers. "We're dropping down to the anchorage off Staten Island. These papers have to be ready. A boat from the *Amazon* will pick us up and this all has to be ready if the admiral or the captain ask for them." They went to work. Jeffrey would make a draft and then Elizabeth would make two clean copies, one for use and the other for the journal as a permanent record. There could be nothing crossed out or erased in the journal or the log.

Mr. Lawton, a man Elizabeth didn't know, knocked on the door frame and came in. "We've divided the men into watches, sir. We have two master's mates, a bosun, a cook, twelve seamen and two boys. And yourself of course. That is a scratch crew but it is all they would let us have. We're a dispatch vessel and not expected to fight."

"Very well, Mr. Lawton. And this is my cousin, Miss Elizabeth Troyes, who is acting as clerk." Jeffrey's hand indicated the mass of papers.

Mr. Lawton bowed to Elizabeth. His eyes didn't indicate whatever he was thinking. She guessed that in the British navy it didn't matter what anybody except the commanding officer thought. She nodded and smiled at Mr. Lawton. She didn't know if that was the proper thing to do but she didn't want to get up and curtsy. Mr. Lawton left with the remark that Mr. McLeod would return soon after taking the cutter back to the *Amazon*. That would give the *Phoebe* three watch keeping officers, counting Jeffrey.

Soon they were interrupted again. A slight, blond child stood at the door. He couldn't be more than ten years old, Elizabeth thought, maybe less. "The cook sent me, sir. He wants to know when to serve your midday meal. And he says he has only two more days of fresh food aboard."

"Tell the cook we will have our meal after the men have had theirs. In about an hour." The boy headed out.

"You, boy!" Jeffrey's voice was almost a roar. "Come back here."

"Yes, sir." The boy's voice shook.

"The next time you leave without an aye aye, sir, you will be in trouble. Real trouble. Understand?"

"Aye aye, sir."

"Did you have to shout at him?" Elizabeth asked after the boy left. "He is only a child and meant no harm."

"Now look here, Elizabeth. On board ship there are officers, petty officers and men. The men are called hands and are treated as such. Boys are the lowest of the hands. Some of them came here from the poor houses or the jails. They were given the choice of jail or the navy. Most of the time they don't even know who their parents were. Hard discipline is the only language they understand. On this ship you will not talk with them and you will not smile at them. Try your republican ideas here and you will find yourself ashore. This is a navy ship and there will be discipline aboard her and I am here to see to it." Elizabeth could see that Jeffrey meant it. He wasn't putting on an act. Yet the statement troubled her. There were servants in Carolina, even slaves, but most people treated them decently. You didn't threaten them with a whipping for not saying "aye aye, sir." At least most people didn't. There were always a few brutes. In the British navy things were obviously done differently. She didn't want to pick up that harsh attitude. And the boatswain had gotten back her miniature for her. Was he just a hand too? Obviously something beyond the fear of whipping kept the crew together. Curious, she ran her eyes down the crew list. Yes, there was a boy, John James, age ten. Further down was another boy. Pat McManus, age eleven, from Bristol. She noted that Mr. Guerney was also from Bristol and was fifty. Her name wasn't on the list. Officially she didn't exist. Probably she should add her name. She decided against it without consulting Jeffrey. The requisitions and such signed with E. Troyes were honored by the officials and didn't show that she was a girl. Elizabeth didn't really want to be an official member of the British navy anyway. She went on with her copying.

They had a hasty meal. Then the *Phoebe* dropped down river to the navy anchorage off Staten Island. Elizabeth was too busy to watch the sailing but Jeffrey was up on deck.

"Who said girls were useless creatures?" Elizabeth told herself. "It wasn't true in Carolina and it isn't here." Talking to herself out loud made Elizabeth feel better and there was nobody below deck to hear her. Mr. Emmons, the cook, was in his cubby.

A short time later Jeffrey came back into the cabin. "It's time to dress for the admiral's supper. I haven't anything fit to wear. I'll look like a poor relation."

"You told me that dress didn't matter, remember? So we will both do the best we can."

"We can't back off," Jeffrey said almost to himself. "Captain Hartman doesn't accept excuses." Elizabeth went to her cabin and ran a comb through her hair. She looked at herself in the small mirror that had been in her toilet case. "At least my hair is naturally curly." She saw that she was pale and knew that she was scared. She just hoped that there would be other ladies present so she could copy what they did. Elizabeth had never attended any formal dinners with her parents so here she would be on her own. Jeffrey wouldn't be able to help her either. Soon there was a knock on the door and a voice saying "The *Amazon's* barge is alongside. You're wanted on deck, miss."

On deck she realized she would have to climb over the side of the *Phoebe* alone and lift up her skirts to do it. The sloop was too small to have a boarding ladder. Jeffrey couldn't help her. He was behind her as a commanding officer should be. One of the sailors on the barge steadied her. He didn't smile as he touched her bare leg but he was obviously keeping his face straight with an effort. She wondered what the sailors thought of her being aboard with Jeffrey and no chaperone. Maybe they thought she was a prostitute like so many women who were seen with sailors. When they reached the *Amazon*, Captain Hartman and Lieutenant Younge descended with the glitter of gold lace and the sound of the bosun's whistles. Jeffrey introduced Elizabeth and the Captain took the seat next to her. "You lived near the ocean, Miss Troyes?"

"No, our home was inland, near a river."

"You seem to take to ships well. You are not afraid of the sea?"

"No, I'm not afraid of the ocean but I admit I was a bit afraid when the *Amazon* surged next to our little *Phoebe* with her guns pointing right at us."

"The British navy is to be feared. If your Rebel captain hadn't hauled his wind we would have sent a broadside into the sloop even if we would have seen your charming shape on deck. War can sometimes be hard on civilians, you know." Elizabeth didn't need Captain Hartman to tell her that. She had already experienced the brutality of the British navy.

Jeffrey was surprised that Captain Hartman was making an effort to be pleasant to Elizabeth. An effort to exert himself to be pleasant and human. That was a side of his character that he hadn't shown much to his midshipmen on the frigate. It was Captain Hartman, not Jeffrey or the lieutenant who handed her out of the boat at the Battery landing. He obviously expected her to walk with him. The two lieutenants followed behind. Rank counted in the navy even on social occasions.

At the "Royal Arms" there was a glitter of uniforms. The blue of the navy predominated but there were also men in the scarlet of the army and the green of the Tory regiments. Elizabeth's russet dress stood out by its very plainness. Captain Hartman introduced her to some of the men including that hard faced captain she had seen at headquarters. Brathwaithe was his name. She curtsied politely to him and the others. She didn't feel at ease. Well, she hadn't expected to be comfortable here. When the innkeeper announced supper she found herself seated between Captain Hartman on her right and an officer of the Highlanders on her left. This was obviously by arrangement since there were little cards with their names at each setting. Jeffrey was at the foot of the table quite far away from her. There were only a few lieutenants and only three civilian women. The women were the only other civilians and were obviously the wives of some of the officers. Being the relatives of an earl apparently gave Jeffrey and Elizabeth standing. Admiral Gambier, a dark visaged man, with his flag captain beside him, occupied the head of the table.

The soup was excellent and Elizabeth was hungry. This food was much better than that served by the *Phoebe*'s cook. The wine glass next to her plate was full. She had barely started eating when she heard the admiral say "Mr. Vice, the King."

Jeffrey, by far the most junior officer present, rose with the wine glass in his hand. "Ladies and gentlemen, the King." Everyone rose, catching Elizabeth by surprise when they all drank the toast. While she was still hesitating whether to get up the chance was over. Everyone was sitting down again. The admiral's brows drew together in a frown.

"Your sympathies are with the rebels, Miss Troyes?"

"I am an American as are many who are fighting both for and against the King." Elizabeth had heard this answer before and had decided to use it if she was asked for her political opinions.

"And being an American is an excuse for rebellion?" That was Captain Brathwaithe's voice.

Elizabeth flushed but she couldn't back down now. Everyone was staring at her. She could almost hear her father speak and she used his words. "I have heard much about the 'Glorious Revolution of 1688',

Captain. And in our part of Carolina there are many men who fought against King George and for Prince Charles Stuart some thirty years ago. Flora MacDonald lived in our section. Not so long ago, it seems, there were rebels in England as well as in the Colonies."

"Many of those men are fighting for King George now." That was the Highlander to her left. "Flora MacDonald is raising troops for the King."

"Yes, I know." Elizabeth had to bite her lips but then her voice was clear. "My father died at the Battle of Moore's Bridge fighting those Highlanders for what he considered his rights."

Jeffrey saw what was happening. These senior officers were treating Elizabeth just as he had been treated by the senior midshipmen when he had voiced an unpopular opinion. They were ganging up and bullying her. He did what little he could to help her. He could only hope she wouldn't break down. These were fighting officers who admired strength and had no pity for weakness.

"Both Miss Troyes' and my grandmother came to England from France as refugees because they wouldn't become Catholics as the King of France decreed. I guess he considered them rebels as well."

Admiral Gambier raised his glass. "I propose a toast to Miss Troyes' courage standing up to both the army and navy." The toast was drunk amid general laughter at Elizabeth's expense but the grilling stopped.

The tension had been too much for Elizabeth. Too much had happened to her today. She felt the room spin in front of her. In another minute she was going to faint in front of all these officers and Jeffrey. She heard Captain Hartman's voice as from far away. "Here, take a sip of this. It will steady you." He held a wine glass to her lips and she managed a swallow. The room stopped spinning. She managed somehow to get through the meal. She even ate something. She really remembered nothing of that meal except Captain Brathwaithe's hard voice and all of those staring faces. She was at the mercy of those officers of the British armed forces who knew no mercy. They made up the rules of war to suit themselves. Everyone was helpless before them.

There was a small gleam of hope for her. Jeffrey had stood up for her and even Captain Hartman had helped her a bit. Now she wanted to see no one and speak to no one. Once on the ship she went down to her cabin, crawled into her bunk and pulled the cover over her head. Curled up into a ball, her body shook in reaction to what had happened.

She heard her door open. "Go away. I don't want anything from anybody," she cried out desperately.

"Please miss," came the voice of little John. "The captain sent me with a glass of grog. He told me to help you, he did."

"Just leave me alone."

"Please miss. Don't take on so." It was hard to resist that childish voice. "It don't help none. I know." She sat up and drank some of that rum and water mixture that was the navy's remedy for all ills. Her stomach revolted and she was just able to get up on deck before being violently sick over the side. That did help clear her head. She went over to the scuttlebutt and rinsed out her mouth with clear water. She washed the tears and sweat off her face and hands. Suddenly she realized that Jeffrey was standing there, not touching her but ready to help.

"I'm sorry," she told him. "I think things just got too much for me."

"I know how you feel," he told her mildly. "I have been joked with the same way. Except in the midshipmen's berth they kick feelings out of you. All your feelings. They laugh at you, they bully you and if you complain you get bent over a table and beaten with a cane. You're spread-eagled and held down by the others. You learn to keep your feelings inside of you, all your feelings. It's supposed to harden you into a good officer."

"Did I embarrass you in front of all those officers?"

"No, I don't think they even noticed how upset you were. As I said most officers aren't very strong on feelings. After all you didn't break down until you got back here. The fact that the admiral toasted your courage didn't hurt either. That's what everyone will remember. Nobody will say a word against you now and the admiral will probably give you a cartel when the time comes."

"What's a cartel?"

"A letter giving permission to cross the lines of both armies without let or hindrance. It's a convenience for both sides and is used fairly frequently."

Elizabeth didn't want to think whether she wanted a letter signed by a British admiral to go to Boston with. Right now it was sufficient that she was on the *Phoebe* with Jeffrey. They stood for a while together on the quiet deck until Elizabeth went back down to her cabin. She fell asleep quickly but her dreams were troubled and she woke unrefreshed.

The next morning she had breakfast with Mr. McLeod and Mr. Lawton, the petty officers. The *Phoebe* was too small to rate more than one comissioned officer and Jeffrey was only an acting lieutenant at that. Right now he was up on deck with the carpenter from the *Amazon* and Mr. Guerney discussing what had to be done to turn the *Phoebe* from a merchantman into a warship. The admiral had decreed that they had only a short time so the alterations would have to be limited to what could be done on board and not at a shipyard. The ten days of hard work together turned the crew into a unit instead of being just a bunch of men. Elizabeth found that she had become part of that unit. The work that she was doing, checking supplies, signing requisitions as well as handling minor purchases was not so different from what she had done at the farm in Carolina. Elizabeth endeared herself to Mr. Emmons, the cook, when she firmly rejected a shipment of cheese.

"I won't sign for these. They are rotten and full of maggots."

"Now, miss, they are fresh out of the king's stores."

"And they undoubtedly been in the king's stores since the days of Sir Francis Drake and the Armada. I grew up on a farm and know rotten food when I can smell it."

"They are proper supplies. We furnish them to all the king's ships."

"Then I will serve them to Captain Hartman and Admiral Gambier and tell them from whom they come."

The victualler withdrew defeated. The next shipment was somewhat fresher. Elizabeth knew that some of the food in the barrels was rotten too. There was little she could do about it. After all the commander of the *Phoebe* had the lowest rank and least seniority of all the ships on the New York station. Their pursers were backed up by full captains and commanders. She also knew nothing about cordage, gun powder and other supplies so she signed for those as Mr. Guerney told her to sign.

The carpenters were making changes on the sloop. Mr. Guerney, the two master's mates and the crew were helping. As an acting commissioned officer Jeffrey was supposed to check on their work but not touch a tool himself. Since he knew nothing about carpentry he just nodded wisely and left them to it. He did know something about the larger guns that were replacing what the *Phoebe* had been armed with. The two swivels were left clamped on the quarterdeck rails but the four pounders were replaced by bigger ones, six pounders, Elizabeth was told. With them came new cannon balls, swabbers and rammers. Elizabeth found that she had trouble when she tried to carry one of the new cannon balls. They were heavier and clumsier than she had thought.

Jeffrey did a little arithmatic when he drew up the list of the crew at action stations with Mr. McLeod. With his crew of twelve he could just man the guns at one side adequately and have enough men left to handle the sails. The two boys would carry up fresh powder from the magazine and he needed two men to handle the steering tiller. True, they were only a dispatch vessel not expected to fight, but that would only make them fair game for any enemy.

One day Elizabeth found that the walls of her cabin had been replaced by flimsy partitions and the doors by curtains. Her bunk had been replaced by a hammock. "Splinters from wood can be as dangerous as cannon balls," Mr. Guerney told her. "Even the flimsy partitions and the door frames are struck below when we clear for action. The hammocks are rolled up every morning and placed into hammock nettings along the rail. That airs them and they also protect the men from musket balls in battle. You will be expected to carry yours up too when you hear the call of 'lash and stow.' Everybody except the captain does."

She saw some of the sailors make the diamond netting to stow the hammocks and promised herself to learn that skill but she had no time for that now. The amount of paper work that had to be done was staggering.

Jeffrey had little patience for clerical work. He wanted to be in the open, on deck and preferably at sea. He grew irritable when he had to sit in the wardroom making out lists. He was glad Elizabeth was on board. She had a neat hand and he could trust her. There was little time for the two of them to talk except on duty matters.

Elizabeth did take time to watch them bring the new six pounders aboard. It was a ticklish operation since the *Phoebe* bobbed one way on the waves of the bay and the barge another. Each one of the gun barrels weighed several hundred pounds. The wooden gun carriages came up seperately. Each gun was fastened to bolts in the deck by ropes. Rammer, cannon balls and a small powder bucket was placed next to them. No one wanted a big supply of gunpowder on deck. Fresh charges would be brought up by the boys, the "powder monkeys." Muskets, pistols and cutlasses as well as the boarding pikes were also stored below in the newly built magazine. Gun powder was in a separate space that had no candles and no metal to strike sparks.

All this work was supervised by Mr. McLeod who had been designated their gunnery officer. He now told Elizabeth what to sign for. She found him easy to work with, quiet and very firm. He would talk about guns to her but nothing about his private life. The crew list told her little about him. He was thirty-five years old and had signed on in Glasgow. He had been in the navy for twenty years and had risen from boy to able seaman and then master's mate.

Finally on a Saturday afternoon, all had been accomplished. Sunday morning Jeffrey made a formal inspection of the ship. He must have found time to have a lieutenant's uniform made up for him and wore a sword instead of a midshipman's dirk. After inspection came church service. Elizabeth's soprano blended in with the sailors voices. Then Jeffrey read the thirty five Articles of War to the crew as had been decreed by the Lords of Admiralty. Article Seventeen dealt with the handling of seized articles and Elizabeth realized why Jeffrey had been so careful about handling her chest. Only after all the formalities were completed did he have time to talk to Elizabeth.

"We're sailing in the morning," he told her. "They must be short of dispatch vessels to have pushed us so fast. Guns, supplies, almost everything we asked for was sent to us. Captain Hartman didn't even take back the crew members from the *Amazon* so we have experienced hands instead of green men from here. Ebb tide will be at four bells of the morning watch."

Elizabeth was thinking hard. Tomorrow morning she would be alone again. When Jeffrey sailed she would be alone in New York or making her way to those unknown cousins in Boston. Neither place would be good. In New York she would be a ragged refugee scorned by the British navy captains as a rebel sympathizer and at the mercy of thieving sergeants of marines. In Boston she would be scorned as a "Tory lover" if she arrived with a letter signed by a British admiral. She might even be suspected as a spy. In any case she would be a lowly servant and nursemaid. At least Jeffrey and the *Phoebe* offered some safety. All of this came into her mind as a flash. She hadn't thought it through. Not only did she have little time for thinking but she had been afraid to think about the future.

"Could I sail with you?" she asked.

Jeffrey showed his surprise. "Would you want to? I mean with all your ideas about the justice of the American cause and all that."

"I don't know," was Elizabeth's frank admission. "I am just scared of starting all over again. I don't even know those cousins in Boston. My uncle wanted to send me there because there was nobody else to send me to. He has no room for me. He has his wife's two daughters to raise and his wife didn't like me. She wanted me bound out to a farmer as a field hand. That way I wouldn't have bothered her or him. Besides there is heavy fighting in Carolina what with Tarleton and his Tories riding and burning all over."

"And in Boston?"

"I don't know," Elizabeth repeated. "I suppose they are worthy people, coopers and carpenters. They have three children, little ones. They want me to take care of them and help around the house. I don't like taking care of small children." Elizabeth was thinking things out hard now. There was no one who would tell her what to do. Before now there had always been someone who told her what was the right thing. Now she was on her own. There was no father, no mother, no uncle to turn to for advice. Nobody.

"You know, Elizabeth." Jeffrey was also working things out as he went along. "This is a warship now with orders to capture, sink or destroy. That means we could be sunk, burned or captured ourselves as well. There might even be the matter of killing or being killed. Maybe I could send you to my family in England or you could stay here in New York." He stopped for a moment. "No, that is out. There is no telling whether I would ever get back to New York from where ever I am going. They haven't sent me my orders yet."

Elizabeth shook her head. "I'd rather go to Boston than go to your family alone. I would be a poor relation and I know how they are treated. They're just servants without the advantage of even being paid wages. No, that's no good. I guess it will have to be Boston and being a nursemaid if Admiral Gambier will give me that cartel you spoke about." Elizabeth's voice was flat. She would be a poor relation in Boston too, now that her hard money was gone. Hard money was scarce in the colonies and she had been given a considerable sum left over from the sale of the farm and their house. That money would have made her acceptable. That was all over and done with. She now knew she didn't want to go to Boston. She had made her decision what she wanted to do. "Jeffrey, what happens if I sail with you?" she repeated again.

"Just that. You would be on the *Phoebe*, sink or swim. Can't stay on forever of course. Sooner or later you would have to go ashore. It takes money to live ashore and you don't have any. I haven't much either. But it is dangerous to sail with me. I don't mean only battles. There are fevers and there is always the sea. Fevers are the worst. Some ships lose half of their crews to fevers in the West Indies or the African coast. There is scurvy too."

"There is smallpox in New York. I'll take my chances if you will let me."

"All right, but look here Elizabeth. If you sail with me you must remember that I am the captain. No arguments from you. You obey, on the jump if it comes to that. You behave yourself and keep your republican

ideas to yourself. You can talk to the petty officers as you have been doing.
No fraternizing with the crew in the forecastle. Understand?"

"It's that or Boston, isn't it?"

"Yes."

"Very well. Mr. Lieutenant Kent, meet Elizabeth Troyes, clerk on the
sloop *Phoebe*."

"His Brittanic Majesty's sloop *Phoebe*," Jeffrey was looking straight
at her.

"As you wish, sir. His Brittanic Majesty's sloop *Phoebe*." They shook
hands formally. It seemed the proper thing to do. Jeffrey suddenly
laughed. "I am going to have you sign the Articles. Nobody needs to know
that E. Troyes is a girl. You will be entitled to wages, rations and a share
of prize money if we capture any Rebel ships." Then he remembered.
"Sorry, that last remark was uncalled for. But it might happen anyway.
Yes, it will be a good thing if you sign the Articles of Enlistment like the
rest of the crew."

Jeffrey remembered that Captain Hartman had told him to use his
judgement in this matter and that he didn't want to hear anything more
about the matter. Well, Jeffrey Kent was using his judgement and Captain
Hartman needed to hear no more about the matter.

Smoke Of Battle

Orders came early the next morning. The papers were addressed to Jeffrey Kent, master and lieutenant. Jeffrey let Elizabeth read them over his shoulder. "You are hereby directed and required to proceed immediatly to the port of Halifax and return expeditiously." She didn't understand the next few paragraphs about recognition signals, rationing and some other matters but the last paragraph caught her attention. "For your information a French fleet including ships-of-the-line is rumored to be sailing northwards from the West Indies under the command of Admiral d'Guiche. Should you encounter any of the French units you are to use your judgement whether to engage or avoid and report." It was not going to be sailing to Europe, West Indies, India or Africa, all of them places where the British navy was engaged. America, anywhere in America, was at least partly familiar to Elizabeth. She was glad. She also remembered Jeffrey's warning that they were on a British warship with orders to capture, sink or destroy. Now there was a French fleet out with orders to capture, sink or destroy the ship she was on. Somehow she wasn't afraid of that.

Jeffrey went below to put the papers away. Then he checked that the tide was at ebb. He had three hours to get out of the harbor. The wind was favorable, coming out of the southwest. His orders rang out. "Mr. Lawton, prepare to make sail."

"All hands, all hands, stand by to make sail." Mr. Lawton had a fine bellow, loud enough to wake the dead. His shout was reinforced by Mr. Guerney's whistle. The crew came pouring up from below. Elizabeth noted that some of them were unsteady on their feet and caught the smell of liquor on their breath. Obviously Jeffrey's effort to keep liquor off the ship had not been wholly successful. Four hands put their backs into heaving on the windlass which hoisted the anchor. The cable was thick and the anchor too heavy to hoist by hand. Four more men wrestled the wet, heavy cable aft to the main hatch where it was lowered and coiled in two tiers under the onlop deck.

"Stand by at the fore sails." Mr. Guerney was standing there. "Now break her out." Mr. Guerney had a knotted rope in his hand to start up laggards. Jeffrey hoisted a string of signal flags which were answered by the flagship.

"Anchor clear," came the call from forward.

"Hoist the staysail. Up mainsail." The mainsail was a huge sheet of canvas but it rose steadily. "Belay halyards and sheet home." The *Phoebe* moved gracefully down the bay. Elizabeth was impressed by the speed with which sail had been set compared with the way it had been done when the *Phoebe* was a merchantman. The large crew and the way Mr. Guerney used the knotted rope in his hand may have had something to do with it but it was more than that, she thought. There was a pride and a joint purpose that had turned this body of men into a crew. Captain Abner had never done that.

"Mr. Lawton, the course is north by northeast. Set the jib and topsail. Elizabeth was surprise to see the sailors climbing up the shrouds to the top of the mast. A square sail blossomed there. That was something new. She hadn't paid attention to what the riggers were doing above deck. Now she saw that there was another smaller mast fitted to the top of the mainmast. The yard with the topsail was fitted to that. She now noted that there was an additional jib forward as well, put there since the *Phoebe* became a warship. She sailed differently too. The motion felt less like a tired rocking horse.

"Course is north by north-east, sir"

"Dismiss the watch below." Most of the sailors went down but a few stayed to watch the sea. Mr. McLeod went below as did Mr. Emmons. The wind was fresh and the bow wave gurgled underfoot. The *Phoebe* was swooping easily over the Atlantic rollers and the sun sparkled on the water. Elizabeth sent a grin over to Jeffrey. They both felt good. Both were glad to be clear of the city and Jeffrey was especially glad to be on his own with no superior officers on hand.

"I am glad I am not an oldest son," he told Elizabeth. "The oldest son gets the land, the house and all but he can't do this. Older sons have to worry about getting married right and producing heirs. They are responsible for the carrying on the family name. I have to make my own way but I have more freedom. Of course girls don't have those problems. They don't have to make their own way. All they have to do is avoid fortune hunters and marrying well." He grinned mischievously at Elizabeth. Here he felt free to tease her. Her own problems were about right now, not some future. She had nothing left to inherit anymore either.

There wasn't much writing to be done while they were at sea. Jeffrey kept the log himself. She had time to stand on deck and just watch the ocean. She tried to make friends with Mr. McLeod but found that he was not much of a talker. He had left his native island of Skye at the age of thirteen and gone to Glasgow to enlist in the navy. He had never looked back. Hull or Halifax, Cape Horn or Cape of Good Hope, Java or Jamaica were all the same to him. The navy was his home. He was content with his position as master's mate. He never would be a commissioned officer and "gentleman" and didn't want to be. Mr. Lawton was somewhat similar. She never did learn where he came from. She made friends with Mr. Guerney and Mr. Emmons, the cook. Despite Jeffrey's prohibition she also became friendly with Pat McManus, the cook's helper. He treated her like an older sister. Little John, who was listed on the ship's books as captain's servant, was too shy to be a friend. He almost worshipped her and tried to do little things for her. Perhaps he also thought of her as a sister.

The peaceful time came to an end on the second day. The shout came of "All hands, all hands, clear for action." The shout was reenforced by blasts from Mr. Guerney's whistle. Jeffrey was on the quarterdeck with his hat on and his sword at his side. He noticed Elizabeth behind him. "You are assistant surgeon's mate," he told her curtly. "Your station is below with Mr. Emmons." She had promised to obey so she went below. She would have preferred to stay on deck and watch. The cook had opened the medecine chest and laid out saws, forceps and knives. Bottles of alcohol and laudanum were set out on the wardroom table. Elizabeth had handled cuts and sprains on the farm but nothing really serious except her mother's illness. This looked different. She saw a pristine book lying in the chest.

"Can I look at this, Mr. Emmons?"

"Go ahead. Don't do me any good. Can't read nohow." The chapter headings sounded gruesome. "Fevers and fluxes, amputations, gangrene and festering wounds." The illustrations were worse than the chapter headings. Despite her shivers she decided she would have to read up on those things if she was going to be an assistant surgeon's mate as well as a clerk. She just hoped she would never have to really deal with these things. She read while listening to the clatter of the ship being cleared for action. She heard the rumble of the guns being run out but they did not fire them this time.

After two hours the command of "secure from quarters," rang out. "All hands muster abaft the mast." The command of all hands included her and Mr. Emmons so they went out on deck. She slipped the book into the front of her dress. She didn't think she belonged with Jeffrey and the two mates on the quarterdeck so she stood between Mr. Guerney and Mr. Emmons.

Jeffrey's voice was strong but he didn't shout. "That was badly done and you know it. You're sailors and not some green landsmen just brought aboard by the press. It took ten minutes to clear for action." The crew shifted uneasily. Words like that from the captain often meant floggings or at least deprivation of the rum ration. Young officers were especially liable to resort to the cat-of-nine-tails to reenforce their authority. "We'll do this again and again to get it right. Five minutes, no more, should be sufficient." Then his tone moderated. "Any enemy we meet will probably be bigger with heavier guns. So we will be faster and better. This ship has no room for losers. We'll probably burn some powder too. That's so you learn to lay the guns accurately at long range. We can't rely on weight of metal to overwhelm an enemy. That's for frigates and ships-of-the-line." The crew gave Jeffrey a cheer when he ended, as much from relief that there were no punishments than anything else. Then they were dismissed.

Jeffrey and the two mates discussed the problem of possible action over the dinner table as well. "With all due respect, sir," Mr. McLeod opened the discussion, "you aren't going to do much good with that pig sticker you carry. You're too light for sword work. If we are ever board to board with an enemy you should carry a pistol. So should Miss Troyes here, Mr. Emmons and the two boys. That's a quarter of our total crew and we would need them. That's especially true in a close action. They should be able to hit what they aim at too. I can rig up a target to use after our guns have had their say."

"Very well. You are our gunnery officer, Mr. McLeod. Make it so."

Elizabeth found that she enjoyed pistol practice and was quite a good shot. So were Jeffrey and Little John. Mr. McLeod had found some short barreled pistols in the arms chest for her and the boys. Mr. McLeod had his own rifled double barreled pistol. He seldom missed the bulls eye with it. Mr. Emmons and Jeffrey used the standard sized weapons. Despite the fact that the target was man-shaped Elizabeth never thought that she was practicing killing. To her it was a sport like horseback riding.

Jeffrey seemed to be wrapped up in himself these days. He was disinclined to speak of anything but duty matters. Elizabeth remarked on it to Mr. Guerney.

"He's the captain, Miss Elizabeth. All the responsibility is on him. What sails to hoist, what course to sail, drill, rewards and punishments and when to serve dinner, the decision is always his."

"But he is only a boy," she objected.

"Age don't matter, not in the navy. He is in charge, all alone. Some officers can't take the loneliness. They take to drink or turn vicious like chained dogs. Him, he'll do. I've seen his kind before. The men will follow him."

With that Elizabeth had to be content. When Jeffrey did want to talk she would walk with him on the quarterdeck, back and forth, sixteen feet each way. The quartermaster at the tiller and perhaps some of the sailors would be on the quarterdeck too but that was all the privacy there was. As on all warships everybody left the weather side free for the captain to walk. At meals she talked to Mr. Guerney or the mates. The rest of the time she sat on deck or watched Mr. Emmons in the galley cook the simple meals. She also studied the medical manual. There was sail drill and gun drill and the continous cleaning and polishing that a ship required. Mr. Guerney explained that in the navy not only was cleanliness next to godliness, it kept the equipment from rusting and the wood from rotting.

Elizabeth had established a special relationship with the boatswain ever since he had gotten her miniature back for her. Now he was her guide in all naval matters. He had explained the question of rank to her. Commissioned officers were addressed by their rank and "sir." Petty officers rated a "mister" in front of their names and hands were addressed by their last names or a simple "hey you." Ship commanders, even if they were lowly acting lieutenants, were always addressed as "captain" and their words were the law from on high.

The voyage took eighteen days. They passed over the Grand Banks with their riches of cod but they didn't do any fishing. Jeffrey's orders had said "expeditiously" and he took that seriously. Besides Mr. Emmons explained to her that the men hated being served fish instead of their salt beef or pork. They didn't see any fishing boats but as she found out on the *Phoebe* under Captain Abner, no merchant ship wanted to meet anything that even looked like a warship. Elizabeth also noted that as they travelled northwards fall advanced and it was getting colder. Soon her linen dress and a cloak wouldn't be warm enough.

Mr. Guerney was also watching the weather. "It's near the equinox, September 21. With the equinox we will be getting storms out of the north-east, like as not. Elizabeth realized that September 21 was also her birthday. She was now all of thirteen years old.

Despite Mr. Guerney's prediction of storms they sailed up Chebacco Bay to Halifax in brilliant sunshine. There were a number of warships as well as merchantmen in the harbor, she noted, as they tied up at the dockyard.

Halifax was a garrison town despite the large number of refugees, the occasional French Quebecquois and Indian. Elizabeth was surprised by the large number of Blacks, many of them speaking in the accents of Carolina and Virginia. She heard that since Britain had abolished slavery, the Blacks preferred the government of the crown to that of the American colonists. This was despite their declaration of equal rights for all men. It gave Elizabeth something to think about. At the moment however she was more concerned about the state of her clothing than about politics. The dress she had on most of the time was showing signs of wear and the dress she kept for more formal occasions wasn't suitable for shipboard. Borrowing some money from Jeffrey, an advance against her wages he called it, she went shopping. She looked at the copies of the London fashions but didn't buy them. She had seen similar things in New York. She also didn't want the fancy dresses refugees offered her from their former wealth. They were also not suitable for shipboard. She needed something practical.

Jeffrey was horrified when she showed off her purchases to him. A wool lined buckskin jacket decorated with moosehair embroidery and a simple blue dress set off with a colorful sash was not his idea of what a lady should wear. "I am not going to a ball," she explained. "This is an American frontier outfit. It is warm, can be brushed off easily and won't tear."

"But it looks strange. You could never wear it in London."

"This isn't London. It will do well aboard ship or in New York. After all I can't wear sailor's trousers out of the slop chest."

Jeffrey wasn't convinced. He had to admit though that aboard the *Phoebe* without servants and with only a gallon of fresh water a day, silk was not practical. After all he wore seaman's trousers and not his dress uniform on board.

Jeffrey had other problems as well. He had delivered his dispatches to the local admiral or rather to his assistant. He had been told that he would get dispatches to take back to New York plus a load of firewood and ship timbers. However since the *Phoebe* was part of the New York squadron, the Halifax commander saw no reason to supply the *Phoebe* with fresh provisions even for their stay in port. "Nova Scotia is a poor province, lieutenant, and the only food we get locally is fish. Wood we have in plenty, but practically everything else comes by convoy from Britain, just like yours in New York," Jeffrey sent Mr. Emmons to the local market. He wasn't going to serve his men salt pork while in port. Mr. Emmons came back with fresh onions, carrots and turnips. He had also arranged with a local farmer to slaughter a cow or two sheep a day for the *Phoebe*. The locals had also reccomended "jerky", dried and smoked strips of venison or beef, to add to the traditional pea soup of the navy. Pat, who had accompanied Mr. Emmons, found a dealer in West Indian goods who sold sugar, spices, coffee and limes for juice that was served out to crews to prevent scurvy. Those things, together with a tub of fresh butter and rasberry jam in jugs completed the purchases. They weren't much but then Jeffrey had not been able to draw much money from the paymaster in New York.

They spent a week in Halifax. Load after load of firewood was delivered to the ship as was a deck cargo of ship's spars. The *Phoebe* was not long enough to carry the tall logs used for masts. He was also given a barrelful of live lobsters to be given to Admiral Arbuthnoth. The deck cargo prevented Jeffrey from shipping some live sheep for slaughtering while they would be under way. That was usually what had been done on the *Amazon*.

There were plenty of longshoremen available so Jeffrey was able to give some shore leave to the hands. Some would probably come back drunk but there was no place they could desert to. Everyone in Halifax was too afraid of the shore patrols to give shelter to deserters. The refugee camps didn't shelter deserters either and beyond Halifax there were only the deep woods.

For Elizabeth Halifax was a vacation. Her clerical work took only two hours a day. Being a relative of an earl proved to be a powerful talisman for her. She and Jeffrey were invited to dinner by the local admiral. Sir Parker was a gourmet and she was served lobster for the first time. She wasn't sure she liked the dish. It was sort of slithery especially when it was served cold with mayonnaise. The rest of the meal was good though and she found that she could drink one glass of wine without getting sick. Jeffrey had a harder head. He not only had wine with dinner but was served brandy after the ladies had retired from the dining room and the table cloth had been removed. The ladies, wives of officers and Tories, accepted Elizabeth as one of themselves. No one asked her political opinions or about the details of her past life. The men talked about the progress of the war and their chances of advancement. Their toast was "to a bloody war and a sickly season."

The weather was still beautiful when they left Halifax. The trees along the shore were a blaze of color where they were touched by the sun. On the third day out the weather began to change. A thin haze covered the sun and it set like a brass ball sinking into a gray-green sea. "Storm coming," was Mr. Lawton's laconic comment.

"Barometer been dropping," Jeffrey answered. "Guess we had better shorten sail." The outer jib was hauled down and orders given to reef the mainsail if the wind increased. Mr. Lawton cast anxious eyes at that big mainsail. "I would suggest getting all the easting we can while we can, sir. We need all the sea room we can get with a rocky shore under our lee. The rebels hold all the harbors around here as well." Jeffrey nodded. He wanted to be further east so as to give Nantucket and Cape Cod a wide berth. His map showed many sandbanks and sandbanks had a habit of shifting. He also wanted to avoid the privateers sailing out of Salem and Boston. The *Phoebe* was supposed to be a dispatch vessel, not a fighting cruiser. Besides she had cargo aboard.

Mr. Lawton gave the necessary orders to shift course. The wind was shifting too, blowing now out of the northeast. Elizabeth felt the uneasy motion of the ship as it began its clawing to the windward. The waves seemed to be bigger as they swept against the starboard bow. Occasionally the top of one came over the bow and drained out again through the scuppers. The wind blew spray over the quarterdeck. She went down for supper.

"Eat all you can," Mr. McLeod told her. "A full stomach is the best preventative for sea sickness."

"I know you haven't been sick yet but a big storm can unsettle anyone," Mr. Lawton added. "Besides, in heavy weather, we put out the fires. Then it's cold food until it quiets down again." Elizabeth was surprised and pleased by the talk. Up to now neither of the men had shown any concern for her as a person. She wasn't afraid of the coming storm and she liked the attention from the two mates.

After supper Elizabeth took her cloak and went back on deck. The wind was stronger and the mainsail was being double reefed. Jeffrey was standing by the tiller but she didn't want to bother him. Mr. Guerney was supervising the double lashing of the guns. He saw her standing there with the cloak fluttering uncomfortably around her. "You have a waterproof and a southwester?" he asked her.

Elizabeth shook her head. "This cloak is pretty waterproof."

"Now, miss, you better come along with me and we will fit you out proper. And see that you are holding on to something at all times now. A good cap of wind would pick up a lightweight like you and you would be over the side before anyone would see you go. Not that they could do anything if they did see you go. You'd freeze to death in this water before you could drown." He led her forward and down the companion way. Mindful of Jeffrey's orders, she had never been in the crew's quarters. Hammocks swayed in the semi-darkness filled with the sleeping bodies of the watch below. A few sailors sat on the forecastle floor playing cards with a greasy deck. It smelled of unwashed bodies and stale tobacco smoke. The men nodded to her as she came down behind Mr. Guerney. The bosun's locker was all the way in the bows. Mr. Guerney rummaged in it and drew out a tarpaulin. Using a knife he cut off a piece of it and then used his sailors needle and a rope to tighten it so she could use it as a collar. Another rope served as a belt. A southwester, a wide-brimmed hat with a chin strap came out of another chest. Elizabeth put them on and thought she looked like a candle snuffer. "There that will keep you dry and the weight won't let it blow loose either. Put it over the blanket when you are not using it. The deck will leak like as not."

"Thank you, Mr. Guerney. Won't Mr. Kent object you using ship's stores like this?"

"Captain won't mind. He'd probably ordered it himself if he had thought of it. It just slipped his mind. He's worried, this being his first command and he being so young like."

Elizabeth heard the watch being called to shorten sail during the night. While she lay awake she felt the waves pounding the bow of the *Phoebe*. The ship rolled so much that she nearly fell out of her hammock. She was only held in by the restraining rope that went across her body. The hammock swayed so much that she almost hit the wall but whoever hung her hammock knew his business. She never quite banged into anything.

Her clothes swung from their hooks in rhythm with the hammock. In the morning she tripped painfully when the ship climbed over an extra large wave. Walking was difficult. Breakfast consisted of water with a bit of lime juice squeezed into it and hardtack. The sailors didn't call it that for nothing. It looked and tasted like old, hard cardboard. Elizabeth was glad her teeth were good and took small bites. She was also glad that she had seen to it that the *Phoebe's* food was fairly fresh. There were only a few weevils in the biscuit. The mates assured her that the hardtack was often full of them. They simply rapped it on the corner of the table to convince the bugs to leave. Elizabeth overcame her distaste. There was nothing else to do and nothing else to eat. As Mr. Lawton had warned her, the cooking fires had been put out. Fire was always a risk on a wooden ship. Holding on with one hand she made her way topside. She needed the fresh air. A wild scene met her eye. Giant waves, each more than twenty feet high and a hundred feet long threatened to sweep over the little sloop. The wind was blowing spindrift off the top of the waves into her eyes. Green water was often coming over the bow. The *Phoebe* climbed over each wave painfully and creaking. Elizabeth held tightly to the rail as she climbed up to the quarterdeck. Once there, she braced herself against one of the swivel guns so the wind couldn't blow her away. The wind also made each rope hum to add to the noise of the storm itself. Talking was difficult so she contented herself with a smile and a nod for Jeffrey and Mr. Lawton. She noted that tiller tackles were rigged and there were more than the usual one man at the tiller. As the spray blew against her body she appreciated Mr. Guerney's concern for her. The tarpaulin kept her partly dry and its weight prevented it from turning into a sail. The officers were all wearing oilskins and southwesterns too. Only a bit of one jib was showing but she could see Mr. Lawton pointing to it. Then the sailing master's voice bellowed above the storm calling for all hands and something about heaving to. There was a rush of sailors coming up barefooted from below. Nobody was getting much sleep anyway. A bit of the mainsail rose and the tiller was put over, Jeffrey helping. For a moment it looked as if the *Phoebe* was going over on its side but it came upright again. The sloop now faced directly into the wind. The sail came down again and was lashed tight. The motion was even wilder than before but Elizabeth could no longer feel the waves pounding the bow. Jeffrey came over to her, balancing himself on the rolling deck.

"Can't fight the wind anymore. She'll ride easier now but we are drifting. Can't take a sight in this either to check where we are."

Elizabeth nodded. She didn't understand the words but she wanted to encourage Jeffrey. She didn't know how long she stood there being pounded by the storm. Thinking was as hard as talking. She finally went below, walking slowly and carefully. In her cabin she stripped off her dripping tarpaulin and after it had dried a bit laid it over her blanket. Mr. Guerney had been right again. The deck did leak.

The storm lasted two days. It seemed forever to Elizabeth. She tried sleeping in her hammock but the motion was too wild. She drowsed rather than slept, rousing herself only to eat the unappetizing meals. She remembered Mr. McLeod's warning about keeping the stomach full and forced herself to down the cold salt meat and porridge. Jeffrey and the two mates hardly left the deck during the storm. She wondered how they could take it. Pat brought in a sailor with a gashed arm while the storm was blowing. Elizabeth managed to sew up the deep gash using a black silk thread from her sewing box. She didn't want to open the medecine chest and Mr. Emmons was busy. That the thread was black didn't seem to matter. She was so tired that she didn't even think about the fact that she was sewing up human flesh. It was simply something that had to be done. She did rouse herself to get some rum out of the wardroom locker to clean the wound. The sailor didn't moan when the raw alcohol touched the wound. He thanked Elizabeth politely when she was done. She didn't know whether that was for sewing him up or for the tot of rum she let him have after. She was too tired to care. She didn't even care whether the *Phoebe* floated or sank. She just endured the tiredness, the wild motion and the constant noise.

When the storm blew itself out she slept for eight solid hours. She woke refreshed and very hungry. The sun was shining again although the waves were still high. Everyone looked cheerful, even Mr. McLeod and Mr. Lawton. The men nodded to her when they passed. She didn't know whether that was because of the assistant surgeon's mate work she had done or just because they had come through the storm together. She was even a bit proud of herself. She hadn't been sea sick once.

"Were you afraid?" Jeffrey asked her when they had a chance to talk.

Elizabeth thought it over. "No, the storm was so big and powerful one couldn't be afraid of it. Awed," she added slowly, "might be a better description."

Jeffrey laughed. "You'll make a good sailor. There are some people who like gales and the exitement. I don't, particularly when I am in command. I just want to get it over with."

The wind had shifted again and was now blowing out of the south. That made it dead foul for Jeffrey to make a straight run for New York. He had to tack or zig-zag to make any progress at all. Elizabeth didn't mind. She wasn't in a rush to get anywhere. She had a place to sleep, food to eat and work she was able and willing to do. The company was pleasant enough. Some of it was more than pleasant. She smiled to herself as she thought of Jeffrey. She had gotten used to ship time with its bells and watches instead of hours. The days flowed into each other. She was usually up at dawn to watch the sun rise before going down for breakfast. That's why she was on deck in the morning when she heard the lookout's cry of "Sail Ho!"

"Where away?" Mr. McLeod was officer of the deck and grabbed his telescope.

"About three miles off the port bow. Lugger by the looks of her."

Now it was light enough for Elizabeth to see the other ship from the deck. It's sails looked strange, like they were on a tilt. She saw them swing around.

"She's coming about," came the hail from the masthead.

Jeffrey was already on deck with his jacket hastily thrown over his night clothes. He had been on deck for the middle watch. He cursed as he examined the other ship through the telescope he had taken from Mr. McLeod. "Frenchman. We don't use luggers around here and the Yankees don't either. He has the weather gauge on us so he can either fight or run. Clear for action, if you please, Mr. McLeod and put us on the starboard tack. I want all the sea room we can get."

He raced below as Mr. McLeod turned up all hands and came back shortly fully dressed. Jeffrey saw that he had no options if the Frenchman wanted to fight. The enemy had the weather gauge and luggers were usually faster than merchant sloops like the use the *Phoebe* had been built for. At least the two ships were about the same size. The strangers sails came around again and he matched the *Phoebe*'s move. "He's going to fight."

The mates shouts and Mr. Guerney's whistle had turned the sloop into a disturbed ants nest. The deck load of spars went overboard and the admiral's barrel of lobsters followed. Mr. McLeod spat after the spars as they were heaved over. "Hope no one runs into them. They'll go through a side like a lance. Sink them sure."

Sailors were bringing up arms chests and stacking pistols, boarding pikes and cutlasses around the mast. Jeffrey went over and picked up a pistol that went into his waistband. John and Pat were bringing up gun charges and stacking pyramids of cannon balls by the guns. There were buckets of water by each gun to wet the swabs for the guns and to fight fires. Mr. Emmons was spreading sand on the deck for a better foot hold before going below.

Jeffrey looked over the placement of his men. They were too few for muskets and even to handle the swivels. Mr. Lawton took the tiller. Mr. Guerney and three sailors were available to handle the sails. Three men instead of the usual four were available for the guns if he only manned one side. It was silly to call two guns a broadside, Jeffrey thought to himself. The two boys and Elizabeth were too light to handle any of the ropes and he had no reserves to replace casualties. As Mr. McLeod had said in New York, it was a scratch crew but at least these weren't green hands. They would give a good account of themselves.

Mr. McLeod touched his hat to Jeffrey. "Ship cleared for action, sir. Five minutes and thirty six seconds."

"Very well." Jeffrey touched his hat in turn. "Keep the gunports closed and the men behind the bulwarks. No sense letting that Frenchman see what we have but load all the guns with ball, both port and starboard."

Jeffrey knew that this was what his years of training had been about. He was being given his chance and he had to seize it. Every officer in the British navy dreamed of getting a chance like this, of being in command in a ship-to-ship action. Now he, Jeffrey Kent, midshipman with an acting-lieutenants commission and all of fourteen years old, was being tested. If he won he would be hailed by the entire navy. If he lost, he and his family would be shamed and all his associates would discard him. Also if he lost, naval regulations demanded that he be court martialed. If the judges at the court martial decided that he hadn't done his utmost he would be shot. They had shot Admiral Byng for that. The fact that he was risking his life didn't matter. The lives of his crew, including Elizabeth, didn't matter either. He had to win, cost what it may.

Jeffrey seized his telescope again and looked over his foe. There was a gleam of gold at the foreshrouds, probably a bronze long gun of some sort. The rest of the armaments didn't look like much of a muchness: swivels to throw scatter shot and probably lots of muskets. A privateer or a letter-of-marque, a merchant ship equipped to fight, rather than a regular warship, but a formidable foe for all that. A crew larger than his too. Some of those luggers carried thirty to fifty men.

Elizabeth looked at the lugger too. She hadn't expected to be in a battle and now she was going to be. She looked along the deck as cooly as if she was appraising a harvest crew on the farm. She too saw that they were short of men. She had been told that there were to be four men at each gun in normal practice and she saw only three.

"She's head reaching on us," came Mr. Lawton's calm voice. "Closing too."

"Very well," came Jeffrey's answer. "The closer the better. We can't do much with our six pounder pop guns except at close range." Elizabeth could see him walking about. He glanced upwards. "Loosen the topsail, Mr. Guerney. We need more speed."

"Aye, aye, sir." Two sailors raced up the shrouds to loosen the square sail. The *Phoebe* pounded harder into the waves.

Jeffrey saw Elizabeth standing by the rail. He had been too busy before this watching the Frenchman to see her. "I've got to fight. Outgunned or outmanned, I've got to fight. We have a hostile shore under our lee if I tried to run. Besides I've got my orders to capture, sink or destroy. I can't put your safety above my duty. You know that, don't you?"

Elizabeth swung around so he could see the pistol she had stuck in her sash. She had carefully seen to the loading and priming too. "You told me that I could stay aboard the *Phoebe*, sink or swim. Well, here I am."

His face cleared. "Even though that ship is on the side of the Rebels?"

Elizabeth laughed. She was scared but she still saw the situation as funny. "I can just see myself yelling across to the Frenchman that I am an ally, with me standing behind a cannon at a mile range."

"Very well. Your station is below. Go there. At least you will be safe from musket balls and I think we will soon be in musket range."

"But I want to see. It's worse if you can't see."

"Your station is below. We need you there."

Elizabeth didn't want to go below. She didn't like enclosed spaces at the best of times. Being below, hearing but not being able to see would be bad. She didn't want to think what she meant by bad. It was too frightening. But she had given her word when she had signed the Articles that she was part of the crew and her word was good, she decided quickly.

"Men, that Frenchy wants to give us a bit of prize money. Let's go get him." Jeffrey was answered by a cheer from the fourteen men on deck. The spirit on the *Phoebe* was high enough. Jeffrey concentrated his attention on the lugger, his eyes narrowed. He now had turned into a fighting machine where the crew were just parts of the fighting strength.

If he tacked now he might get behind the Frenchman so that the Frenchman's gun wouldn't bear and the *Phoebe*'s would. He sprang for the shrouds. "Hands to wear ship. Mr. Guerney, put her on the port tack."

"Port tack, aye, aye." The hands sprang for the lines that controlled the sails. Mr. Lawton put the tiller over and Jeffrey sprang to help him. The prow of the *Phoebe* now pointed at the lugger's stern. The French captain didn't want the sloop at his stern where her guns could rake his ship from bow to stern. He followed Jeffrey's maneuver. That put the ships closer to each other. Suddenly a gun boomed from the lugger and a fountain rose out of the water not twenty yards from the *Phoebe*.

"A nine pounder. He outranges us."

"He's got only that one long gun on his forecastle. The rest is nothing. Our guns outweigh his if we can only close." Jeffrey's response was quick. "Hoist our colors. Let him see who we are." Elizabeth saw the ensign rise to the gaff. It was the white ensign of the British navy, not the red one of the merchant service. It was answered by the French flag of the golden lilies on a white field. There was another shot and a hole appeared in the mainsail. The Frenchman was firing high to cripple rather than to sink his enemy. The Frenchman fired a third time but there was no answer from the *Phoebe*. Jeffrey was holding his fire until he was in effective range. He wanted to hit back properly. Elizabeth remembered that even at gunnery practice the *Phoebe*'s gunners had not been able to hit at anything like the present range. They would be under fire for a while before hitting back. She went back into the wardroom. Her help might be needed there.

She nearly tripped over a bucket when she came into the dim light from the bright deck. "What is that thing doing there?" It hadn't been there when she had gone on deck.

"We don't want loose legs rolling about when we amputate," Pat told her, grinning. He didn't mind teasing Elizabeth. "The bucket will hold them." Mr. Emmons was methodically laying out bandages, knives and saws. The dining table had been covered by an oiled cloth and had now become an operating table. There were pallets laid down around the walls of the room to lay out the wounded. Elizabeth could do nothing except wait. The Frenchman's long gun boomed out again and again. There was a sound like a dog crunching a bone. "Hulled us that time. Now that he knows we are a warship he is trying to sink us. Must have thought we were a coastal merchant sloop and easy game." Mr. Emmons and Pat went out to check for wounded, leaving Elizabeth alone. Twice more she heard the enemy cannon boom. Then she saw Pat helping a bloody figure aft. A splinter had laid open the man's arm. Elizabeth helped Mr. Emmons sew and bandage. The man went back outside. It wasn't considered a disabling wound. Another man came in with a large splinter sticking out from his thigh. They took it out with forceps and bandaged. Elizabeth remembered being told that wooden splinters were as dangerous as cannon balls. Suddenly a rumbling sound filled the cabin. The *Phoebe's* guns were being run out. They thundered, the Frenchman's cannon boomed. Acrid powder smoke began to fill the cabin and set Elizabeth coughing. She saw Pat trying to drag a man in and went out to help. The deck was a wild scene. The lugger was a lot closer now. There was noise and smoke from the guns. The crackle of French muskets cut through the booming of the cannons. Elizabeth saw a dead sailor laid out next to the mast while she was helping Pat drag the man with a crushed foot in. Mr. Emmons was right there, tied on a tourniquet and prepared to amputate. That was the only treatment available for such an injury. Elizabeth worked automatically. Her eyes saw the horrors but her mind refused to record them. Pat staggered in. A musket ball had made a mess of his shoulder. She tried to stop the bleeding with pads and tight bandaging but she remembered all too well the illustration in the manual showing all the blood vessels that ran through the shoulder. Pat's face was gray but he was still trying to grin. Then he asked for some water and she held the dipper to his lips and wiped the sweat of shock off his face. There was a crash and a smacking sound behind her. A cannon ball had come through the side of the ship and smashed Mr. Emmons against the opposite wall. One glance showed Elizabeth that there was nothing she could do for him. Then another horrifying thought hit her. She was the only medic left on her feet and she knew so little. She only knew what she had read in that manual and the little nursing she had done on the farm. She started to go outside for help when she realized that there was nobody to help her.

Jeffrey saw that the high quarterdeck was protecting him and Mr. Lawton from the French musket fire. It was higher than the deck of the lugger. On the main deck he was losing his crew to both cannon fire and musketry. Mr. McLeod and Mr. Guerney were taking the place of men shot down at the guns. The two boys were gone too. He would have to get Mr. Emmons to help at a gun and Elizabeth to carry powder. Just then a lucky shot from one of his guns brought down the foremast of the lugger. The sail brought the head of the Frenchman around like a sea anchor and also masked the big gun.

"Grape," he yelled, "a load of grape to sweep that deck." Mr. McLeod just had time to fire one load of grape shot when someone on the lugger saw that their situation was hopeless. They couldn't clear the wreckage under fire from the *Phoebe's* guns. Down came the flag with the golden lilies on a run. The British navy had won another engagement.

Elizabeth still had her head out of the gangway door when she heard Jeffrey yell something. Then she saw the lugger swing around helplessly. The whole battle seemed a nightmare to her, a nightmare that would never end. She went back inside when she realized that the guns had stopped firing. She heard the crew screaming like hungry panthers. Jeffrey on the quarterdeck was screaming too. So he was still alive, she noted dully. Mr. Guerney came in, his head bloody with a dirty rag wrapped around it. Elizabeth removed the rag, bandaged and stitched. "What happened?" she asked.

"We took her. Smashed her foremast and that masked her long gun and she struck. French letter-of-marque named *Nymphe.* We're alongside and Mr. Lawton is taking posession now." He went back outside.

Elizabeth didn't care about winning. She was glad the battle had ended but Pat was dying. His eyes were closed and his breathing was uneven. As she went over to his pallet his last breath went out with a sigh. Mr. Guerney had said something about prize money for all so the wounded were trying to cheer. She gave everybody a tot of rum. It was a stimulant and might help temporarily and that would be good.

A while later, a good long while, Elizabeth heard the cry of "Sail Ho." She didn't care anymore about what would happen to her, to Jeffrey or to the *Phoebe.* Her world was reduced to the wardroom. Jeffrey came in. His voice was elaboratly formal. "What are our casualties, Miss Troyes?"

Cold formality was the only support Jeffrey had left. The crew had cheered him. They expected him to act like an officer and gentleman so he couldn't just crawl into a corner and howl. He had seen the price of victory. He had seen the sodden bundle that had been the hard working Mr. Emmons. He had seen the sweat slicked face of George Sullivan who would never walk properly again. He had seen the gray faced corpse of Pat McManus who wanted to grow up to become a real sailor. Yet the crew, many of them with bloody bandages themselves, had cheered him.

Then there was his cousin Elizabeth. He saw her in that stinking wardroom with her arms covered to the elbows with blood. He had also seen her on the open deck, disregarding the musket bullets and cannon balls, dragging the wounded to shelter. She certainly had not done that for the glory of the British navy. She probably hadn't done it for him either. She had done it because she had given her word to be part of the crew and they needed her help. And he had promised to protect her. He would remember that. She had kept her word. He hadn't.

Her voice cut through his thoughts. "I have four badly wounded here, sir. I would like to have some help to carry out the two who have died."

"Very well. The *Amazon* is coming up. Soon you will have a surgeon to assist you." He went out again but Mr. Guerney came in with two sailors. They lifted the corpse of Mr. Emmons, Mr. Guerney took the body of Pat McManus and they carried them out. Elizabeth checked the remaining wounded. She knew that one of them would surely die. He had been hit in the abdomen and there was no cure for that. The other three, including the man with the amputated foot, would probably recover. When the surgeon from the *Amazon* came in he showed no surprise to find a girl in charge.

"I will have the wounded transferred to the sick bay of the frigate. We have better facilities there. You can rest now, miss. You might want to wash up a bit first." Elizabeth looked down. Her feet and her arms were covered with blood. She had kicked off her shoes so as to have a better grip on the bare planks. The front of her dress was all bloody as well. She staggered to her cabin. The partitions hadn't been put up yet but someone had provided a bucket of water and rehung her hammock. She did manage to clean her hands and feet before falling into her hammock and being drowned in the blackness of exhausted sleep. She didn't even dream of anything.

Mr. Guerney's voice roused her some hours later. She staggered as she tried to rise. "Easy, miss." His arm supported her. He picked up the pistol she had dropped on the floor. "You won't be needing this anymore." Then he answered the question she had never asked. "I have a daughter back in England about your age. I would be proud if she did as well as you did." Then he dropped back into his role as boatswain. "We will hold funeral service in a few minutes. The captain said to wake you and that he would appreciate it if you were on deck." Elizabeth managed to strip off her dress and put on her new one and the buckskin jacket before appearing in public. She had managed to learn to dress very quickly. On deck she was surprised to see the *Amazon* near by with her sails any which way, cock-a-bill it was called. Her sailors were lining the rail. A boat was coming over with Captain Hartman's gold braid flashing in the sun. He was received with the honors due to a captain. A lieutenant and four sailors followed him. Then the *Phoebe*'s crew was called to attention. Elizabeth lined up next to Mr. Guerney. She didn't think she belonged on quarterdeck with Captain Hartman and the other officers. There were seven shrouded bodies by the hatchway, two smaller than the others. She didn't need to ask who the small ones were. She knew that the powder monkeys, the small boys carrying cartridges to the guns on the open deck, were good targets for the enemy muskets. The gunners were shielded to a certain extent by the bulwarks and the rolled up hammocks. Elizabeth's mind recorded the facts. Her emotions had frozen.

So that would be all that there would be to these boys lives. From the poor house to the navy and now slid into the sea with a cannon ball at their feet so they would sink. She promised herself that somehow she would make it up to Pat. To little John too. Jeffrey read the burial service in a clear voice and then the bodies slid into the sea, one after the other. She made another horrifying discovery. There were only eight men of the *Phoebe*'s crew standing at attention. They had sailed with nineteen. Many of those who were left wore bandages too.

"That's all that is left of us?" she whispered to Mr. Guerney.

"Four with Mr. Lawton over on the *Nymphe*, as prize crew." His chin indicated the French lugger. There the British flag flew over the golden lillies. That meant that half of the crew of the *Phoebe* were casualties, she realized.

The men were dismissed back to their work. Captain Hartman and his men returned to their ship and the small flotilla set sail. *Phoebe* was in the lead, followed by the *Nymphe* with the *Amazon* in the rear should a ship of force be needed. She had hoisted the broad pennant on her main mast that indicated that her captain was a commodore in command of other ships besides his own. He gave orders to the other ships by flag signals.

Captain Hartman had spoken to Elizabeth. "I have suggested to Mr. Kent that he mention you in his dispatch to the Admiralty. It will look well in the *Naval Chronicle*. Officially there will be no mention that E. Troyes is a girl but the navy will know. It is not every day that a woman rescues casualties from the open deck under fire. Or for that matter that she is under fire at all instead of hiding in the cable tier."

"Pat McManus died doing the same thing."

"That was his duty. It wasn't really yours."

Someone had managed to get the galley fire started. There was pea soup and corned beef for a midday meal. Elizabeth ate without tasting anything. She was very concious of the raw wood board nailed over the hole where the cannon ball that had killed Mr. Emmons had entered. The wardroom floor had been scrubbed clean of blood but despite the open stern windows the smell of blood and death still lingered. It was no better on deck. Raw wood had repaired smashed bulwarks and holystones had smoothed out the gouges and splinters. The old mainsail had been lowered to patch the holes made by the cannon shot and a new mainsail bent to the gaff and mast hoops. In another day the ship would look normal.

Jeffrey called her below for paper work. There was always paper work to do, but right now both of them were glad to have something to concentrate on: reports on the expenditure of powder and shot, bosun stores used, casualty lists and new watch bills. The report on the battle needed fair copies. Elizabeth stopped short when she came to the last paragraph. "Acting surgeon E. Troyes rescued wounded from the open deck under fire. Her conduct has my total approbation."

"Is that necessary?"

Jeffrey nodded. "Captain Hartman also told me that the glorious battle was in the best tradition of the British navy. I got a third of my crew killed," he added bitterly. "Besides there is the matter of prize money."

"Prize money?"

"Yes. According to the regulations the winners get to divide the value of the capture plus five pounds for each enemy killed or captured. The captain gets two eights, the lieutenants get an eight to divide between them, the petty officers get an eight and the men get an eighth. The commanding admiral gets an eighth. As an acting surgeon you get a petty officers share instead of the pittance the hands get."

"Mr. Emmons?"

"A petty officer's share as the cook. He wouldn't get a penny more if he was acting surgeon as well. And the *Amazon* wasn't in sight when the Frenchman struck so we get to divide the whole prize. That's the way the navy works. It's better than the way the army does things. They loot. They also sell commissions, sometimes to incompetents or young boys. We don't." Mr. Guerney added another shock to Elizabeth.

"Captain, sir. John James and Patrick McManus told me that if anything happened to them they wanted their wage and share to go to Miss Troyes here. They had no relatives, either of them. On the poor rates before they joined."

"Very well. I will enter it into the log. I will require you to sign as well."

"I'll make my mark. Never did learn to write. I'm no scholar." The trip to New York took another five days. It wasn't a pleasant voyage. Jeffrey kept wondering whether it wouldn't have been better for him to run rather than fight. Elizabeth couldn't help him. She had her own troubles. She saw and smelled the carnage in her mind's eye every time she entered the wardroom. She was glad it hadn't been her decision to make whether to fight or run. Jeffrey's decision affected many. So far all the decisions she had made affected only her.

She was now considered a full member of the crew. Even Mr. McLeod included her in the casual conversation. At the Sunday inspection she stood with the men but she ate her plum duff with Jeffrey. Their relations had changed as well. He now considered her his equal instead of someone he had to protect. Of course he still issued her orders but they were as a member of the crew, not as a younger relative.

When they got to New York they were told that the *Phoebe* would be temporarily taken out of service while she was being rebuilt as a schooner and had her bottom scraped free of sea weed and barnacles. That would take a while. Meanwhile that meant they couldn't stay aboard but would have to find quarters ashore. Jeffrey was also worried about his position. Captain Hartman had reclaimed the entire crew of the *Phoebe* for the *Amazon* but he had no room for an acting-lieutenant. Jeffrey didn't want to return as a midshipman where he would face the jealousy of the rest of the midshipmen's berth. To return would also mean that there would be no chance for him to command the *Phoebe* when she was returned to service and there would be no place for Elizabeth. Elizabeth was glad. She wanted to leave the *Phoebe* which now had so many bad memories for her.

They did have some money. The paymaster had released their wages and an advance on the prize money. The admiral had pressed for a quick sale of the *Nymphe* so he could collect his share of the prize money. Jeffrey had nearly seventeen hundred pounds due. Much of this was his captain's share of the capture of the *Nymphe* and the rest was the midshipman's share of the captures the *Amazon* had made, including the *Phoebe*. Certainly no officer could live on his wages alone. The *Nymphe* had been a letter-of-marque, a merchant ship with permission to capture enemy vessels but not a privateer, a privatly owned and armed warship. The French captain had been carrying a valuable cargo of sugar from the West Indies to France. The captain had been greedy and wanted to capture a weak seeming opponent as well. He had paid for his greed and stupidity with his life. Now even Elizabeth had several hundred pounds due since there were so few petty officers to share. Naturally the paymaster had not paid out anything like those amounts to them. Only a small portion, the rest to be paid at their discharge or transfer. There were specialists who handled negotiations over prize money with the paymaster for a commission. That Elizabeth had money coming at all was due to the insistence of Captain Hartman and the implied influence of her relative, the Earl. She was also officially discharged from the navy. With that she could collect the rest of the prize money. Mr. McLeod went with her to collect the money and turned almost black with fury on hearing the insults of "doxy" and worse she had to endure. They didn't fight back. Mr. McLeod had warned Elizabeth that clerks had all sorts of sneaky tricks to get back at you and that all government clerks stuck together. Elizabeth noted that most of the clerks were Americans, Tories, and wanted nothing to do with them. Nor did she want to explain how she became a regular member of a warship's crew. She wanted to be away from the navy, the war and everything except Jeffrey and she still wasn't sure what her relationship was with him.

THE CITY

Jeffrey simply assumed that he and Elizabeth would stay together, at least until a more permanent solution for her could be found. He had managed to find two rooms for himself and her on the north end of the city near the shipyards. It had been a private house but was now a small inn. It hadn't been easy to find something. The city was terribly overcrowded with the military and refugees. Since the war had dragged on so long, five years so far, many of the military had brought their wives and children here. The generals and admirals didn't approve of that but with such a long war they couldn't stop it. No one knew how much longer the war would last. Jeffrey was lucky that the landlady had preferred him and Elizabeth as tenants to a Hessian officer with a large family. Meals were served in their rooms since it was not considered proper for a young lady to appear in the common room which also served as a tavern. Elizabeth was expected, however, to add to the food supply by shopping in the market. "You have the time and the money for it," the landlady told her bluntly. "I don't have either." Jeffrey, of course, had to report for duty at the headquarters on lower Broadway every morning.

Two days after they settled in a midshipman showed up at their rooms while they were having breakfast. Obviously this midshipman had money and influence. His breeches gleamed in their white newness and his coat fitted snugly. Unlike Jeffrey's hastily made uniform, this midshipman must have had his uniform made by one of the best tailors in London. Jeffrey could have written to his family for more money for clothing and other expenses while waiting for his prize money to be paid out but he told Elizabeth he hated doing that. My brother Robert has enough desire for fine clothes, fine horses and gambling for the two of us. I prefer to have the money spent to improve the house and improving our farm in England."

"Mister Kent, the admiral sent me, Admiral Graves. He would like your presence at headquarters as soon as it is convenient." Jeffrey knew that when a superior officer said "as soon as it is convenient" it meant right away if not sooner.

"I will be with you as soon as I freshen up and get my sword and hat."

The midshipman had been gazing superciliously at the simple meal, the small room and Elizabeth. Now he smiled and the smile made his face more pleasant. "Don't worry about your appearance, sir. You have made the admiral a few hundred pounds richer by your capture of that French lugger. That will be more important to the admiral than the name of your tailor."

"I will be with you in a moment," Jeffrey repeated. "In the meantime I make you acquainted with my cousin, Miss Elizabeth Troyes from Carolina. She will make you comfortable while you wait."

"My apologies, Miss Troyes." The boy's bow was polite but bored. "I am James Smythe, very much at your service. I am midshipman-aide to Admiral Graves." Suddenly the boredom dropped away. "You are the girl on the *Phoebe* when she engaged *Nymphe*. All the service is talking about that brave fight. I envy your experience and would like to hear the details of that fight."

"I saw very little and did less. I was below attending to the wounded."

"So I understand but it is amazing what stories spread in the navy. Lots of people are not only envious of you but of Mr. Kent. There are so few chances of ship-to-ship engagements in this war and for prize money. There are even fewer chances for junior officers. It is Admiral Graves' belief that the *Amazon* was not in sight. That can be taken as a compliment. It would be easy to claim that she was and split the prize money. Of course if the *Amazon* would have been in sight Captain Hartman instead of Admiral Graves would get the commanding officers share. There is bound to be talk."

Jeffrey came in. He had brushed his coat and was carrying his hat and wearing his sword. Elizabeth saw the two officers leave and her thoughts were uncomfortable. People were envious and were talking, Mr. Smythe had said. Among other things they were probably talking about her and Jeffrey living together. There might be trouble for Jeffrey because of her. She didn't want to cause him any trouble. Maybe it would have been better for everybody if she had been killed along Mr. Emmons and Pat. Maybe then Jeffrey would think of her with fond memories instead of thinking about the trouble she caused him. Maybe it would be better if she left now while he was gone with that very well dressed midshipman. That midshipman probably didn't like her either despite his politeness. She went and counted her money. She still had twenty five guineas left from the advance on her prize money. The portrait of King George the Third stared at her from the coins and he didn't look very friendly. Still twenty five guineas was a fair amount of money. It was almost a year's wages for a craftsman and almost as much money as she had left Carolina with. But where could she go? The Colonies were closed to her since it would be known sooner or later that she had served with the British. Nobody would believe that she hadn't turned Tory. If the Patriots won, and Elizabeth considered that likely, they wouldn't be the forgiving kind, not after more than five years of war. She couldn't stay in New York. Jeffrey and the officers of the British navy would find her. England? Would the money be enough to take her to England? And what would she do when she got there? No, she had no way out. She would have to stay with Jeffrey whether she wanted to or not. And she did want to. She felt better when logic and facts confirmed her emotions. She just hoped that Jeffrey felt the same way about her.

Jeffrey came back to the inn about two hours later. "They confirmed my warrant as acting lieutenant," he told Elizabeth. "They took away my command of the *Phoebe*. The admiral told me that I would have to give somebody else a chance for glory. He probably has a favorite he wants to give a command to. I am attached to headquarters. Captain Hartman has no opening for another lieutenant and nobody else wants one with only an acting warrant. So I am a glorified messenger boy." He sounded disgusted.

"My fault?" The question was half a statement. She had brought nobody any luck.

"No, although having a woman aboard probably didn't help. Not even if she was a heroic woman mentioned in dispatches or my cousin. There were all sorts of flattering remarks about you but that still doesn't help me get a ship. I am too young. That's the main trouble. I can't get a regular commission until I am eighteen and have passed the examination. They couldn't revoke my warrant after my victory. That is something anyway. I just have to sit and await a ship. A headquarters assignment is nothing."

A tremendous surge of relief went through Elizabeth's body. She would never have to go aboard *Phoebe* again. She never would have to see the planks where her friends died. She didn't want to be brave. She probably would still have her nightmares, but she could wake up now and know they weren't real. She could let her pictures of blood and twisted bodies fade. She could hope there never would be another ship to twist her fate. And Jeffrey would be with her. She just managed to restrain herself from telling Jeffrey that she was glad he had lost his ship. "What are you going to do?" she managed to ask him.

"Don't know. Probably run errands for the admiral and copy papers. Hope they don't send me out to one of the signal stations on Staten Island. I'd be completely forgotten there." Elizabeth could see that he was trying to stay cheerful but it was an effort. "At least I have been in action and everybody knows it. Having money from captures helps too. I hate to write home for more funds. Lots of officers do it but I think letters should contain news, not be requests for more money."

"Are you going to write home about me?"

"Yes. I want to tell them about finding an American branch of the family. I want to tell them about you. I am going to write to my uncle too. He is very much interested in family."

"Won't they mind? About me, I mean."

"Not really. I'm not the heir. My brother Robert is. And the line of the earldom is safe too. My uncle has two sons. They are in school now but they are in the line of succession. Younger sons are supposed to make their own way and that is what I am doing."

Elizabeth had to be satisfied with that. She wasn't worried about what Jeffrey would be doing as a navy officer as long as it was something. She was worried about the other thing. She did want to belong to a family, very much, but she was scared what they would say and think about her. It probably would be months anyway before an answer came to Jeffrey's letters. Only a few ships braved the Atlantic during winter from England. Meanwhile there were things to do in New York. For one thing she would have to buy another new dress. The old one had blood stains on it that wouldn't wash out. She had wrapped it around a six pounder cannon ball and dropped it overboard. Her shift had gone the same way. She would be glad to have a new dress. It wouldn't be anything fancy. Something practical.

None the less Elizabeth found the atmosphere in New York depressing. There were few places to go. She had no friends once the *Amazon* had sailed with Mr. Guerney and the others on board. Jeffrey had made friends with James Smythe but that friendship didn't include her. The lower end of Manhattan swarmed with troops and refugees. Many of the houses had been taken over by military departments and generals. There was no pleasure to be found walking there. Much of the rest of the island had been taken over as camp grounds for regiments, English, Hessian and Tory. She supposed she should call them "Loyalist" now that she was behind British lines but to her they were still "Tory". The houses everywhere looked unkempt and most of the trees had been chopped down for firewood. The Hudson River looked beautiful but one couldn't make excursions to the other side. That shore had been raided by both sides. Recently the Americans had even temporarily stormed the British fort on Paulus Hook in Jersey. Brooklyn and Long Island were a little safer, but again, one always ran up against army campgrounds. The few working farms were guarded by fierce dogs. North of Manhattan was the "Neutral Ground" raided by pro-American "Cowboys" and pro-British "Skinners" where nobody was safe. Nor was the company she found in New York pleasant. The British officer's and senior enlisted men's wives were lonely and stand-offish. The Americans were refugees driven from their homes because of their political opinions. Many had been important people in their communities; lawyers, judges, merchants. Now some of the men had found employment in the many military departments or enlisted in Tory regiments. For their wives there was nothing to do except to talk how important they had been before the war. Now they complained about everything around them. They were not happy about the food, the climate or how the British snubbed them as "Colonials". Elizabeth could understand why they were unhappy but that didn't make them any more fun to talk to. Even the woman who sold Elizabeth her new dress told her that she would never have lowered herself to be a dress maker before this awful war. Nor was it really safe for Elizabeth to walk the streets of the city. She had heard a good bit about incidents of robbery and rape. There were patrols of provost guards around but not enough to insure safety and order. Both Jeffrey and James Smythe had suggested she hire a maid. Elizabeth felt shy about hiring a ladies maid. She felt that a maid would sneer at her for her backwoods manners and her unladylike experiences. In the meantime she carried the pistol that Jeffrey had given her on the *Phoebe* in the pocket of her skirt.

Then she ran into Anna. Elizabeth had been shopping at the Fly Market, near the docks. "Would your ladyship be needing a strong girl to carry her packages?"

Elizabeth laughed. "Do I look so weak that I couldn't carry a few pounds of vegetables myself?"

"No, but you look like you have been having enough to eat. That's more than we have had for many a day. You also don't look like the kind of officer's lady who would have us whipped for the asking. You're no servant, but you are shopping without having a servant with you."

Elizabeth looked the speaker over. This girl was Irish, as Irish as Pat had been. She had the same blue eyes and snub nose. She was the same age as Pat had been too. Elizabeth remembered that she had promised herself to do something for Pat's sake since she had been unable to do anything for Pat himself. The girl looked reasonably clean. "Who are you and what do you do?" Elizabeth asked the question as much to gain time as for the answer.

"Name's Anna. Do just about anything to get food into my stomach. There is a whole bunch of us living on the docks." Her hand indicated the piers just to the north.

One of the stall keepers called over to Elizabeth. "Don't trust her none, miss. That gang of hers cleaned out half of my stuff last week and she helped." The vegetable dealer's voice annoyed Elizabeth. She wanted to talk to Anna. Besides she was tired talking to the ladies and would-be ladies back at the inn. The pistol in her pocket reassured her. She surreptously cocked it but she realized that nobody would attack her in so public a spot in broad daylight.

"Now look here, Anna. I want to talk to you. Might have something for you to do."

"Could you buy me something to eat before the talking? Then we can sit at the end of the dock. Provost don't chase you none there."

Elizabeth fished out a few of the copper half-pennies in her pocket. She gave them to Anna. It was a test of honesty. If the girl ran away with them that would be that. If not they could talk. Shared food always helped talking. "Go ahead. Buy some buns. They sell them at the next stall. Then let's go over to where you live. The end of this pier is too public." Anna left at the run. When she came back she already had one bun crammed into her mouth. The rest were in her hands.

"Right you are, miss. Follow me and watch your step. Some of the boards are rotten."

Elizabeth handed Anna the basket of vegetables and kept her hand in her pocket where she had the pistol. Anna led her to the next pier where there was a lean-to made of old lumber. There were two boys hanging around but Anna waved them away with a gesture. She didn't share the buns with them either. The two girls sat down on an old blanket. Anna started on the second bun and Elizabeth ate the third. "What do you want, miss? Someone beaten up or to go across the lines?"

"Can one get across to the American lines?"

"That's easy, the getting there. Got to know someone to stay though. I tried it once. Nothing to eat. They take anything you got of value and send you back as a Tory, quick as quick. Lucky to get back from the Neutral Ground or the Connecticut shore with your whole skin. Real tough people there now, all of them."

Elizabeth hadn't made any plans. She had half a notion to make her way back to Carolina. Anything was better than sitting in New York rotting and depending on Jeffrey's charity. She'd miss Jeffrey, miss him badly, but she had made up her mind to do something. Doing something, any thing, was better than just sitting here waiting for something to happen to her. She hardly knew this girl but she found herself telling her the whole story. She told about her parents, her uncle, Jeffrey and the *Phoebe*, everything. Somehow it made her feel better, getting everything out. Anna was a good listener. She sat silently opposite Elizabeth, chin in her hand, just listening. She shook her head at the end of the talk.

"Nope, you can't go back. Even if the lobsterbacks win. You can't go back, ever. The people, they'd treat you like a Tory, officer's doxy too. My father, he enlisted in the Orange Rangers, Tory outfit. Deserted and tried to cross the lines. The Rebels sent him back after stripping him. Lobsterbacks sentenced him to five hundred lashes. He died after." Anna stopped for a moment. "That's when I tried to get back to Connecticut. They wouldn't have me. Sent me back. Didn't hurt me none. Just made me go. Been in New York since. Got to stick with the British. Nothing else to do."

The two girls sat there. Anna finished her second bun. Elizabeth realized that she had heard the Word, as firm and unalterable as a text from the Bible. She had thought so already but now she heard it confirmed by this experienced street girl. There was no going back. She didn't think the British would win the war here in America. Not with the French, the Spaniards and the Dutch allied with the rebellious colonists. She had heard there was also fighting as far away as India but that didn't concern her here. Even should the British win, her neighbors in Carolina would drive her out. She could never go back there. She would have to make new plans. Perhaps she could go to England. She would have to talk with Jeffrey about that. Maybe there was someplace else in the world to go to. Maybe Canada—Halifax—not the French speaking Quebec. She would have to see. In the meantime she was here in New York City. She would start her new life here. She wouldn't be like those Tory ladies who dreamt of past glories and hoped to return behind British bayonets. For her the past life was completely gone, finished. It hadn't even been that good a life, not recently. "Anna, would you come with me? As a maid or companion or something. I don't know why I trust you but I do. Do you know anything about being a maid?" Elizabeth knew it was her loneliness talking. She was taking a chance, taking up with this unknown waif. But she had been doing nothing but taking chances the last few months. She had little left to lose taking another chance.

Anna stared at Elizabeth. "Why would you be wanting me? I am nothing and nobody. Don't know polite talk. Don't know nothing about fancy lady things."

Elizabeth's thoughts were now in order. This was a turning point in her life just as it had been when she had chosen to stay aboard *Phoebe* with Jeffrey. "I'm nothing either, not really," she told Anna. "I wouldn't know what to do with a fancy ladies maid. I need someone to talk to. Someone who won't laugh at me or my American ways. The other things, the polite things as the British call them, those we can learn about together. Jeffrey and that James Smythe always tell me I need someone just to walk in this town safely."

Anna helped Elizabeth to her feet. The basket of vegetables hung on Anna's arm. "Try it anyway," was her curt comment. "You'll have to explain me to your lieutenant though, and buy me something clean to wear so I look respectable. I was decent once."

Elizabeth looked around. "Don't you want to take your things?"

"Nothing left to take. All I own is this blanket and the clothes on my back. One of the others will use the blanket."

Jeffrey said nothing about Anna except that he was glad Elizabeth had found a maid. He was sure the landlady would find a cot for her in the attic. Right now he was too disgusted with his own affairs to worry about anyone else's troubles. "They've attached me to the supply yard to check on supplies for the ships," he told Elizabeth. "There is an old guy in charge there. Real old, old enough to have sailed with Noah on the Ark. He told me that I could learn something from him. That there were other ways to make money in the navy besides winning prize money." Jeffrey described the inefficiency and outright corruption that prevailed in the navy yard.

The old man had told him that it was that way all over. Jeffrey wasn't surprised by the shortage of supplies. After all New York was a besieged city. Except for the few things from Long Island everything had to be brought in by sea. Convoys got through despite the French navy and the American privateers. However some of the shortages weren't necessary. They were caused by sloppiness or by corruption. It was Jeffrey's first contact with that sort of thing and it shocked him badly. He had always considered the British navy an honorable service. "I found some barrels of beef in a warehouse," he told Elizabeth. "The meat was so rotten I could smell it right through the sealed tubs. I wanted to dump it in the river but I was told I couldn't do that unless it had been condemned by a properly constituted board of inquiry. So I went to headquarters to get a board convened. A commander, a full commander, took me aside and told me not to press the matter. To put the barrels aboard a ship that wouldn't be back soon to complain about the sailors' rations. Told me that someone with influence was interested in the matter and there should be no scandal about supplies. The old man told me that the commander was paid to keep his mouth shut. A commander, a British officer, taking bribes. I can't believe it."

Elizabeth could, easily. She remembered the cheeses and other rations she had sent back from the *Phoebe*. She remembered her chest and what had happened to it. She remembered Captain Brathwaithe and his indifference to her complaints. She couldn't say that to Jeffrey, not the way he felt about the navy. It wouldn't be fair.

James Smythe just laughed when he heard the story. "Been happening that way all through history. Julius Cesear complained about his supplies. The Lord High Admiral Howard complained to Queen Elizabeth that his sailors were starving after they beat the Armada. If the Rebels ever get a real navy their admiral will undoubtedly complain to General George Washington about the quality of his supplies."

"But our officers are gentlemen," Jeffrey objected.

"Gentlemen need money too, lots of it. They maintain houses and families on shore. The Admiralty doesn't supply cabin stores or uniforms or things like that. That's why there is the system of prize money."

Jeffrey remembered how prize money was distributed. The captain took two eighth, the commanding officer of the squadron or fleet took an eighth even though he wasn't even there. All the sailors together only divided an eighth between them. With the small crew on the *Phoebe* that still amounted to something. On a frigate or a line-of-battle ship each sailor got only a couple of shillings. Still Jeffrey's face showed his dislike for what he had seen of the navy in New York. This wasn't what he had joined the Service for.

Anna was helpful in managing their money. She used her reputation on the market to have the stall-keepers keep their best goods for her and Elizabeth. She helped Elizabeth get around more in New York. She also helped Jeffrey. She washed his shirts and mended his stockings. Even with Anna's help there wasn't much food to buy in the markets. The admirals and other high officers could afford to order pineapples, sea turtles and other delicacies from the West Indies. They couldn't. The landlady did the best she could with the meager fare. She stretched the small amount of stringy meat available into soups and stews. Eggs, butter and good flour were also expensive and hard to find. The landlady kept tea locked up in a tea caddy and they had coffee or cacao very occasionally.

The winter was a cold one and there was much illness in town. So far all three of them managed to avoid infections. Both Jeffrey and Elizabeth had been innoculated against smallpox and Anna had survived a bout of that dread disease. Just hearing about all the sickness added to their depression.

Through Anna, Elizabeth got to know a different part of the population of New York. She met the apprentices and clerks, the servants, river rats and prostitutes. They were a welcome change from the Tory and British wives with their constant complaints. However, when her new acquaintances heard that she had been rated as a surgeon's mate, they brought their illnesses and injuries to her. There weren't many civilian doctors in the city and the army doctors only took care of members of their own regiments. The few civilian doctors were expensive. Elizabeth couldn't say no and thought that she could face anything after her experience in the wardroom of the *Phoebe*. Anna also had some experience in nursing. Their patients paid what they could but that barely covered Anna's keep. Elizabeth began to buy drugs and medicines but only bought imported drugs when she had to. She relied heavily on the herbs she got from old Sarah Tantequidgeon, a Native American herb gatherer from Connecticut that Anna had known before the war. Sarah showed the girls the use of sassafras and willow bark and other native herbs. Anna was pleased with their increasing medical practice but Elizabeth was still depressed by the many patients, especially babies, whom they couldn't help.

One day when they were buying some laudanum, an opium derivative for pain, and mercury salve from a downtown pharmacy Elizabeth heard a sharp voice behind her. "Those are not things to sell to little girls."

Elizabeth swung around. The man behind her was portly with gray hair and wore the uniform of the Hessian corps. Judging by the quality of the uniform and the gold braid on it he was a major or even a colonel. His English was clear even if strongly accented. "I am rated as a surgeon's mate by the Royal Navy, sir," she told him stiffly.

"A girl doctor? That I do not believe. Your name and ship at once, miss."

"Elizabeth Troyes, late of HMS *Phoebe*, honorably discharged. I do not claim to be a doctor falsely, as you seem to imply. I am told that the Baroness von Riedesel helped with the wounded in Burgoyne's army. She was no doctor either."

"She does good," Anna broke in fiercely. "That's more than you Hessians do. You only serve for the money."

"Anna do quiet down." Elizabeth was afraid that this high officer could do her or Jeffrey harm with his influence even if he didn't belong to the Navy. She was scared of his age and obvious rank. He didn't look like a man who would stand much nonsense either.

The German bowed and clicked his heels. "Your servant is quite correct, miss. We are professional soldiers who go where we are sent. It seems sometimes we do no good to the people of this land but we serve as best we can." Then he introduced himself. "Doctor Johannes Schmidt, late of Heidelberg University and now on General von Knyphausen's staff, your servant." Then Elizabeth heard him mutter to himself. "The physicians oath: You shall teach by precept, by lecture, by all means of teaching. There is nothing in that oath that says it applies only to boys." He looked sharply at Elizabeth. "You have been innoculated? You have a navy medical chest? You have been taught?"

"The surgical kit stayed on His Majesty's ship. I have studied the manual as best I can. I do not do surgery but we do the best we can with medicines and herbs."

"Come to the hospital with me and we will get you what you need, you and your servant. You have been innoculated, both of you? We have cases of smallpox in the hospital."

"Yes, I have been innoculated and Anna has had the disease." Doctor Schmidt turned to the druggist again. "You will not sell poison to children. I will tell General Robertson who is in command of this city otherwise. Understand!"

Dr. Schmidt was as good as his word. They were now able to get instruments and medicines. With them they were able to set fractures, extract rotten teeth and lance boils. They still used native herbs against fevers. They worked as well or better than some of the European drugs. They still didn't attempt major surgery and left childbirth to the midwives.

None the less they had more people calling for them than they could handle. Elizabeth was glad that she no longer had to pay for all the medicines out of her own purse. Best of all they could consult with Dr. Schmidt and learn.

"You are the luckiest girl in the world," Anna told Elizabeth. "High Hessian officers listen to you. The officer who captures your ship turns out to be your cousin. You win prize money. Are you sure you are not a witch?"

Elizabeth didn't feel lucky. She was still a poor refugee without a home, without a real family and most of all, without a real future. Unfortunatly, Jeffrey was just as depressed as she was and their irritation turned into their first real fight.

One evening Jeffrey walked into Elizabeth's room without knocking like he usually did. "I've had it," he announced. "I've got to do something to get out of here, to get on a real ship somewhere or back to England."

"What happened? Today, I mean."

"I was sent to the *Jersey* over in Brooklyn. She's a hulk condemned even as a hospital ship and turned into a prison. She's still a ship so she is the navy's responsibility. They have prisoners packed into her real tight. It is worse than on a receiving ship. There are no medical facilities and there is almost no food. Some of the prisoners are nearly naked. Now, in winter. They must be dying like flies in her. I was checking supplies for the crew and the marine guards. I wasn't supposed to do anything about the prisoners. They are the provost marshall's responsibility but I couldn't help seeing. I know that there aren't always enough supplies for our own men but someone is stealing the little that is allocated for the prisoners. Our own officers don't care. The ones who are sent to serve on prison ships weren't probably good officers in the first place. It is considered a kind of punishment to be sent to serve on a prison ship. The lieutenant in charge of the *Jersey* is probably no worse than the officers on the other hulks but I have seen him operate. I've seen what is happening there. Everyone seems to know about it. They tell me there is no sense protesting. Nobody will listen. I've got to get away, to sea, to England, anywhere where it is clean."

It was hard for Elizabeth to make sense out of what Jeffrey was saying. She tried to listen sympathetically but finally her patience snapped. "Go ahead, it's easy for you! All you have to do is to transfer someplace else and you can forget all about the misery that comes with war. Those are only things that happen to other people like my father, my mother and me. Ordinary, decent people. What do you expect me to say to a British officer like you or to Captain Hartman or Admiral Gambier? You can talk of glory or taking prizes. You have clean uniforms and food and steady pay. What did you think war was? It's burnt houses and starving people driven from everything they knew or held dear. It's children left without parents or homes or hope like me and Anna!"

Suddenly she stopped and stared at Jeffrey. Jeffrey stared back at her. They were both horrified at the bitterness that had come pouring out of Elizabeth. All that they had shared since *Amazon* had taken *Phoebe* was swept away. They were back to what they had been then, strangers and almost enemies. This thing between them now was like a lead curtain, a thing of weight and substance. It seperated them. Both knew that the next words they said would determine their future relationship. All of it. Neither knew how to say the right thing to break the silence. Jeffrey was the first to recover his voice. "You hold me personally responsible?" he asked quietly.

Elizabeth took her time answering. She hadn't known she still had all those bitter feelings inside of her. But she couldn't take her words back. They were what she honestly felt deep inside her. "No," she answered slowly. "I don't hold you personably responsible. At the same time, you wear the uniform. You are a British officer. You chose to join the British navy in this war. To me, I guess that uniform represents the entire war and what it has done to me. Before the war I had a home, a family, a place where I belonged. Now?" Her hand swept around to indicate the small room. "Is this a home? Is this a place where I or anyone else belongs? My neighbors who are still alive think I have become their deadly enemy. I can't go back to where I came from, ever." Her own honesty forced her to go on and weaken her own argument. "Anna's father took the other side from mine. Yet she is no better off than I am, worse if anything. The war has ruined her life too. Perhaps she could blame the Americans who rebelled against the King because his ministers misgoverned.

"It's not that easy for me either," Jeffrey said. "You say I joined the navy for glory. That much choice I didn't have. As I told you I am a younger son. My brother Robert will inherit the house, the land, everything. That's why they call it "real estate." Maybe my father will leave me some money but it won't be much. That is the way it is under British law. The eldest son gets everything so the estates aren't broken up into small lots that can't support a family. Our land isn't enough to support my parents and the two of us. Certainly not support two sons the way my brother chooses to live. I am a gentleman's son. My father even has a title. So the gentlemen's professions are open to me. I probably could have become a lawyer or a churchman or an army officer. The navy was my choice since I like the sea. I like adventure, yes. But the navy is my occupation just like the carpenter or the tailor has his. That's why I can't quit. I can just ask for a transfer if I am disgusted. If I want to advance in my profession I can't even do that too often. As you know I've broken the rules once or twice or at least bent them. I am lucky because my victory over the Frenchman has covered my eccentricities, as I have heard them called." All of this came out slowly. Jeffrey had never really thought out the why he was in the navy. Then his voice strengthened. "Also I am an Englishman. Now we are fighting not only the rebellious Americans but all the old enemies of the English: the Spaniards, the Dutch and the French. That was not an American ship that we took. Maybe if there was no British navy the French would land a force on English soil, burn our house and kill my family. It has happened before you know. The French burned Teignmouth about a hundred years ago. That is something for me to think about, too."

They were interrupted. Anna came into the room carrying a pot of tea. She had obviously heard them but she saw their faces and said nothing as she went out again. The silence between Jeffrey and Elizabeth stretched longer and became heavier. Finally Elizabeth asked: "What can I do? What should I do now?"

"I can't give you back what you have lost. That's gone. I can say that I am sorry and I am, but that doesn't help you now. It won't end the war. And even if the war ended today, thing's wouldn't be as they were. That's gone too. Things won't be the same for me either. You were with me on the *Phoebe*. I can spend the rest of my life regretting those lost lives. Maybe I could have run away, escaped combat. I didn't, but I don't forget what I did do. We can spend the rest of our lives wishing things were different. You can spend your life weeping and hating. I guess there will be plenty of people who will do just that. Some of the Loyalists in this town will, for instance. You have heard them talk about how things were so much better before the war. You've heard them often enough right here in the inn. You don't want to be like them. You want to go on, to live a life. We both do, I guess."

"What can I do? What should I do?" The words were the same as before but the anger had gone out of Elizabeth's voice. She was asking for help, for advice. She was asking for an answer to her problem.

"You could go to England," Jeffrey's answer was prompt. "You have family there. It's not close family but family none the less. I think they would welcome you."

"I could go there? You would take me?"

Jeffrey laughed a little bitterly. "It has been hinted in certain quarters that a request for transfer by me would be welcome in certain quarters. I have said some things that didn't please certain people. I have even done some things. That didn't make me popular. They were kind enough to put it down to my youth."

"You would take me? You would come with me?" Elizabeth wasn't interested in the ways and doings of the British navy. She wanted Jeffrey's promise for herself. She couldn't face another strange place and more strangers by herself. Maybe with Jeffrey along she could find a place that she could make her place. Maybe she could start over again. It depended on Jeffrey and whether he could accept her as she was now.

"I will come if I can and when I can. I am in the navy, remember. I don't write my own orders. You could sail on the next packet boat with Anna. We have money enough for that even if I can't get the admiral to give you a travel warrant. I think the admiral would give me one. They are always trying to reduce the number of dependents in New York. My father and my uncle would welcome you in England."

"I need you, not some unknown uncle." Elizabeth knew she could trust no unknown uncle. She had been down that path before. It had ended on the river road in Carolina and the *Phoebe*. It had hurt too much to ever trust such promises again.

Jeffrey heard the desperation in Elizabeth's voice. He knew that he would have to keep any promise he made to her now. Elizabeth trusted him. His crew had trusted him too and had willingly gone to their death at his word. This time it would be worse if he made the wrong decision. Elizabeth would be just as dead as they were. Her body would go on living but she would be dead inside and this time he had no time to think. He had to make his decision now. He offered her his hand to shake. Elizabeth flung herself at him. Her arms were around his body. She held on to him hard. His arms came up awkwardly and patted her hair. Then something welled up in him and he held her just as hard as she held him. Their lips sought each other. It was the first time for both of them and they kissed clumsily.

It was a while before they could break from each other and sit down. It was hard for both of them to accept their new relationship but they both knew that this was something new and good that they had found. Elizabeth saw the pot of tea that Anna had brought in and poured Jeffrey a cup. The tea was cold but even cold tea was good for both of them. It was something normal. Elizabeth found that her stomach muscles were loosening up bit by bit. She had nearly thrown up from the tension. Now she felt warm, really warm inside for the first time since her mother had become ill. She took another sip of tea. Jeffrey sat there with a sort of a smile on his face. "You know, you're a pretty girl, Elizabeth."

"Thank you. I like your looks too." It sounded silly even to Elizabeth herself. She searched for other words and found none. Suddenly she was being held tightly by the shoulders. Jeffrey's hands were very strong. His fingers dug in and it almost hurt but Elizabeth liked the hurt. It was good to be held by someone strong who cared, really cared.

Finally Jeffrey's hands dropped. There was nothing left of his light tome. "You belong to me. You." His voice slowed and his shoulders slumped. "I don't know how to say things. It comes out silly and all wrong."

"I know. It does for me too. Maybe we no longer need words. I guess we have belonged to each other ever since we met on the *Phoebe*. Only we didn't know it then, and we do now."

Jeffrey and Elizabeth now could talk freely to each other. They talked about serious things and unimportant things. They talked about the sea and ships. They talked about the foods they liked and those they didn't like. They talked about New York. It was late when they went to bed, each in their own room.

The next morning Elizabeth woke up still feeling good. The sun was shining through the window and making bright spots on the floor. Elizabeth got out of bed and carefully stepped on each sunny spot. She hadn't done that since she was eight years old. She hadn't wiggled her toes like she had this morning either. She was glad to be alive. She, Elizabeth, all of thirteen and a half years old, was in love. Anna brought in some hot water for washing. There wasn't very much of it and it wasn't very hot. Wood to heat water was expensive. Neither of the girls spoke much to each other beyond the conventional good morning. Elizabeth washed herself all over. She wanted to be all clean when she met Jeffrey for breakfast. She didn't think about why she wanted to. She just did.

Jeffrey was already eating some oatmeal when Elizabeth came in. "Sleep well?" he teased.

"Very well. I feel like a young girl."

"And at other times you were an old woman? Look out or they will burn you for a witch."

"I felt very old, witch or no witch. But today I am young enough to sit down and have breakfast with a young boy."

"By all means. This young boy is hungry. He has been up for hours already and he has to get downtown to work as well." Elizabeth curtsied formally. He got up and bowed just as formally. Then he pulled out the only other chair in the room for Elizabeth to sit on. Anna brought in some fresh tea and bread, toasted to make it taste fresher. Somehow that set them laughing and they couldn't seem to stop.

Anna's reaction was surprising. She looked at the two of them and burst out crying. Elizabeth stopped laughing. Anna wasn't the crying kind of girl. "What's the matter Anna?"

"You'll be going away together. You will leave me all alone again."

"No, we won't. If we leave here we will take you with us."

"You won't be needing me. There will be trained servants to do the cooking and the sewing where you are going. The gentry won't let you be friends with the likes of me. Not in England they won't."

Elizabeth felt that cold black area spread across her middle again. Anna, clear headed Anna saw the truth. It would be difficult to find a place for Anna as a friend in England. It wouldn't be only Anna who would find herself out of place. What room would there be for the American orphan girl in a English gentleman's home? She knew that orphans were usually shipped out of England to the Colonies. She had heard about such girls in Carolina. They were bound out to farmers. That's what her uncle's wife had wanted for her as well. Her uncle's cousins in Boston wanted her to take care of their children and help in the house. That would have been only a little better. She thought about that now. It stopped her laughter completely.

After Jeffrey had left Elizabeth sought out Anna. It was a cold day but the two of them walked out to the docks anyway. It was where they had met and it seemed the right place to talk. The lean-to was gone. After all, fire-wood sold for something in New York. There was nobody about either. The two girls sat on the bare planks and let their legs dangle over the edge of the pier. "You love the lieutenant?" Anna asked bluntly.

"Yes, I think I love him, love him very much. But he is a English gentleman, a navy officer and sometimes I am afraid of him."

"You love him." Anna's voice was flat.

"I guess so, I never loved anybody before. But I went with him before I even knew or liked him. I had no choice. No place else to go or anybody to go with."

Anna wouldn't accept that. "Always a choice. I had no one to go with either. I am still alive and in New York. You love him. That's different. You don't need me."

"I do need you, especially now. I need someone to talk to besides Jeffrey, to give me advice. A fancy ladies maid would laugh at me."

Anna shook her head. "I wouldn't be able to help you none. Don't know English ways. Don't know English dress. They'd point at the two of us. With an English maid you could be more like them, on the outside at least."

Elizabeth tried to dodge the issue. "How did you know we planned to go to England?"

"You didn't keep your voice down. Heard you tell his lordship off too. You did good."

"I want you with me."

"Wouldn't do you any good. Wouldn't do the lieutenant any good either. People would say things about a lieutenant travelling with two young girls and they would think worse. Would myself if I didn't know you. They'd take it out on me. Maybe on you and the lieutenant too." Elizabeth had noted that Anna never used Jeffrey's name. It was always 'the lieutenant'.

They talked for a while longer but Elizabeth knew that Anna was right. For Jeffrey to bring one poor American girl home would be bad enough. Two girls would be too much all together. "I'm sorry Anna. But you will stay with us until we go, if we go? It isn't decided yet. It would take a while to make arrangements in any case."

"No reason to say you'll be sorry. You've been nice to me. You didn't need me. Not really you didn't. I'll make out. I'll miss you. Miss the lieutenant too."

Elizabeth looked sharply at Anna. Anna looked down. "Yes I love him too. He never saw me, not really, only saw you. That's another reason I can't go with you." There was nothing more to say. The two girls couldn't even cry together because tears would no longer help them. They walked home sadly. Elizabeth felt she had lost a friend. Anna was the only friend she had besides Jeffrey. She had tried to help Anna and instead she had hurt her more. There wasn't anything she could do about it. Her good intentions didn't matter at all. The hurt was there. She agreed with Anna that with the two of them in love with Jeffrey they couldn't go to England together. That would never work. Anna agreed to stay with them until they left for England. Of course she would never tell Jeffrey why she couldn't go with them.

Anna wasn't the only friend who made difficulties. James Smythe didn't approve of Jeffrey's plans at all. Jeffrey told Elizabeth about the discussion afterwards. "You don't want to tie yourself to a penniless girl," the midshipman had argued. "Send her to England if you must. Your father will find a place for her. She probably would make a good companion to an old woman. She is too young to be a tutor or a governess."

"She won't go unless I go with her."

"Of course she'd say that. They all do. I can't even blame them, but we have our careers to think of. Making ourselves agreeable to our superiors is one way. Taking up with a rich and well connected girl is another. Elizabeth would be of no use to you what so ever. I know she is a nice girl but she wouldn't be able to bring you any wealth or influence in the navy. You can't always expect to meet and defeat a French lugger with a rich cargo."

"She is my cousin. I can't just ditch her even if I wanted to and I don't."

"Who is talking about ditching?" He stopped talking suddenly and then started again. "Wait a minute. I just got an idea. You're the nephew of the Earl of Severn, aren't you? And Elizabeth is also some sort of relative of the Earl?"

"Yes but not a close relative. He's never even met her. Just knows about her from my letter."

"Doesn't matter as long as you let people know she is a relative. It will do. All admirals need influence behind them. Admiral Rodney needs it now that his capture of St. Eustatius is being discussed in parliament. The Very Honorable Admiral Graves will think your uncle might be useful to him. Admirals need appointments, just like us junior officers."

"I can't pledge my uncle's influence."

"That's not the way these things are done. I've learned that much in the navy even if I haven't learned as much navigation as I should have.

You will tell him that you want to take this long lost relative back to your uncle. Bet he will make out a travel warrant back to England. That doesn't cost him anything but it will save you passage money. In England your uncle will know what to do with her. You will have done more for her than she can expect."

ATLANTIC TRANSFER

It didn't quite happen the way James Smythe said it would but it came close to it. In late winter two letters came for Jeffrey by way of a ship that had taken the southern route across the Atlantic. Jeffrey turned a little pale when he saw his mother's writing. This letter would be in answer to his letter about Elizabeth. He cracked the wax seal and read the letter to Elizabeth after hastily scanning it himself.

> Dear Jeffrey
>
> Your father told me to write you that your brother Robert was killed instantly when his curricle slipped on the ice and overturned December 18th. His fiancee, Miss Venetia Burnthurst, was fatally injured as well. We both feel the loss of your brother very much. The house feels empty even though Robert spent a good part of his time in London. Your father is busy settling Robert's affairs and dealing with the Burnthursts. They feel we owe them part of the settlements since the betrothal had already been printed in the papers. They also want you betrothed to their younger daughter Lily. We are not really in favor of that. She is only seven years old and no one knows into what kind of a woman she will develop into. You only knew her when she was barely out of leading strings

and she has only a limited dowry at best. As you know we are neighbors of the Burnthursts but not close friends.

Please come home soon and bring your new cousin with you.

Mother

P.S. We understand your uncle is writing you about your return here as well.

His uncle's letter was even more brief.

Dear Nephew

You will have been informed of your brother's unfortunate death. Since you are now the oldest son and heir it would be good if you returned here as soon as possible. I have written to Admiral Graves to ask him to release you from your duties as a personal favor to me.

Lord Sandwich, who is still First Lord of the Admiralty, was kind enough to interrupt his gaming when we met at Brook's to show me the dispatch in the Naval Chronicle. It reflects credit on you and our new cousin but one such exploit is enough for a lifetime. We are not swashbucklers.

When you arrive in England I would like you and Miss Troyes to visit me in my townhouse after you have paid your respects to your parents.

I have arranged with my bankers, Coutts, so you can draw on my account to settle your affairs in America as I do not believe you will return there. Settle any debts our cousin has as well and pay her fare to England. I understand she is not wealthy.

Severn

Jeffrey sat still and stared at the bulkhead for a while. "So Robert is dead and I am the oldest son." He stopped and turned to Elizabeth. "You'll come with me, won't you?"

"Yes if you think I will be welcome. The letters seem kind of cold."

"We English are not good at showing our feelings and even less comfortable writing them. Uncle's invitation to you is formal and complete, He signed it with his title, not his personal name. I won't have to draw on his bank account. You have no debts and I don't either. I feel good about that. My brother gambled, liked fast horses for his curricle and to be part of high society. I don't. I like to ride well enough but I don't need high steppers. You ride, don't you?" he asked suddenly.

"Ride yes, race no. I guess we both have other ways to risk our necks. Never played cards for money either nor did my parents. My mother always said that farming was enough of a gamble for her. Won't you miss your brother at all?"

"Yes and no. He was five years older than me. There was a sister between but she died when she was a baby. Robert taught me riding and encouraged me to go into the navy but we were never close. He was always very much the elder brother and the heir. I never wanted to copy him." He picked up his mother's letter and read it again. "I don't understand this business with the Burnthursts. I certainly don't have any intention of offering for Lily, now or ever. I didn't know Venetia very well either but she suited my brother. She wouldn't have suited me. She shared his passion for fast horses and fine clothes." He turned to Elizabeth looking a little helpless and confused. "I never wanted to be the heir. I don't know anything about farming or polite society. All I know is the sea. Will you help me? I need you." There was nothing for Elizabeth to say. They threw their arms around each other but it was for need, not love.

James Smythe helped Jeffrey arrange things with the Admiral. The Admiral made no trouble about the travel warrants. Jeffrey noted that Admiral Graves had his uncle's letter in front of him. He recognized the handwriting. It was James Smythe who told them about the packet, the *Sophia of Hanover,* that was preparing to sail for England in a week. The Admiral had made no trouble about the warrants but Captain Nordstein was not so enthusiastic. "He told me that he didn't want a jumped up snotty to tell him how to run his ship," the midshipman told them. "Then he wanted to know why a surgeon's mate thought himself too good to share a cabin with a lieutenant." James Smythe had explained to him that E. Troyes was a female and that both she and Jeffrey were relatives of the Earl of Severn. Then the captain had wanted an extra fare for her. James Smythe had settled that matter by promising the captain to provide him with a cargo of sugar from the *Nymphe* to carry back to England. Cargo from New York to England was scarce and the *Sophia* would have had to sail in ballast. Packets were under government contract and couldn't wait to have a full cargo like ordinary merchantmen.

Jeffrey tried once more to convince Anna to come with them. "No thank you, lieutenant. We couldn't be friends in England. It would be Master Jeffrey and Miss Elizabeth upstairs and Anna the maid downstairs. It wouldn't be proper to be anything else. I have talked to Dr. Schmidt and he will let me work with the women and children that are attached to the Hessians. He'll teach me too." Jeffrey kissed Anna good bye. It made Elizabeth uncomfortable. She was suddenly glad that Anna was not coming with them. Jeffrey also realized that it would be better if Anna stayed in New York. When he kissed her something had welled up in him that made him see what would happen to him with two girls around. He wasn't immune to Anna, not at all. None the less the parting made Elizabeth feel like a Judas. She needed something to ease that feeling. She suddenly realized that she had a gift for Anna that would be personal and useful as well as a good remembrance. Anna would take their medical kit if she was going to work with Dr. Schmidt but Elizabeth's pistol would be a good gift.

"I won't be needing it anymore. The British are law abiding, in England anyway." Neither Jeffrey nor Anna had a gift to give each other. Elizabeth was glad. She now knew she could be jealous of Anna. That was an uncomfortable thought but it was real anyway. To build a relationship with Jeffrey would have enough problems without additional complications. She wasn't sure it could be done as it was.

Jeffrey and Elizabeth made arrangements to have their baggage taken to the ship by a carter and to come aboard the next day. James Smythe had laid on a farewell dinner at a fashionable eating house on Queen Street. Elizabeth was glad because she knew that the food aboard the *Sophia* would be sea rations and she knew all about those.

At the inn, Elizabeth remembered the dinner with Admiral Gambier and all those British officers. That had been only seven months ago and so much had happened since. She also knew that she and Jeffrey were considered people of influence by James Smythe, persons who might help him in his career. She realized even more how she was considered when the midshipman said "Mr. Vice, the King." Elisabeth would be considered the junior officer present and knew what was expected of her. She rose, wine glass in hand. "Gentlemen, the King, long may he reign as King in England." The two boys laughed at the joke but to Elizabeth it was not quite a joke. She would be living in England. She had even fought against the king's enemies but she hadn't changed her opinion of the King or of his ministers.

When they reached the gangplank the next morning she suddenly froze. She couldn't put one foot in front of the other. It wasn't only that she was leaving her country, although that was there too. Every time she had gone aboard ship disaster had followed. In Carolina she had gone aboard the *Phoebe*. On her she had lost all her posessions. It was also true when she had gone aboard again in Halifax. In her mind's eye she saw the cannon ball smash Mr. Emmons and the look of Pat's shoulder. She hadn't even been able to be with him as he died. Now she was going on a ship again and she was afraid, very afraid, of another disaster.

Jeffrey felt her body shake but he couldn't help her much. Captain Nordstein was watching and he would think that Elizabeth was afraid of the ocean. That would be a bad beginning to the voyage. All Jeffrey could do was to help Elizabeth to her cabin. She knew why she was afraid. She had lost her father. She had lost her mother. She had lost friends when they had fought the French lugger. Now she was leaving her only friend behind in New York. All she had left was Jeffrey. He would be a sea officer on the ship and then would be with his family. Reason enough to fear the future.

There were no other passengers and they got acquainted with Captain Nordstein. He had been born in Stralsund in Swedish Pommerania and drifted into the British merchant service. His hair was grizzled, his face square and he spoke little. The first mate was of the same type. The captain also had old-fashioned ideas. When he saw that Jeffrey assumed no airs as a naval officer and truly wanted to learn Captain Nordstein was glad enough to make him a watch standing officer as second mate. Like most merchant ships the *Sophia* was short handed. Jeffrey not only stood watches but also turned out at the call for "All Hands."

On the other hand Captain Nordstein treated Elizabeth as he thought a lady should be treated. He suggested strongly, very strongly, that she should have as little contact with the crew, including the cook, as was possible. He also suggested that she should be on deck only during good weather. Unfortunately the North Atlantic didn't have much good weather in early spring. Elizabeth would have liked to rebel. She remembered herself on the *Phoebe* and Mr. Guerney making a tarpaulin for her. Unfortunately, that also brought up the memory of the shambles in the wardroom and when she stood with the crew on the deck for burial services. Besides, she didn't want to interfere with Jeffrey's position as a temporary second mate. So she stuck mostly to the great cabin and her bunk. Her cabin did have a bunk, not a hammock, and even had a folding shelf that served as a desk and dressing table.

Jeffrey was learning a lot. Many of the officers of the British navy were satisfied to be fighting men, leaving navigation to the master and his mates. Jeffrey wanted to be able to navigate as well as fight. Captain Nordstein was paid a bonus for a quick passage so he drove the *Sophia*. The men were called out often to handle sail. The cloud cover prevented the use of a sextant to determine their position but Captain Nordstein taught Jeffrey the value of the long line, dead reckoning, how to judge the wind and the action of the birds. They made the entrance to the British Channel in a mere four weeks.

For Elizabeth the voyage was troubling. Being below deck so much with no one to talk to allowed her to think about her position. She was cut off from America, from her only friend, and even from the sailors she had known who were now on the *Amazon*. In England, she would only have Jeffrey. He had made it clear in New York that his freedom of action was a result of his being a younger son. Now he was heir to a considerable estate. He was also a member of the nobility, to be addressed as "the Honorable Jeffrey Kent." That might make a difference in his attitude.

Then there was his uncle, the Earl of Severn. He was obviously a very powerful man. Admiral Graves, His Majesty's Commander of all the Ships and Stations in North America, had hastened to do him a personal favor. The Earl had written that he was willing to acknowledge Elizabeth as a member of the family, to have Jeffrey pay her fare and any debts. What did he have in mind for her when they got to England? They had never met in person.

In England her father would be considered an active rebel. Maybe that would be forgotten in view of her meritious service on the *Phoebe* or maybe not. At least she wasn't a follower of the Jacobites, as the adherents of the Stewart kings like Flora MacDonald were called.

However, first and foremost of all would they allow her to continue her relationship to Jeffrey? When it came to it he was still a minor. He would have to obey his father or his uncle. Or they could have his naval superiors send him off to India or someplace else far away. She was helpless in England and knew it. That was a thought as bleak as the green-gray waves of the Atlantic. She couldn't even run away. They, the Earl or Sir Kent, could claim guardianship over her. They were her closest relatives, even closer than her uncle in Carolina. Maybe she could disappear, dress as a boy. She did know some medecine. Maybe she could ship aboard a merchantman. If she did that she would lose Jeffrey anyway. There weren't many jobs that were open to women and even fewer without references or powerful friends. That thought was even bleaker.

Elizabeth was on deck on one of the rare sunny days when the *Sophia* was ordered to heave-to by a British sloop-of-war near the Scilly Islands. As the midshipman climbed aboard Elizabeth had the feeling of having been through all this before when the *Amazon* stopped *Phoebe*.

"All right captain, line up your men. You don't need this many to navigate to port. We need sailors for the navy and will take five under the law for impressing seamen. I'll take them as "volunteers" so they get a bonus instead of being listed as pressed men. If I don't get enough that way I'll just "press" them." Captain Nordstein suppressed a curse and started lining up his crew. Suddenly Jeffrey came up on the quarterdeck in full uniform and with his sword at his side and his cocked hat on.

"What seems to be the trouble, Captain?"

"This officer wishes to take some of my men."

Jeffrey swung on the midshipman. "Your name and ship, Mister." Elizabeth had heard Jeffrey use that tone before when he gave orders to engage the *Nymphe*.

"I am Midshipman Sidney Gardner of his Majesty's ship *Swift*, sir." The "sir" was reluctant but Jeffrey was in the uniform of a lieutenant and thus the midshipman's superior.

"This is a ship under orders of the government carrying urgent dispatches from Admiral Graves to their Lordships of the Admiralty." He saw the midshipman glance at the figure of Elizabeth on the quarterdeck. "And I am also conveying my cousin to my uncle, the Earl of Severn. That should satisfy your captain." He turned to Captain Nordstein. "Set sail immediately, Captain. Mr. Gardner is leaving, now!" The voice cracked like a whip. The unlucky midshipman went back over the side with his men, followed by the laughter of the *Sophia's* crew. Jeffrey knew that he had made an enemy of that midshipman and possibly of the commander of the sloop-of-war as well but he didn't care. He had done something he just had to do.

Jeffrey wasn't laughing or accepting any thanks. He swung around and went back down the companionway. Elizabeth followed him into the great cabin. He was sitting at the table with his head in his hands. "I went against the good of the Service, Elizabeth. I had to. Those were men

I commanded, my men. They trusted me. I couldn't let them be taken." There was nothing for Elizabeth to say. She naturally was on the side of the men. In the merchant service sailors got decent if monotonous food and decent pay. In the navy they got neither. She didn't have Jeffrey's loyalty to the navy. She wasn't loyal to the Revolutionary cause either and she hadn't even been very loyal to Anna.

When they got to a spot off the Island of Wight Jeffrey had Captain Nordstein signal a lugger which took Jeffrey and Elizabeth into Portsmouth while the *Sophia* continued on her way to London. Once ashore Jeffrey looked around Portsmouth warmly. "It's good to be home, Elizabeth."

She felt cold and empty. Here in England she felt truly in exile. The houses seemed strange. The English as it was spoken here sounded strange to her ears. Even Jeffrey, standing straight in his uniform beside her, seemed a stranger. He seemed so at ease. His head was up as he surveyed the scene outside the brick gate of the navy yard. He so obviously knew his way around town. Without hesitation he took Elizabeth to the "Admiral Boscawen", a public house down the street. He took two rooms and inquired about the schedule of the mail coaches. The parlor maid took them up to their rooms and lit a fire in the grate. "There, that's good," Jeffrey told her. "Now bring up some tea and scones. That's the ticket for a brisk British day." Only then did he notice that Elizabeth was still sitting in a chair all huddled up in her wet cloak. He helped her get her cloak off and noticed that her hands were cold as ice. "Here, move up next to the fire and warm up." She nodded and moved next to the fire but it didn't help. Neither did the tea the maid brought up and the scones tasted like sawdust to her. Her hands and feet felt like frozen clumps. She answered Jeffrey's talk automatically but she only remembered that they had some supper before she crawled shiveringly into her bed. The room closed in around her.

Jeffrey got her up early the next morning for breakfast. The mail coach left at six, before it was really dawn. Elizabeth had gotten washed and dressed somehow and now sat huddled up in her cloak by the window of the coach. There were some other passengers but they were only a blur to her. The sun rose as they rumbled out of Portsmouth and the dew sparkled on the grass. Jeffrey talked enthusiastically about the landscape and about his home. After a while he noticed that Elizabeth wasn't answering him. "What's the matter? Are you sick? You are as pale as you were when we left New York."

"No, I'm not sick. I never get sick on a boat or in a coach. You know that. I guess I am scared. This is home for you. It is all foreign to me. I shouldn't have come. I should have stayed in New York with Anna. I don't belong here.

"We'll make you belong. You'll see. You'll love it too. Just look at this rich country. Just look at the Downs." His hand indicated the hill visible through the window.

"Downs? Even the language is foreign. What you call the Downs is a big hill."

"Just give it a chance. Naturally you are nervous but just wait until I get you home."

Elizabeth knew that she should show some enthusiasm. She should be thankful that Jeffrey was taking her into his home. Instead she felt dull and empty. Nothing was going to help that. She couldn't even bring up the energy to wonder what his father would think of this moneyless American girl and what his mother would think of the stray he was pushing into her household. This was all wrong. Anna had been right to stay in America. Together they would have made out some way.

They stopped at some roadside inn. Jeffrey and the guard helped her down the steps which had been let down from the side of the coach as if she was a great lady. Then the post boy took her baggage out of the boot. The coachman blew his horn and the coach rumbled on. "There goes my last link with America," Elizabeth thought as the coach drew out of sight around a hill.

The landlord came out in his green baize apron and welcomed Jeffrey warmly. Elizabeth was introduced to him. She didn't know what to do. Did one curtsy to an inn keeper or not? She just stood still while the landlord gave her a sharp looking over. Apparently standing still was the right thing to do. Then they were invited in and the landlord suggested something to eat and a warm-up. Jeffrey wouldn't have it. "You'll hear all my stories soon enough, Mr. Morley. I promise to come down soon for a glass. As soon as I can. Right now I just want to borrow your gig so we can get up to the house. Father didn't know when we would come so he couldn't send down the carriage for us. I want to get Miss Elizabeth settled too." The inn keeper laughed and had his hostler bring out a small two seater vehicle and hitch up a single horse. Jeffrey confidentially took up the reins and settled Elizabeth beside him. She was still in her daze.

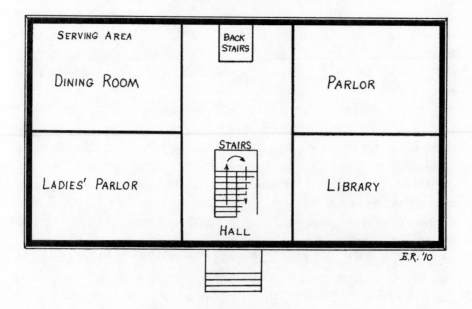

Upstairs Floor Plan

| GUEST | BATH | GUEST | BATH / TO ATTIC | JEFFREY BEDROOM | JEFFREY PARLOR |

HALLWAY

| ELIZABETH BEDROOM | ELIZABETH PARLOR | BATH / DRESSING | | BATH / DRESSING | MASTER BEDROOM |

OAKDALE MANOR

| SERVING AREA / DINING ROOM | BACK STAIRS | PARLOR |
| LADIES' PARLOR | STAIRS / HALL | LIBRARY |

E.R. '10

OAKDALE MANOR

GENTRY

As the gig swept up the driveway Elizabeth came out of her daze enough to examine the house. It seemed reassuring, not much different from the plantation houses she had known in Carolina. There were the familiar red brick walls set off by white stone lintels under the windows. There were additional windows set under the slate roof in the dormers. Beds of yellow daffodils nodded on each side of the steps. More buildings seem to be hidden under trees to their left. A groom came out from that direction to take charge of the gig and the horse. Another servant in livery opened the door for them after allowing Jeffrey one blow of the knocker. Elizabeth just had time to note the wide stairway sweeping up from the front hall as Jeffrey's parents came out of the room to their right. Now Elizabeth was in Jeffrey's house, his home.

There was no question of the warmth of their welcome. Jeffrey's father kept his well-bred composure but his voice was warm as were his brown eyes. "You are welcome in this house, Miss Troyes, and I hope you will make it your home as well," he told her after she curtsied formally.

Mrs. Kent was less restrained. She had tears in her eyes as she threw her arms around Jeffrey. Then she loosened a flood of questions without giving Jeffrey time to answer. "Why didn't you tell us when you were coming? Have you eaten? Was the voyage rough?"

Jeffrey was finally able to break in with answers. "Both you and the Earl wrote me that I was needed here. We took the first ship that was available. A letter would have reached you no faster than we did." Elizabeth was able to use the time they talked to get her bearings. Jeffrey's father was a tall man. He wore a blue coat over a flowered waistcoat., tan breeches and highly polished boots. His hair was unpowdered and turning gray. His wife was a small woman with blond hair under a cap and cornflower blue eyes. She had the superb complexion of the British. Her dress was a flowered muslin with a wide skirt. Elizabeth was well aware that her own skirt was unfashionably narrow but a wide skirt would have been an intolerable nuisance aboard ship. It would have billowed like a sail. She hadn't needed a fashionable skirt in New York either and hadn't had the money to buy one anyway. The butler brought in food and drink on a silver tray. Elizabeth found that she was hungry and Jeffrey piled in with the enthusiasm of youth and a long spell of monotonous food. The *Sophia of Hanover* didn't feature fine cooking. "I can reccomend the food." Sir Kent told them. "It is mostly of our own raising."

Elizabeth agreed that the food was fine. She had relaxed enough so that she could taste again. The roast beef with just a touch of mustard practically melted in her mouth and she took a second slice of ham with the bread. The cider complemented the food. Sir Kent contented himself with a glass of wine but Jeffrey's mother joined in the eating for courtesy's sake. Jeffrey needed to talk and Elizabeth was content to sit back and watch the conversation flow. The room was wonderfully homelike. The fire was just enough to take the chill off. The chairs were comfortable and the furniture gleamed with polish. It would be good to live here, she thought. Jeffrey was very much at ease and told his parents about the *Phoebe*, Elizabeth and why he had brought her. He stressed the hard conditions in America and her courage. Then it was her turn to answer questions.

"You didn't think to write us, Miss Elizabeth?" Sir Kent asked. "After the death of your parents, I mean. From what Jeffrey tells us we are closer relatives than even the man you call your uncle or those people in Boston."

"No, I didn't. I wouldn't have even if I had known you existed. Appealing to people in Britain would not have been a good idea, even if I could have gotten a letter through. The British, any British, were not considered our friends after the war began. There had been too much blood shed. My father was killed in battle fighting against the King but there had been many murders committed by the Tories. Most of the Highlanders in our section were for the crown. They copied the methods learned from the Duke of Cumberland to suppress the rebels in Scotland. First disarm the potential enemies and then kill them and their families. From what I have heard the Duke did not get his title of "Billy the Butcher" for nothing. Elizabeth knew she was being harsh and should frame her talk in politer terms but she was too tired to be very polite.

"Yes, wars seem to banish clear thinking." Sir Kent didn't seem to be disturbed by Elizabeth's harsh account. "However, we do not think of the Americans as enemies. Perhaps that is because the war is not so close to us here. We are your relatives and we would like to make you welcome if you will let us."

Jeffrey looked at her. He seemed hurt by her recital but came to her defense anyway. "I think Elizabeth is very tired. We have been on the road since dawn and only arrived in Portsmouth yesterday." Elizabeth was thankful to him. Tomorrow she might be able to think better and frame her answers in a more tactful way.

"We have been thoughtless," Mrs. Kent apologized. "We should not have submitted you to all those questions today. There are rooms ready for you and have been for weeks. Sleep yourselves out." She rang for the housekeeper while Elizabeth made some sort of polite response. The bedroom she was taken to looked wonderful to her. However she was glad she had refused the services of a maid. She wanted no more new people. There was a feather comforter on the bed and a blaze in the grate. A nightgown and a robe had been laid out for her. She managed to get undressed and snuggled under the covers. She just had time to realize that a warming pan had been passed over the sheets and that the wall paper was green with silver stripes. Then she was asleep.

She woke up with the sun shining on her face through the window panes and realized that it was morning. She had been asleep for eighteen hours. She slipped on the robe. Neither the robe nor the nightgown were hers. They probably belonged to Jeffrey, she thought. It was kind of someone to get them out for her. There was a pitcher of really warm water next to the wash basin and it helped her to wake up fully. She washed herself quickly and combed her hair. It still felt salty and dusty. She would wash it properly when she had the chance. Then she stepped to the window and opened it. The smells that came in weren't so different from those in Carolina. Oak wood smoke, a whiff from the stables and the smell of bacon frying were all familiar. Someone was gently knocking at her door. "The family are having breakfast in fifteen minutes if you would care to join them, miss," came a woman's voice.

"I'll be ready," Elizabeth cried out cheerfully. She realized that she was hungry, ravenous in fact. Well, of course, she thought. I slept through supper and lunch wasn't that heavy. It was a very good lunch though. It didn't take her long to brush her teeth and get dressed. She didn't need anyone to show her to the breakfast room. She just followed the sound of voices and the smell of food. She went down the stairs, noting the hand-painted Chinese wallpaper that lined the wall. The handrail was burnished so smoothly that she really wanted to slide down it. Jeffrey and his parents were standing at the entrance of the parlor. Sir Kent pulled out a chair for her and Jeffrey did the same for his mother. "Good morning. I hope you slept well?"

"Very well, about eighteen hours I guess. I apologise."

"No apologies needed. From what Jeffrey told us it has been a while since either of you slept in a really comfortable bed."

Elizabeth enjoyed the breakfast very much. The fine china, the well polished silver all indicated a well run household. It was quite different from the inn they had lived in when they were in New York or the great cabin of the *Sophia of Hanover*. And it was much finer than her uncle's house. Even her own house, where she lived with her mother, had not been as well kept. They hadn't had the time for the niceties. She glanced out of the windows and had a view of the stables and outbuildings behind the trees. Sir Kent noticed her glance. "Would you like a ride around the estate with Jeffrey and me, Miss Elizabeth?"

Jeffrey laughed. "Father is proud of his scientific farming. He can't wait to show it to us. He shows it off to anyone else who visits as well. I've been shown it every time I came home on leave or on vacation from school."

"I would be very much interested in seeing it. We were farmers in Carolina." Elizabeth was not just being polite. She really was interested how farming here differed from what she was used to. "It will have to be a gentle horse though. I haven't ridden in quite a while." She remembered how long it had been. She hadn't been in the saddle since her mother became ill. Her uncle didn't have any riding horses. There were just the two work horses to pull the wagon and some oxen for the plow.

Sir Kent had noted the 'quite a while'. "Do you hunt, Miss Elizabeth?"

Elizabeth was puzzled. What did hunting have to do with riding. "We hunt but I am a little light for a musket, even a Pennsylvania rifle."

Jeffrey explained. "He means fox hunting on horseback. They do a lot of it as well as coursing for hares even though this isn't as good country for it as the Shires."

There it was again, the difference between America and England. It was just like calling a hill 'the Downs' and maybe it was even more than that. She tried to answer Sir Kent's question. "Oh, like that. I believe

General Washington is an enthusiastic fox hunter in Virginia and they do some of that kind of hunting down-country on the big plantations. In upland Carolina we hunt for the pot. Come October you will hardly find a man at home. They are all out after deer, turkeys and sometimes bear. That's our winter meat. Of course we all club pigeons."

"Club? That's hardly sporting, is it?"

"Don't know about it being sport. Those pigeons come in flocks of thousands. They'll clean out a grain field if you let them and break the branches of the trees they roost on, they are so many. They are very good eating though. That's our revenge for the damage they cause. We salt them down in barrels." Her answer seemed to satisfy Sir Kent.

At the stable a groom brought out a small russet mare for Elizabeth. She stepped in front of the mare, fed her some fruit she had taken from the breakfast table and blew into the horse's nostrils. She knew that was the way to make a horse acquainted with its rider. Sir Kent nodded approvingly from the back of his grey gelding and Jeffrey mounted his own horse. They trotted through the orchards fragrant with blossoms and by fenced meadows with black faced sheep. Elizabeth was glad Sir Kent kept the pace down. She suspected that Jeffrey was glad too. After all he hadn't been on a horse for a while either.

Their path led by several tenant farmer's houses and Sir Kent stopped by each one. He introduced Jeffrey to the tenants as "My son Jeffrey, who will now make his home here." Elizabeth was also introduced. "Miss Elizabeth Troyes from Carolina in America. She helped manage an estate there after her father died." Her father's farm hadn't really been an estate but she didn't argue. Elizabeth forced her mind to function. This ride was more than a casual exercise. The introductions never varied. Sir Kent and Jeffrey shook hands with each farmer but they didn't dismount. Jeffrey was now introduced as the heir to the estate and she was being given the status as a landholder. So far she had not been introduced as a member of the family but obviously birth and status mattered here. She suspected that her family status was being left for Sir Kent's older brother, the Earl, to decide. The Earl had acknowledged her as a member of the family in his letter, she remembered.

They rode by a field of hops, a crop that Elizabeth didn't know and by a structure that she was told was an oast house used to dry the hops. They also rode through some woods which Sir Kent inspected as carefully as he did his fields and orchards.

That evening the Kents and Elizabeth discussed the differences between farming in England and America. The subject of the forests came up. "You don't value your trees in America?" Sir Kent was surprised.

"Hardly. The first thing a farmer has to do when he wants more land is to chop down the trees. Then he has to clear out the stumps before he can plant anything."

"Aren't you afraid you will run out of timber? Sir Jervis always carries acorns in his pocket to replace the oaks we take to build our ships. I do the same thing."

"We've got hundreds of miles of trees. Beyond the Carolinas is Kentucky and the Ohio country. That's almost all trees with cougars, bears and wild natives. That's one of the grievances. The King wanted to restrict settlers to the east side of the mountains and even chase out those who had already settled west. The land was to be left to the tribes and a few Quebecquois fur traders."

The discussion about farming ran on the next day. "You managed the plantation with your mother?"

"Nothing so grand. We had two hundred acres cleared, mostly in corn and tobacco. We ran some cattle as well. That's all we could manage with the labor we had available. I helped with the tobacco stripping and corn shucking but I am too light for the plowing, of course."

"You did the work yourselves?"

"In America it is said that a man must be able to geld a pig, build a ship and shoot a gun."

"And you can do all those things?"

"Well, I helped when a cow had difficulty calving. I can cook and sew. According to the British navy I am an adequate clerk and served as surgeon's mate. I didn't handle a gun on the *Phoebe* but there were plenty of muskets firing at us."

Jeffrey cut in. "She was mentioned in dispatches for carrying wounded from the open deck under fire. She carried a pistol in New York. She isn't afraid of anything," he finished proudly. Elizabeth remembered how scared she had been on the *Phoebe*. Carrying in the wounded was just something that had to be done. She remembered that it hadn't been enough for Pat McManus.

That evening she caught Jeffrey alone in the parlor. "Why am I being questioned like this. It hurts to have to remember everything."

"Father is trying to place you. He never met anyone like you." Then he put his arm around her and kissed her. "I never met anyone like you either. By the way, Father is very impressed by your knowledge of farming," he went on slowly. "They want to know about America but remember, you home is now here, in England." Elizabeth swallowed hard. She was hard to place. She didn't know where she belonged herself. She felt her tears start up but she had sworn to herself that she would never cry again, not now and not ever. She was going to look forward and not back. She had told Sir Kent that every house in America had a gun. In Carolina they were using those guns on the British and they would use them on her if she ever tried to go back there. She had served in the British navy.

She knew that in order to live here she would still have to meet Jeffrey's uncle, the Earl. Well, that could be no harder than facing Sir Kent's questions and she had done that. She had faced Admiral Gambier and Captain Brathwaithe in New York. London and the Earl could be no more difficult.

LONDON TOWN

Before Elizabeth and Jeffrey left for London at the end of the week, Mrs. Kent told Elizabeth something important. "My husband and Jeffrey need you here. You care about the land. Robert never did. He only saw it as a source of income and Jeffrey is a navy man first and foremost. He really never had a chance to learn anything about the land or agriculture. When he was a boy he always hung around the village and the fishermen. I need you too. It is lonely to have only men and servants to talk to. They think differently." That gave Elizabeth enough peace of mind to actually look out of the windows of the mail coach. The green of the grass did seem greener than grass had been in Carolina and the landscape had a less straggly appearance. She could live here, Elizabeth decided, but she would always remain an American in England, not an English girl. Probably her grandmother had always remained a little bit French even after she landed in England.

Elizabeth had also made things clear to Sir Kent when he suggested she should buy some things in London. She was a poor girl. "I don't have much money left," she told him. "What I had from home was seized by the British navy as prize of war. My father was classed as a 'rebel' so I couldn't even try to get it back." She left out the story of the theft by the dock workers and the sergeant of marines. "I have lived on what I got from the navy as wages and prize money and that isn't much except for captains and admirals. Jeffrey helped me but I do not like to accept charity. I own three dresses, a jacket and a cloak, my sewing box with a gold thimble and an ivory miniature of my mother framed in gold. That is all. The navy would have seized those if they had found them. Oh yes, I also have eight guineas, earned money."

"You seem to have done marvelously well, but you are now a member of the family. My brother will probably give you an allowance. That is the way family members who have no land of their own are taken care of here. Jeffrey had an allowance from me while he was serving in the navy. Robert had an allowance too."

Jeffrey also talked to her about money. "Father has made the estate profitable. He inherited some money too. Mother also came from a wealthy family. Neither of them have expensive tastes like Robert had. Father is a country squire and that is enough for him. The Burnthursts, who are our neighbors, do have expensive tastes. They are probably in dun territory burdened in debt with their land mortaged. That is why they want me to marry their daughter Lily. I would have to settle money on her. The Burnthursts couldn't give her much of a dowry either. That's one of the reasons my parents don't care for the match. Often things are the other way around and men are on the lookout for rich wives, preferably well born, with influence as well."

Elizabeth had a lot to think about. She didn't have any money and there was nobody from whom she would inherit any either. She wondered what Sir Kent thought about that. She already knew what James Smythe had told Jeffrey. He should ditch her and look for a rich wife. If the Earl thought the same way she would be sent away from Jeffrey. It wouldn't matter if she was good looking and had been brave. Jeffrey would have to obey the head of the family. Of that she was sure. Sir Kent would defer to his older brother as well. I survived New York, she told herself, I can survive in London.

It was raining now. The coach bucketed along the muddy road. The horses slipped on the down grades and threw clumps of mud on the up grades but so far the passengers had not been asked to get out and walk to lighten the load. Inside the coach it was stuffy and it was crowded with passengers. They didn't talk to each other or to her or even Jeffrey so she could ignore them. There was only time to grab a snack at a roadhouse while the horses were being changed. Then the guard blew on his horn and the uncomfortable trip continued.

They rolled into London after dark and all Elizabeth saw of the city were a few flickering lamps. Some of the foot passengers carried lanterns or had link boys light their way but the pedestrians were only shadows to her. The "Crown and Anchor" that Jeffrey took her to smelled of horses and coal smoke. However the food was decent and the sheets had been aired. It was better than the inn they had lived in when they were in New York and better than on the *Sophia of Hanover* but Elizabeth missed Anna. Jeffrey would not be the right person to talk to about her fears.

The next morning, not too early, they called on the Earl at his town house in the newly fashionable West End. Jeffrey seemed just as tense as Elizabeth was. Both had taken care with their appearance. Jeffrey was in his best uniform but wore no sword. Elizabeth wore her best dress but knew that it really wasn't that good anymore. Luckily it had stopped raining and she wouldn't look like a drowned rat. She did have a hat that Mrs. Kent had given her and she had a silk scarf over her shoulders pinned with the miniature of her mother. She could do no more for her appearance.

A liveried footman ushered them to the Earl's parlor on the second floor. The first thing Elizabeth noted about her relative was his clothing. His bottle green coat fitted like a glove. He wore a flowered brocade waistcoat with lace at the throat and cuffs. He wasn't old but his hair was powdered and carefully arranged. It was only when she noted his clear eyes and powerful hands that she realized that this was no fop or playboy. The clothing was only that of a man who followed fashion. Underneath the appearance was a man of strength.

"So you are from the American branch of our family. We know little about them once they left for the colonies."

"There is little left of us. My father fell in battle. My mother died of lung fever brought on by over-work. My aunt died in childbirth and the baby with her. Her husband has re-married and was sending me to Boston to some cousins of his but that didn't work out. So here I am without home or money, a refugee from war." Elizabeth was proud that her voice didn't shake through the telling of that brutal tale.

"You could go back now that Earl Cornwallis has destroyed the rebel army at Camden."

"No, sir. I don't think I can ever go back. I have served with the British. I wouldn't be welcome even if I had a whole British regiment at my back and Washington was defeated. Anyone who tried to go back would find his cattle hamstrung and his barns burned. That was how it was when the war started. It will be worse now. Besides I have no home anymore. The house and the farm were sold. Some of the money went for taxes and some my uncle used for my upkeep."

"And the rest the Rebels stole?"

"The British navy took it. All of it."

"Elizabeth's chest with her money in it was seized when the *Amazon* intercepted the sloop she was travelling on," Jeffrey told his uncle. "As a matter of fact I was prize master. Didn't know who Elizabeth was at that point, of course, but it wouldn't have mattered. I couldn't have done anything else anyway. A prize is a prize, and so are the goods of any passengers travelling on it. The sloop was definitely enemy, travelling from a rebel port to a rebel port."

"Sounds like quite a tale. Maybe it will be better with some nourishment. Some ratafia and macaroons," he told the servant who answered his bell. "Would you like something stronger, Jeffrey?"

"No sir. It is still morning."

Elizabeth found that ratafia was a sweet drink. She didn't like it. Clearly the Earl didn't like it either and kept sipping his wine. After the servant had withdrawn the Earl indicated that Elizabeth should continue. The Earl was a good listener, almost as good as Anna. His questions were very much to the point. "So you don't believe we can win this war? One might even still call you a rebel at heart."

"I am sorry if my opinions offend you, sir, but you asked for my opinions. They hold even though I have served in the British navy. The English have won many battles: Brooklyn, Chad's Ford, Charleston, Camden. Despite those victories they are only able to hold a few cities. America is just too big to be conquered by a few regiments and the Americans always come back after a defeat. According to the journals Sir Kent showed me, the Loyalists," and she didn't call them Tories here, "couldn't even hold their posts at Ft. Motte and Ninety-six in Carolina."

"I am not offended by your opinions but I suggest you do not voice them here in England. People don't like to hear political or military ideas expressed by young ladies. That is especially true if they disagree with those opinions. It doesn't matter if your opinions are true and they might not be, you know."

"I'll try but it is hard when you hear some of the nonsense that you hear expressed about America and Americans. Some British officers have said that all Americans are barbarians, even the ones loyal to the King."

"You are a guest here and guests don't contradict their hosts. It isn't done."

Elizabeth nodded. There was nothing else to do. She resented being told what to say none the less. Children like Pat or Anna could be hurt or killed by politics. That didn't seem to matter to the Earl as long as good manners were observed. Children were not allowed to have a say about what happened to them. That was reserved to their elders. The Earl wasn't done yet. "Now to come back to you. My brother probably told you that we considered it better if I were your guardian." He noted Elizabeth's rebellious expression and nodded grimly. "You will find having a powerful guardian is useful at times. You have had experience what it is like to be an unprotected girl. You have been lucky so far, partly because of Jeffrey. It isn't always so." Mentally Elizabeth agreed with him. She remembered Anna and some of the other street kids she met in New York. However she didn't like the statement even if it was something meant for her own good. She didn't like that some one could tell her what to say or do, not at all.

"As I said," the Earl went on, "we don't know much about your family in America. However I have had my secretary do some research here. We were unable to find a portrait of your grandmother, your mother or you but we did find out some facts."

"I have a miniature of my mother here." She indicated the brooch on her shoulder. "It escaped the hands of the British navy."

"If you will lend it to me I will have it copied in oils. That is for our family portrait gallery. We like to show who we are."

"Of course, sir." She unpinned the brooch and handed it to the Earl. She was glad she had something of quality to show him. It made her less of a poor relative.

"You and your mother never used your title in America?"

"My title?"

"Yes. You are Elizabeth Troyes d' Raython. Your grandfather was Hubert, Sieur d'Raython. His land was confiscated by the French crown when he got involved in the last Huguenot rising, the Camisards, in 1704. He was killed in the fighting but the title descended in the female line."

Elizabeth felt faint. She was a noblewoman. Her mind raced and she gripped the arms of her chair hard. The title wouldn't have meant much in America but it certainly did matter here in England. It would matter even though she didn't have any land or money. Her title meant that she would be considered eligible for Jeffrey. His parents must have been told that she was of "good birth." That was probably why they hadn't objected to his bringing her into their home. She might be a better match than that little girl of the Burnthursts. That girl would bring in her whole family and their debts. Elizabeth had no family anymore and no debts. Elizabeth's mind was racing but her tongue seemed paralyzed.

"You weren't told?" The Earl's voice seemed to come from a long distance but she was determined not to faint. She could only nod at the Earl. Jeffrey seemed equally thunder struck. The Earl didn't seem to realize that what he said was anything unusual. The title was something usual to him. He kept right on talking and didn't see that he had changed everything for Elizabeth and Jeffrey.

"There is another thing." He surveyed Elizabeth through his quizzing glass. "That dress you are wearing really doesn't fit you anymore." Elizabeth started to protest but he waved her into silence. "You are growing, as is only natural. I presume one doesn't have to dress properly in a colonial town like New York. Here, however, you will dress as becomes my ward and a girl of quality. I will give you a note to Maria, the dressmaker on Conduit Street. She is a woman of sense and will fit you out. At my expense of course. You allowance of two hundred pounds a year would hardly cover it." He turned to Jeffrey. "You will need a civilian outfit as well. I will give you a note to Weston. He doesn't usually bother with boys and he is above your touch but he will do me the favor. You will need some decent boots as well. You aren't sloshing in salt water all the time now. After the two of you order your clothes you should show your cousin the sights of London. Perhaps that will give her a better idea of England than she seems to have right now." He went to his desk and scribbled out some notes for Jeffrey. He also passed over some gold coins. "You will need more than a lieutenant's salary to entertain her. I am relying on you."

When they reached the sidewalk they were still completely in a daze. Jeffrey was groping for some reality and Elizabeth knew that ratafia contained some alcohol but what she needed now was a slug of that strong corn liquor that her neighbor used to make. She needed something strong to unscramble her brain. The Earl had been so casual about her being a noblewoman, about giving her an allowance of two hundred pounds a year. She remembered the five shillings that Jeffrey had offered her in New York and the scrimping of the pennies by her and Anna. There were twelve pennies to a shilling and twenty shillings to a pound, twenty-one to a guinea. She remembered reciting the table of coinage from her arithmatic, farthings, half-pennies, shillings, crowns and the rest of them. And the Earl had told Jeffrey to show her London and for her to get new clothing. All this swirled in her mind without any order. Shopping for clothing would help. It was such a normal activity.

Jeffrey's mind was in no better shape than hers. This waif, this cousin whom he had sort of adopted was of as good a birth as he was. She was acceptable to his uncle and therefore to polite society. She might even be more acceptable than he was. Well maybe not, now that he was no longer a younger son. He was no longer a lowly midshipman, he was a civilian and an heir and he was going to have his clothing made by the best tailor in London. It was too much to think about. One thing he was sure of. He was not going to imitate his brother and enter high society. There was going to be no curricle, no fast horses and no gambling. That was the only thing he was sure of except Elizabeth. She was going to stay with him. She knew about being an agriculturalist and she was going to stay with him. She had told him that she needed him. He felt like throwing his arms around her and kissing her right here on the open street. It wouldn't do of course but he gave her hand a tight squeeze. It wasn't enough at all.

"We're going to have to hustle. Some luncheon, your dressmaker, Weston and the Admiralty. That's a lot to do. Some lunch and your dressmaker first. I am too hungry to wait till dinner."

"I feel all empty inside too. But you go ahead to the Admiralty. I can find a place to eat and then go to Conduit Street. I can take a hack or walk. It isn't far."

"Not alone you can't. You don't go anywhere in London alone. It isn't done."

"Why not. This isn't a wartime town like New York. Nobody will hurt me."

"They'll hurt me or at least my uncle will. Look, girls of birth don't walk alone in London. They go with a male relative, an elderly aunt or at least a servant. The Earl said for you to do as is proper for his ward and a girl of the quality. So we follow the rules. I can't kiss you on the street either and I want to."

"Me too."

"This town gossips. Someone would recognize me and the Earl would get to hear about it. Then I would get to hear about it from him in a quick and nasty manner. Very nasty. So we go to Fenton's for a bite to eat and then to your dressmaker. I will pick you up there later. If I need to, I can go to the Admiralty again tomorrow or skip it for today, go to Weston's and then the Admiralty tomorrow. They are not exactly waiting for an acting lieutenant. The Navy Board isn't either." Elizabeth didn't like getting a lecture from Jeffrey but maybe he was right. Things were done differently in England. She still felt that she was Elizabeth, the refugee from America, but maybe new clothes would help her play this new role as a girl of the quality. She said as much to him.

"No, you are no longer quite the same person as you were. Admiral Gambier and Captain Brathwaithe would not have treated you as they did if they had known you had a title. You might even gotten your chest back with your things in it. You've seen how the fact that my uncle is an earl has helped us get our passage here and everything."

Maria the dressmaker was a small, dark woman with penetrating eyes. She had come out to serve Elizabeth as soon as a shop girl had brought her the note from the Earl. "Miss is from the country, yes?"

"I am from America. I lost most of my clothing due to the war."

"You are for London?"

"She is living in Kent now," Jeffrey cut in. "She will need clothing for the country, not town."

"As you say," Maria answered smoothly. "But her guardian, the Earl of Severn, said that she is to be dressed properly. Isn't that so?"

There was something foreign to this woman but Elizabeth was impressed how she handled Jeffrey. She turned to the dressmaker. "When should my cousin call for me?"

"Perhaps at five. We have much to do."

Jeffrey knew there were times when it is wise to retreat. This was one of those times. When he left, closing the door firmly behind him, both women laughed. "Men, they know everything they think. Even about women's clothing." There was no malice in Maria's laughter, only amusement. They decided that Elizabeth would need a morning dress, a riding dress and something for more formal occasions. Then there would be shifts, petticoats and all the other underwear a girl required. Elizabeth didn't ask about prices but she wondered how girls that didn't have a rich uncle managed. This establishment didn't look like it had anything cheap. The whole allowance that her uncle had said she would get each year wouldn't cover the cost of her clothing. She had been told by the British officers wives that a governess would get about fifty pounds a year and her keep. For a maid ten or twelve pounds plus food and shelter was a good salary. The title and the Earl had put her into an entirely different class of people even from those officers wives who had snubbed her or if she would have to become a nursemaid or companion as she had thought she would have to be.

First came the job of measuring Elizabeth every which way. Critically Elizabeth looked at her body. She had changed physically in the last year.

There was no denying that she was now a young woman instead of a girl. It was a shock for her to see that change in her own body. It had been a long time since Elizabeth had really looked at herself. She hadn't wanted to see how she had changed. Now there was no avoiding it. The full length mirror didn't lie. Maybe with her changed circumstances she could face herself again.

Going over patterns and fabrics with Maria was fun. The dressmaker didn't seem to want to take advantage of the Earl's open offer to try to sell Elizabeth any of the fancy silks or brocades. "High fashion would be out of place for me," she had told Maria. "I'm sure my uncle doesn't plan to introduce me into high society. I won't need high fashion in the country. I might even go back to America." That last just slipped out. It was a remote hope rather than a reality. Life in America seemed so much more real than London to Elizabeth.

When Jeffrey returned Elizabeth's appearance stopped him cold. He faced a young lady instead of his familiar companion. He bowed very formally to Elizabeth standing there in a blue ribbed riding dress with black frogging. The jacket was cut tight but the skirt flared out to one side for side-saddle riding. On her head was a hat with one curling feather. Then Jeffrey burst out laughing.

"What's so funny?" Elizabeth asked him sharply.

"I want to see Mrs. Burnthurst's face when you are formally introduced to her. I have heard that she spoke of you as 'that ill-dressed hoyden of no birth that Jeffrey dragged home like a stray cat.'"

"Your father and your uncle have both remarked on my shabby dress. Now I don't have to be ashamed of how I am dressed. There are two more outfits coming. One is a formal dress in pink silk." Elizabeth didn't feel like laughing at all. How she appeared to others was not a joke. Then she forced her mind away from her own feelings. "How did things go at the Admiralty?"

"They didn't keep me waiting when I handed them that note from my uncle. They put me on half pay as a lieutenant. They granted me that status. I didn't want to resign my warrant. They let it stand almost as if it was a commission. You know why I didn't want to resign. It was easy for them too since they didn't have to find me a ship." Jeffrey stood there considering things. "Let's you and I go out and celebrate."

"Celebrate what?"

"Everything. This shop," he waved his hand around the display of fancy dresses. "My being still a lieutenant. Uncle telling you that you were a noblewoman. Everything."

The dinner was not altogether a success. They were too unsure of themselves. Elizabeth questioned Jeffrey about titles descending in the female line. "It dates back to King Henry V," he told her. "That king claimed the throne of France based on the female line. So now you can claim your title since there is no male heir. I am sure uncle has already had the heralds dig out your coat of arms. He is fussy that way. It will be in the shape of a diamond instead of a shield since you are a female but it is a valid coat of arms. It's not an English title so you can't sit in the House of Lords."

"And your status as a lieutenant?"

"That's a bit irregular since I am not old enough to sit for the examination. I am not on the active list so it doesn't matter. I'll just be another lieutenant on the shelf."

"So now I am Lady Elizabeth and Jeffrey is a British officer and heir to a considerable estate." That didn't sound right to Elizabeth. She had ridden over the estate and saw how big it was and the respect Jeffrey got from the tenants. She would have to think over the implications of those facts. She couldn't change them. And she would have to trust the Earl. He had made his position as head of the family clear.

"Tomorrow I will show you London. That should be a break from all this serious talk." Elizabeth thought she could use some relaxing, lots of relaxing.

The next morning they were ready for sightseeing. Palaces and castles weren't places where real people lived. They were something out of fairy tales or plays. Her father had read her a play about Henry V, she remembered. She never thought that Henry V, a king, would have anything to do with her life. Maybe Lady Elizabeth Troyes d'Raython was also something out of a play and she wondered if the curtain would come down on her.

The noises of London could be heard through the windows of the coffee room. There was the clatter of horses hooves, wagon wheels and apprentices taking down shutters. This was a big city, not a colonial town like New York, Halifax or the backwoods of Carolina. Jeffrey took her first to see St. James palace. She wasn't too impressed. "I expected turrets, towers and dungeons like in the stories. These are just big buildings, nice but nothing special. The park behind it and the fancy carriages are a bit like the stories at least."

"Wait until you see the Tower and St. Paul's. Towers, turrets, gold domes coming up. We will go by water so you get the full effect. That is more than you can see from a closed hack." A shadow crossed his face as he pointed to a curricle being driven through the park, "That's a curricle, the kind of carriage my brother was killed in while driving. It's flimsy and I won't have one. You can go fast in a curricle and see and be seen if that is what you want. Riding or a carriage will do for me."

"No, a boat will be fine," Elizabeth assured him. "We are used to boats."

They walked down to the Whitehall steps. The Thames with its glittering silver gray waters, lay before them. "Oars, sir? Sculls, miss?" The boatmen crowded around them looking for customers. Jeffrey picked out a sturdy waterman sporting a gold earring.

"You've served?" he asked him.

"Maintopman on the *Arrogant*, 74, Captain Cornish," was the sullen answer. "You can't press me, lieutenant. I've got my exemption with me." Jeffrey was still in his uniform.

"Of course you have one or you wouldn't be seen near the water. I'm not looking for men. I want to show my cousin London. She has never been here so row easy."

"Aye, aye." The sullen tone hadn't changed and the waterman conspicously omitted the customary 'sir'.

"Can the navy just grab anyone on land?" Elizabeth asked.

"Press gang can grab anyone. All they have to claim you are 'idle'. Then unless you have your exemption handy or are one of the quality you're on a king's cruiser and out at sea. Nobody will hear what happened to you. Aboard it's rotten food, stinking water and the cat-of-nine tails for them whats objects. You wouldn't want to be aboard a king's ship. Not ever. Jail is better."

Elizabeth laughed. "Thanks for the warning but its a little late for me. Meet the acting surgeon's mate of the *HMS Phoebe*, sloop. I guess I was sort of pressed. Discharged now."

"Always glad to meet a shipmate but I've never met one as neat looking as you."

"She can sew you up real nice too. We were in action against a Frenchy." Jeffrey's voice expressed his pride in Elizabeth.

The waterman's voice had lost its sullenness. "Now step aboard, miss, and I will show you the greatest town in the world. Tide is right to go down to the Tower too." Elizabeth reflected, if she was back aboard a ship she would want to be with the the the crew and Mr. Guerney, not on the quarterdeck with Jeffrey and Captain Hartman, title or no title. She wasn't cut out to be an officer.

Westminster Bridge loomed up ahead of them but the boatman shot safely between the columns. Jeffrey pointed out the sights in competition with the boatman talking but Elizabeth found the river more fascinating than the land. The Thames was crowded with shipping of all kinds. There were big sailing barges, North Country brigs loaded with coal, an East Indiaman getting ready to sail, ships from Hamburg and Sweden. Elizabeth saw the golden dome of St. Paul gleaming above the smoke of the city and other church towers poking through the haze as well.

"There, miss. There is the bloody Tower. Get in there and they chop your head off. Plenty of young girls too. Ther' was Lady Jane Grey and Ann Boylen and Catherine Howard. 'Bout fifty years ago they chopped that Scotch lord's head off. Lovat his name was. Don't pay to get across a king's hawser, not even a king like 'Farmer George.'"

"Lord Lovat led Clan Fraser at Culloden," Jeffrey added. "Now the Fraser clansmen are the 71st regiment. You met them in New York. Lovat's son is their colonel. Guess he learned to change sides. Maybe he has changed his ideas and maybe not, Elizabeth thought. After all she had served in the British navy but she hadn't really changed her opinions. She also liked what the waterman had said. His Britannic Majesty, George III, by the Grace of God King of England, Scotland and Ireland, was simply "Farmer George" to him, a powerful neighbor but just a neighbor all the same. There was nothing divine about him as far as the boatman was concerned.

The boat swung toward the landing. Elizabeth saw the turrets of the White Tower loom above everything. She also saw the batteries of cannon and the sentries everywhere. The waterman pointed to a barred gate just downstream from the landing. "You see miss, that gate down there? That's the Traitor's Gate. That's where they bring in the rebels before they hang them or chop them." Elizabeth shuddered. This wasn't a fairy tale after all. She was a rebel and she could see herself brought here and locked in a cell to await the headsman and his axe.

"Thank you, sir." There was nothing sullen about the boatman now as Jeffrey paid him off. "And good luck, miss."

"You see what service in the Royal Navy gets you?" Jeffrey joked. "You don't get sent to the Tower by the Traitor's Gate."

"That's not very funny. If the Americans lose, they will bring George Washington and Sam Adams here. They might have brought my father here if he hadn't been killed in battle."

"Sorry. But look on this as history. The first walls here were built by the Romans over 1500 years ago. William the Conqueror put up the White Tower in 1068."

Elizabeth couldn't see it that way. The Tower was a jail and a fortress, and it always had been. She felt it and the guards were just waiting for her. She could understand Simon Fraser very well indeed. He might not like everything King George and his ministers said or did but he could live under them. She would have to also. She might not like it but she had to. She hadn't even liked everything William, Earl of Severn, said to her but she could live with it. That was the price she would have to pay for Jeffrey and a place in his house. She found she didn't enjoy the menagerie either. She could see killing an animal to protect her herds or for food but she couldn't see locking them up for life so that people could stare at them.

Saint Paul was more of a success. The soaring dome gave her a feeling of space and peace. Jeffrey led her around to read some of the memorial plaques to the famous men and women. Some were in Latin which neither of them could read and some had very beautiful sculptures around them. In the churchyard were the stalls of the book sellers and print makers. She was glad to see that not all Englishmen agreed with the policies of the King. Some of the cartoons were downright nasty.

She and Jeffrey bought some buns with shrimps that were being sold by children circulating through the crowd. The food sellers included both boys and girls, many of them younger than Elizabeth. It seemed quite a feat to swing around with the big trays but nothing ever spilled. Then Jeffrey and Elizabeth walked down to Blackfriars where the pantomines were being given. "You want to go to the theater tonight?" he asked.

"No, this whole town is a stage. I don't need the theater."

"We must go to the Pantheon. Everyone who is anyone goes to the Pantheon in the evening."

Packages from both Maria and Weston had arrived at the inn while they were gone so Elizabeth was willing to go with Jeffrey. The Pantheon was everything Jeffrey had promised. Mysterious lights were reflected from the ceiling. There were niches with statues lit in green and purple.

Much of the interior sported gold paint. Overdressed men whom Jeffrey called "macaronies" strutted about with women in silk dresses with wide hoops and having their hair dressed in fantastic shapes strutted with them. Elizabeth pointed one man out to Jeffrey. He was indeed something to see. He wore a pink waistcoat embroidered with roses under a long coat of purple velvet laced with silver. His shoes had high heels decorated with small flashing diamonds. He carried a cane decorated with ribbons. White lace cascaded from his collar and cuffs. The woman with him wore her hair dressed in the shape of a crouching dog. Elizabeth stared. She couldn't help herself. The lady noticed and hid her face behind a painted fan with gold ribs. Elizabeth blushed with embarrassment. "They are like painted butterflies," she whispered to Jeffrey. "They are pretty but useless."

"Some of them might be but make no mistake. Some of these here have big estates or are cabinet ministers. It's the same thing with some of the big gamblers. Lord Sandwich, First Lord of the Admiralty, doesn't even takes time to eat properly. He just grabs a slice of meat between two slices of bread while he plays cards. Runs the Admiralty just the same. Makes and unmakes Captains and Admirals. The ladies give dinners and routs while they play politics. There are more decisions made in drawing rooms or over the dinner table than are made in Parliament. Fashion is just fashion but fashion and money alone can't get you into a position of power. You have to have birth and land as well, and the right connections."

"Looks silly. Your father doesn't dress like that."

"Father is just a plain country squire. He isn't fashionable at all. Uncle is fashionable and look how fussy he was about our dress."

Elizabeth couldn't adjust to London. Places like the Pantheon and poor apprentices everywhere. Jails like the Tower and fancy marble monuments. Fortunes spent on gambling and fancy clothes. This was too different from America. She could live in the country well enough but not in London. Jeffrey didn't belong here either. He had told her he didn't want to be in high society. "Let's go home," she told him as they returned from the Pantheon.

Jeffrey looked at her sharply. "Home?" he repeated.

Elizabeth had already considered all the implications of that statement. "Home" she said decisively.

It didn't go quite that quickly. Elizabeth had to try on her fancy dress. Jeffrey had to go to the Admiralty again to try to get his prize money released. Many officers left that to agents but they charged a commission for their services. He also had to open his own account at Coutts, the banker. Both of their allowances would be paid into that account as well. All this would take at least a day.

Elizabeth also had one more thing to discuss with Jeffrey before they returned to Oakdale Manor, as the Kent estate was called. "I don't want to be a drag on your family. I want to do something useful. I know the tenants won't listen to me. I am a girl and a newcomer. Besides I don't know much about English farming. Your mother has a housekeeper. She doesn't really need me either. I can't take a position as a governess or tutor. I am too young. I don't want to be a useless guest forever."

"You can't take any kind of paid position. Neither father nor my uncle would let you. People would think they can't support you or don't want to. Besides the pay is lousy. A housekeeper gets fifteen guineas a year plus room and board. A butler gets the same plus a new suit every two years. A maid gets only five to seven guineas a year plus her keep. He thought for a moment. "You're a clerk or at least the navy thinks so. You did well on the *Phoebe*. We don't talk much about it but father can't read or write his own letters. His eyes get the alphabet all twisted up. That is why mother wrote the letter we got in New York. You could be his secretary."

"He'd let me?"

"I think so. Mother would be glad to give up that part of her work. There are things that get done that we don't tell our bailiff, Mr. Clark, about either. Things that don't concern the Manor. We have shares in the Hudson Bay Company that owns half of Canada. Father and Uncle have shares in some of the independent traders that run ships between India and China. The East India Company allows that as long as the ships don't trade directly with England. That's a company monopoly. Nobody talks about being in trade. It's not considered genteel like farming or government service. Trade is more profitable than farming, but no one admits being in it. They don't admit being in manufacturing either. Only cits do that, people who have only money but no title, never any of the quality. It isn't done. You could be trusted to keep your mouth shut. You're family."

Elizabeth was reassured. The Earl said he had a secretary. She could be useful. Now she could return to Oakdale Manor in good heart.

ADJUSTMENTS

Jeffrey and his mother took on the job of introducing Elizabeth to the staff and all the activities of Oakdale Manor. Jeffrey hadn't followed all the details of what was done at the estate either but at least he was known to everyone. He had left at the age of twelve to join the navy but most of the people here were long time residents. In some cases they had been tenants or staff to the Kents for two or more generations. Now Jeffrey got more respect than before since he was now the oldest son and heir. He and Elizabeth had ridden over the estate with Sir Kent before they had left for London but Elizabeth hadn't realized the full extent of the work that was carried on here or the number of people attached to Oakdale Manor.

First they went to the coach house and stables. The coach house only contained the chaise and a gig. Sir Kent preferred to ride even in bad weather to using a carriage. Henry, the head groom, showed them around the stables. The little mare that Elizabeth had ridden recognized her and whickered. Elizabeth only had some bread in her pocket but she fed her that. She was glad to be recognized, even if it was only by a horse. There were five other riding horses, four coach horses and stalls for the big work horses that were out in the fields. Jeffrey told Elizabeth that the grooms and gardeners slept in the loft of the coach house. Apparently they didn't mind the smell of the horses and the midden outside. The blacksmith, who had his forge near by, also served as the farrier. He repaired the farm machinery, shod the horses and oxen. Talking to him she learned that the iron came from the Weald in the next county, Sussex. Iron seemed to be cheaper than it was in the colonies. Most of the blast furnaces were in the northern colonies and good steel only came from England or Sweden. There was also a grist mill, a carpentry shop and a brew house where they brewed their own beer and ale. There was a big market for the Oakdale brews since no one drank water except as a penance. Drinking water was also blamed for diseases like typhoid. Oakdale made its own cheeses, baked its own bread and cakes and bought its fish from the fishermen of the nearby village where the houses were also owned by Sir Kent. In the old days the women had done their own weaving and spinning but now cloth was cheaper made in the factories up north. Coal also came from Yorkshire by ship to London. Raw wool was a money maker for the estate. Cows and sheep sold to travelling drovers who took them to London's Smithfield market. Pigs were only raised for home consumption either as fresh meat or smoked. Chickens and ducks were also raised for eggs and home consumption as were geese. Pheasants and venison came from the forests attached to the estate. To the east of Oakdale lay Romney Marsh, a region abounding in swamps and fevers. Some of it was now being drained by ditches and canals. Jeffrey told her that marsh people were considered a breed apart. The women were considered to have "second sight," being able to foretell the future and the men were fishermen and smugglers. Jeffrey also told her that the Kents bought lobsters, shellfish and baskets from the Marsh but said both he and his father disapproved of smuggling. Many of the locals, including the gentry, did not. They bought smuggled goods and sometimes even invested in smuggling activities. It was dangerous to flout the law but highly profitable. Untaxed goods cost about a third less than those that had paid custom duties. Of course the navy tried to stop smugglers at sea and dragoons tried to intercept cargoes on land brought in by the "Free Traders" or the "Gentlemen" as the smugglers were called. Jeffrey thought that some of their own villagers were smugglers but smuggling was one of the things known but not talked about.

She was also introduce to Ketham, the Keeper, who was in charge of the woods, hunting and fishing. He was a black haired man with heavy eyebrows and Elizabeth thought him capable of anything. On the other hand Mr. Clark, the bailiff, was the kind of man one would not remember seeing five minutes after having met him. "We are the only ones allowed to hunt according to the laws set down by William the Conqueror, but there are always poachers, aren't there, Ketham."

"I try to keep them down, sir." There was obviously little humor in the dark man. For some reason Elizabeth was afraid of him. She was also beginning to wonder about Englands reputation as a law abiding land. She had heard about the highwaymen, of course, but now she had to add smugglers and poachers to the number of lawless men. Maybe she had been hasty in giving her pistol to Anna in New York because she wouldn't need it in England.

Mrs. Kent took Elizabeth around the orchards and gardens. She was proud of her herb garden but told Elizabeth that fruit grew along the garden walls, espalliert she called them. "Pears and apricots do especially well grown this way. The walls keep the cold winds off and the bricks hold the heat of the sun."

Elizabeth saw that Oakdale employed as many people as had crewed the *Phoebe*, even if she didn't count the house servants. The farm in Carolina had used far fewer. She would have lots to learn and there would be as little privacy here as there had been aboard ship. "I will go riding and walking in the woods by myself," she told herself. "I can even understand why Robert spent so much time away from here and why Jeffrey joined the navy. Of course knowing how to live in a place without privacy helped him do so well at sea." Elizabeth had gotten used to talking to herself out loud. "In America the problem is the other way around. People live all spread out so we have dances and barn raisings to get together. I'm still an American and some people here will resent that."

Elizabeth was right. Neither Mrs. Lundridge, the housekeeper, nor Mr. Clark liked her. They felt she might undermine their authority. They didn't approve of her American ways and that Jeffrey, the heir to Oakdale, obviously was close to her. Jeffrey should marry a girl with a good dowry, preferably one from the neighborhood, they thought. Mrs. Lundridge had approached Mrs. Kent already. "You know, Mrs. Sophia, that girl doesn't have the least idea how to behave. She needs a governess to show her our ways. Yesterday Miss Elizabeth went striding down the village street in that heathen jacket of hers without even a servant to attend her. My cousin told me about it. I was so ashamed I didn't know where to look."

Mr. Clark was suspicious when Elizabeth asked him for a map of the estate and another of the district. "What do you want those for, Miss Elizabeth?" he asked.

"I want to know where I am. People talk of places and I just don't know where they are talking about." That answer didn't reassure Mr. Clark at all. Sir Kent was the squire and he was the bailiff and what they did was nobody else's business. It certainly wasn't the business of this pry-monkey of an American girl. She was much too curious for his taste.

Actually Elizabeth was frightened of all this strangeness. She was frightened of the coming Sunday as well. She would have to go to church with the Kents. All the people of the neighborhood would be there. She was sure that she had been the subject of gossip already. They would look at her as if she was a strange animal. She would have to meet the Burnthursts as well, and they certainly wouldn't approve of her. She tried to get out of going to church by telling Mrs. Kent that she had no gloves and no proper hat for church but that didn't work.

"You can carry a pair of gloves of mine in your hand. They don't have to fit. And I have a cap that should be just right for a young girl. You're a member of our family now and you should feel more comfortable with us. First of all learn to call me Sophia, not Mrs. Kent. Also remember that we have few new people coming to our village. Naturally the people will be curious about you. You are as strange to them as they are to you. You are an American and the story of you having served aboard ship with Jeffrey has gotten around, but a person from Wiltshire would be just as much a 'foreigner' from 'away' as you are. People here are loyal to their own and that term 'our own' only covers a small area. Mr. Clark is not a local either and Ketham is from the 'Marsh'. Those are always considered strangers and keeps to their own. They are a breed apart and even look different than the rest of the people from around here. As far as clothing is concerned we will go to Tunbridge Wells next week and shop. You need new shoes and riding boots and some other things you didn't get in London. Tunbridge Wells is a watering resort and its shops are almost as good as London. It will take us only two hours to get there in the chaise. We should do that before the harvest begins. Then everybody will be too busy. You'll help also, won't you?"

"Of course. I always did in Carolina. Everybody did."

Servants were another ticklish problem. Elizabeth knew she was expected to have a personal maid. Sir Kent had a valet who took care of him and Jeffrey. She didn't want a fancy ladies maid and certainly no governess. Her past experiences hadn't been what was expected from a well brought up young lady. A fancy ladies maid or a governess would sneer at her. After talking it over with Mrs. Kent she went to Mrs. Lundridge for help. That melted some of the ice between them. "My sister's youngest is just about ready to enter service, as it happens. She could help you dress and also keep your and Master Jeffrey's rooms in order. She won't be giving herself airs like those London maids do nohow. They're no better than they should be."

The Sunday church service wasn't as bad as Elizabeth had feared either. The vicar had spoken kindly to her and had wished her good luck in her new home. Sir James Crosby, a neighbor, had invited her and Jeffrey to have dinner with him. She had curtsied to the Burnthursts. It seemed to go well but she overheard Lily's shrill voice telling her mother "she doesn't look like a Red Indian. She looks just like a person." Elizabeth presumed that most of the villagers thought that all Americans worshipped some woodland spirits and scalped their enemies. She hoped that now that they had seen one in church they would modify their opinions, maybe.

The visit to Tunbridge Wells was a big success. Elizabeth didn't think much of the waters which were supposed to be good for your health. They tasted of rotten eggs and smelled like the gunpowder on the *Phoebe*. She did have a lot of fun shopping with Mrs. Kent. The shoemaker measured Elizabeth's feet and promised to send the boots and shoes to her by mail coach. The dressmaker supplied her with gloves and caps. She also took the silks that Mrs. Kent had gotten from some of her friends in the East India Company and promised to make them up into robes. Elizabeth's was a lovely pink with peach blossoms and Mrs. Kent would get one in blue with golden embroidered phoenixes. They had their midday meal at one of the many hotels. They also interviewed Mrs. Lundridge's niece. Jane had helped her two older sisters dress and had spent her life so far in the elegant town of Tunbridge Wells. That seemed to make her ideal for Elizabeth's needs. Elizabeth also hoped that Jane would make up for the loss of Anna but didn't speak to Mrs. Kent about that. She still had trouble thinking about Jeffrey's mother as Sophia. To her she was still Mrs. Kent.

Then it was time for the sheep shearing. England had been famous for its wool for centuries and Oakdale had many of those animals. Elizabeth found that she agreed with her father's opinion of sheep. They were stupid, they smelled, they ate weeds that were not good for them and they had a positive gift for falling into ditches or getting themselves drowned in ponds. The only time they looked good was at a distance in a green meadow or served as a roast on the dining table. Shepherds were nothing romantic either. They smelled too.

Sheep shearing was followed by fruit picking and the beginning of the grain harvest. Everyone was drafted to help. Elizabeth became very adept at handling horses. She could handle and help care for the heavy Suffolk work horses and she loved her little mare whom she called Fancy.

Of course, horses were not very intelligent either, but they were better than sheep or cows. Jeffrey hadn't done much farm work either and had as much to learn as Elizabeth. Both of them worked in the fields dressed in farmer's smocks as did Sir Kent. However the farm work made Elizabeth really enjoy sitting by the fire in her silk robe in the evenings. She and Jeffrey played chess, read or just sat doing nothing. The work in the fields here in England might be hard but over all Elizabeth was more comfortable than she had ever been in her life. Field work was no harder here than it had been in Carolina and here the servants took care of all the household chores. Any letters Sir Kent needed written Elizabeth also took care of in the evenings. There weren't that many.

One job that Elizabeth didn't like was working in the kitchen. It wasn't a matter of the daily meals. Those were taken care of by the cook. It was the boiling of jams and the pickling of vegetables that was supervised by Mrs. Kent that she didn't like. Elizabeth hated the shut-in feeling of the steamy kitchen. She didn't even like the still room where herbs were dried and cheeses prepared. Getting out in the open was better even if the work was harder.

Jane was only a partly successful experiment. She was competent in doing her work. She cleaned Jeffrey's and Elizabeth's rooms. She helped in the bathing, bringing up the tubs of hot water from the basement and helped Elizabeth dress. However she was not the companion that Anna had been. That gap between mistress and servant was too wide as Anna had foreseen. Elizabeth and Jane were polite to each other but that was all. Elizabeth lived above the stairs and Jane lived below with the other servants. Elizabeth could never tell what the servants were thinking either. When she had dealings with any of them except Jane she was expected to go through the housekeeper or the bailiff and she didn't particularly like either of them.

THE SMUGGLERS

Elizabeth got into the habit of getting up very early, sometimes even before dawn. She did it even if there was no harvest work. Jane would bring her a cup of chocolate and a slice of bread with jam. Then Elizabeth would slip out of the side door to the stable where Henry would have her mare saddled. She would ride up into the silent woods or canter down to the village and along the shore. The family had gotten used to the idea that she didn't want a groom or even Jeffrey along. It wasn't quite proper by English standards but Mrs. Kent figured that Elizabeth would come to no harm. She didn't ride into Romney Marsh with its swamps, waterways and strangers, and around Oakdale all the neighbors knew Elizabeth. It seemed safe.

Elizabeth quickly made friends with the villagers and the fishermen who brought their boats up onto the beach beyond the dunes. She was more comfortable with them than she was with the house servants. Occasionally she would stop at the local inn, "The White Boar", for a second breakfast. The innkeeper, Mr. Morley, became her friend. She was also friendly with Mrs. Fowler, the local seamstress and knew most of the other villagers by name.

The woods, though, were her favorite place to be. There was less underbrush here than in Carolina since the villagers had the right to pick up all the fallen branches for fuel and to clear out the brush. Faggots these bundles of brushwood were called. This made the woods quieter than those in America with more tall trees like pillars in a church. There were some grassy dells as well. She also saw the traps for hares and rabbits set by poachers. She never touched them since she had little sympathy for garden pests like rabbits and she felt the Kents could spare the animals that the poachers took. She didn't favor the fox hunts since foxes kept hares and rabbits down but she had heard Sir Kent and Sir Crosby speak of the pleasure of these hunts often. She could not think of the master of Oakdale Manor as Howard or even Sir Howard. He was and remained Sir Kent to her, master of the entire estate.

There was an old lane which she considered her private path. It had been used by peddlers and foot travelers for centuries. Their feet had worn the path so deeply that she could scarcely see over the edges from horseback. She needed this lane as a place to be private and free from all the people of Oakdale.

That was why she was very surprised to see tracks and hoofmarks on the trail one morning. There was fresh horse dung too. It was so fresh that it still steamed in the cool morning air. Sniffing, she also smelled wood smoke. She knew that there shouldn't be any fires in these woods. There were no charcoal burners here. Poachers didn't light fires. The only people allowed in these woods were herb and mushroom gatherers and the villagers gathering faggots. They wouldn't be out this early. Anyone else would be a trespasser. Poachers were out at night but they didn't signal their presence by lighting fires. This was something else. Elizabeth examined the traces again. Most of them were made by small horses, ponies almost, that peddlers and poor farmers used. There were also the hoofmarks of a larger horse, the kind the gentry used, and tracks of people on foot. None of the marks were those of heavy work horses or cavalry chargers such as the dragoons used. She judged that there were about twenty-five of the ponies, the one large riding horse and an unknown number of people on foot.

Elizabeth decided to investigate. After all she was part of the family that owned these woods which were called the Upper Hangers. They were part of the Oakdale Manor. Sir Kent was proud of his woods and wanted them cared for. Trespassers should be warned off. She would go carefully to see what was going on.

Her life in Carolina had trained her in woodcraft. She used that training now. She tied Fancy to a tree far enough off the trail so she couldn't be seen and also wouldn't challenge any horse on the path. She checked that there was a stump that she could use as a mounting block. It is fairly easy to mount a horse if you are riding astride but much harder to climb onto a ladies side saddle. Then she went ahead, keeping low. She knew that the path curved here and would bring her out at one of the grassy glades. If she cut straight through the woods she would save time and be less likely to be seen by any watcher. The sun was straight behind her and would blind a sentry if there was one. The wind was blowing toward her and she hoped that would keep any dog from smelling her. She had sneaked through the woods since she was seven and she used her skill now.

There were trespassers in the woods here all right, about twenty five or thirty of them. They had that many ponies and were unloading them. She saw small barrels, brandy barrels, being stacked under brushwood with some sacks and boxes of other goods. Brandy was the favorite cargo of the "Gentlemen," as the smugglers were called locally. French lace, silk, salt and American tobacco were other goods smuggled in from France or the island of Guernsey. There was a fire at the campsite but it was properly surrounded by stones and presented no danger to the forest. The flickering flames lit up the scene.

Elizabeth knew what she was looking at. This was a smuggler's camp where the cargo brought in by boat was transferred to those who would carry it to London to be sold. The London group would arrive the next day so the two groups would not know each other. Only the paymaster would know both groups so he would be a man trusted by all. He could betray everyone.

With a shock Elizabeth realized that she knew the paymaster too. Mr. Clark's tall horse stood out among all the ponies. Then the light of the flames showed Ketham guarding with his musket held across his chest. Each of the smugglers came up individually, bowed to Mr. Clark and received his pay. Then they took their ponies and went back down the hill.

Elizabeth didn't know what to do. Sir Kent had told her about his dislike of smuggling and the "Free Traders." Jeffrey was a navy man and held the same opinion as his father. If they heard of this camp they would send for Lieutenant Waller and his dragoons. On the other hand the smugglers were poor men from the local village supplementing their meager incomes. If they were asked, they would probably say that they were men who opposed the taxes imposed by King George and his ministers. They were just doing the same thing that the Colonists had done when they dumped the tea into Boston harbor at the "Boston Tea Party." The smugglers weren't hurting anyone except the tax collectors nor were they stealing from anyone. In addition, smuggled goods cost less than half of what taxed salt or tobacco cost. That way even poor people could afford these things.

Elizabeth knew that if she sided with the smugglers she might have to leave England. She would be betraying the Kents and Jeffrey. She wouldn't get an allowance from the Earl either. If she was caught she might end up in the Tower after all, charged with treason. If she went straight to the Manor many of her new friends would end up in jail or "pressed" into the navy. She remembered the London waterman's opinion of that choice. The dragoons would certainly seize or destroy the fishing boats of the village. And if the soldiers found any smuggled goods in the village they had every right to destroy the boats according to what she had heard about the law. At the very least Sir Kent would turn them all out of their cottages. He owned the houses as part of Oakdale Manor. He would consider the cottagers law breakers and that would be that.

Very quietly she crept back downhill, mounted her mare and rode back down the trail. She didn't hurry as she had no desire to meet any of the villagers. She also remembered Ketham and his musket. He was probably capable of using it even on a woman. She rode among the trees rather than risking the trail. She needed time to think out what she would do as well. As she came into the orchard she urged Fancy into a canter. A good horsewoman could gallop while riding sidesaddle but Elizabeth knew her limitations. She drew rein in front of the "White Boar". Mr. Morley was up as she knew he would be.

"Good morning, Miss Elizabeth. You are up early today."

Mr. Morley was a heavy, muscular man from carrying the beer barrels and he had twinkling eyes.

"I would have a cup of tea, Mr. Morley. I was up early riding in the Upper Hangers."

"Oh?" The twinkle died out in Mr. Morley's blue eyes.

"Yes, there is a smuggler's camp up there. I will tell Sir Kent and Jeffrey all about it as soon as I finish my tea. They will probably send for the dragoons. Sir Kent dislikes smugglers and Jeffrey is a navy man. The dragoons will probably search the village as well as the woods."

"You know, Miss Elizabeth, you ought to be careful. Some people dislike interference." He paused for a moment. "Did you recognize anyone up there?"

"There were a number of people up there but the fire light made it difficult to identify anyone except Mr. Clark and Ketham. After all, I know them well. Mr. Clark must have told them all that it was safe to store goods there and Ketham, as Sir Kent's gamekeeper, knows all the paths. They broke Sir Kent's trust as well as the law. They know his opinions. I don't care if they get caught." She laid down a few pennies to pay for the tea.

"Thank you very much, Miss Elizabeth." They both knew where they stood. Mr. Morley had been up in the woods too. His shape made him easy to spot. It wasn't necessary to spell things out. Elizabeth knew he would warn the village although there would be no time to clear the woods before the dragoons came. "Do be careful as you ride home. Them outside people don't have no hem to their garments. They don't know where to stop. Mr. Clark is from 'outside' too. Mr. Morley helped Elizabeth mount and she rode slowly away.

The family was sitting around the breakfast table when she came in. Sir Kent's eyebrows rose when he saw her muddied skirt and her tense face. "What's amiss?" he asked.

"I've stumbled on to a smuggler's camp on your grounds, sir. I sneaked up on it and saw them unloading barrels and sacks of other goods. Your bailiff and the gamekeeper know all about it. They were supervising the unloading and paying off the men.

"You are sure, very sure?"

"Yes, sir. I recognized Mr. Clark's horse first and then saw him and Ketham by the firelight. The place is up in the Upper Hangers. I can show you where on the map of the estate."

"Very well. Jeffrey, you better ride for Lt. Waller and a squad of his dragoons. You know where they stay, at that roadhouse two miles down the beach. It won't take them more than fifteen minutes to get here. Elizabeth, you come with me to the library and show us the place where that camp is. In the library she showed the location to both Jeffrey and Sir Kent. They both knew that clearing. Then Sir Kent went to the gun rack and took out a pistol. He carefully checked that it was loaded and primed. Elizabeth saw Jeffrey pass by dressed in his navy uniform. Elizabeth saw where Jeffrey had gotten his gift of command from. His father sounded just like him. She wasn't offered a gun and she regretted again that she had not brought her pistol with her from New York.

Sir Kent shoved the pistol into his waistband under his coat so it wouldn't show. "Clark and Ketham have eaten my bread and salt. They know my opinions. They should be loyal to me even if they can't be loyal to their king and country." He indicated that he wanted Elizabeth to go with him. She felt strange. She too had accepted food and shelter from Sir Kent, his "bread and salt" as he termed it. She had even accepted King George's pay on the *Phoebe*. Yet she had warned Mr. Morley and all the villagers through him that the dragoons would be coming. Deciding what was right and wrong wasn't always so easy, Elizabeth now had found out. She certainly couldn't be sure that what she had done was right. It was just something she felt that she had to do. There were no rules to follow.

She had seen Jeffrey pass in his uniform. That was his loyalty. She had served in the navy too. "But I wasn't an officer," she told herself. "I took no oath." Then she remembered. She had signed the Articles when she became a crew member. She had accepted prize money that being a crew member entitled her to. The thoughts made her confused. But at least she knew what guns meant and that they could kill. She remembered Ketham's musket and she also remembered what a musket ball had done to Pat's shoulder. There is no backing out here anymore than there was on the *Phoebe*. I have faced guns before and this is not different. Obviously Sir Kent was willing to face trouble although she didn't think he was wise to hide his gun in a way that he couldn't get at it quickly. She didn't say anything. She was under Sir Kent's orders as she had been under Jeffrey's on the ship. She wished she would have stayed in New York but she had chosen what seemed the easier and safer path. It now seemed that it hadn't been but this was what she had chosen.

They walked to Mr. Clark's office. He sat behind his desk as peacefully as if he hadn't been out of the woods this morning. He had changed his clothes too.

"Clark, you are dismissed as of this morning. You can take Ketham with you too." Sir Kent's voice was stern.

"Sir?"

"Elizabeth saw you in the smuggler's camp this morning. The Upper Hangers are on my property and you know my opinions on smuggling."

"There is no contraband here, sir. You cannot accuse a man without evidence."

"I can swear I saw you and Ketham in that camp," Elizabeth told him. "I can probably get others to give evidence as well."

Suddenly Clark had a pistol in his hand. Its muzzle swung back and forth to cover both her and Sir Kent. "You sneaking bitch! You won't tell anyone about anything ever again."

Elizabeth saw the muzzle of the pistol swing to cover Sir Kent. Clark must have noted Sir Kent going for his own pistol. She sprung forward to cover Sir Kent. The muzzle was a black hole. She distinctly saw the flint strike the frizzen and spark. There was a cloud of smoke and she felt a blow against her side. "Smugglers do hurt people," she had time to think. Then the black hole of the muzzle seemed to grow bigger and swallowed her.

HEALING

When Elizabeth woke up it was night. There was a single candle burning near her bed. Sophia, and she thought of her as Sophia now, was sitting there. Elizabeth managed to croak out a request for water. Mrs. Kent lifted her up and let her sip from the edge of a tumbler. That was good because Elizabeth felt like a rat had died in her mouth, foul and furry. Then Mrs. Kent answered the questions that Elizabeth hadn't dared ask. "The doctor said you lost a great deal of blood but you are going to get well. You'll need a lot of rest to recover and it will take a while. And Clark is dead. He tried to shoot Ketham and Ketham dropped him. Probably thought Clark would push all the blame on him." That was as much as Elizabeth had strength to hear. She slid back into that black hole that had held her.

When she woke up a second time it was day and Jeffrey was sitting beside her. "You scared us, Elizabeth, scared us good and proper. You were out for two days and I wasn't even there when you got hurt." Jeffrey was almost babbling with relief. "And I am glad that Clark is dead and Ketham has disappeared. Gone to earth like one of the foxes. And the doctor says you are going to get well but it was a close run thing. The bullet hit a rib and travelled around your side. You will have a big scar but broken ribs heal. The dragoons cleaned out that camp and you will get a third as finder's fee."

Elizabeth tried to smile and absorb all that information. It took an effort. "The smugglers, they got away?"

"You tipped the villagers off, didn't you?"

Elizabeth nodded. "Is your father going to send me away for helping them?"

"No way. Father is going to apologize to you. For trusting Clark and not having his pistol out before that man shot you." Father doesn't want the poor villagers punished. They're small fry. Besides they are *our* villagers. He'll tell you."

Elizabeth felt relieved but she was very tired and she hurt all over. She had trouble breathing too and the bandage was tight and it itched. It was hard to think when she hurt so much. But Jeffrey was here and she wasn't going to be sent away. That was enough.

The talk with Sir Howard Kent, baronet, was harder. He came in the evening and sat beside her. Elizabeth could see that this was hard for him too. "I am a justice of the peace and a magistrate. I believe in law, all the law and not just the laws I like. I let you get hurt because I thought that no one would try to oppose the laws by force. My pistol was only a symbol, not something that I would have to use. You were hurt, almost killed, because I forgot that laws were often brought about by armed force. The *Magna Carta* was imposed on King John by armed men who used force to create a new law. I forgot that men will fight for things they really believe in or for their own advantage. Your Americans are doing it now. And I forgot that even a cornered rat will show fight. I owed you protection and I forgot those things. That is why I must apologize to you." He stopped for a while. "The villagers are poor men trying to feed their families. I forgot that too. Fishing is not a very profitable profession. However they have a warning now about defying the law. They don't want bloodshed. That's a hanging offense. Ketham will probably hang if they catch him."

Elizabeth didn't care about philosophy, now less than ever. "You aren't going to send me away?" She didn't think she could stand to lose her home again, her home and Jeffrey.

"No, and not only because you are family. You are good for us. You are good for Jeffrey. You taught me to think about people and not just the law and my privileges."

Jeffrey sitting by her bed was more fun. He knew how to keep quiet and didn't talk more than she could take. "You are even going to have money," he told her one day. Lieutenant Waller said you are entitled to one third of the money from the sale of the goods in the camp. That's 'informer's share.' It won't come from our villagers. They were paid off before the dragoons came. The dragoons didn't find anything in the village either. They searched. Probably no one will thank you openly but Mr. Morley sent up a bag of lemons and has sent up twice to ask how you are recovering. You will be considered 'one of us.'"

Her recovery was slow. It was two weeks before she was allowed to get out of bed and have her meals with the family. Jane had left. She told Mrs. Kent that she "couldn't abide the sight of blood." Sophie had hired a Mrs. Whitby, a widow of a fisherman from the village. She was a slab-sided woman of undeterminate age with wonderfully gentle hands and a no-nonsense manner. Elizabeth didn't ask whether Mrs. Lundridge approved of the change. Elizabeth approved of it and that was enough. Somehow she didn't mind when she was helped by Mrs. Whitby with all the personal things that an invalid required done. She was still too weak to do them by herself. Mrs. Whitby was more like a mother than a maid. Mrs. Kent was too busy to help much with the nursing. All the Kents did come up to the bedroom for short visits. They were too smart to ask how she felt. The truth was that she felt lousy. Her side ached, her head felt woozy and her legs hurt from lying in bed so much. The worst was that she kept going over in her mind what she had done. Jeffrey told her that she had done well but she wasn't sure. She was unsure about a lot of things. Should she have fought for the British? Should she have left New York for England? Was it right to live in the same house with Jeffrey?

A letter from the Earl helped:

Dear Elizabeth,

When Jeffrey and you were mentioned in the Naval Chronicle I told Jeffrey that one such exploit was sufficient for a lifetime. Therefore I will not say anything about your latest heroic deed. You have my respect for saving my brother's life and your discreet handling of the whole affair.

My sister-in-law writes me that your dress was ruined. I have asked Maria to send you a duplicate. It will probably reach you considerably earlier than they will let you remount a horse. I am also returning your miniature. It has been copied and will hang in the portrait gallery of my country house.

With best wishes
Severn

If the head of the family thought she had done well perhaps she could stop worrying.

It was late August until she could go riding on Fancy. Henry, the groom, rode with her. Sir Kent had put his foot down firmly about riding out alone. "You have enemies now. Whoever heads that smuggling ring knows who brought down the dragoons on the camp. The smugglers like to discourage that kind of thing. And Ketham is still at large. He has nothing to lose by revenging himself on you for costing him his position. You can only hang a man once."

"He might plead self-defense." Jeffrey put in. "Clark fired first, from what Henry says."

"We still have him on a smuggling charge."

"Only if I testify," Elizabeth told them. "I might get a weak memory, like I did in talking to Mr. Morley." She still felt bad about Mr. Clark being killed. She remembered the dead on the *Phoebe* but she didn't blame the French sailors for the killing. Both sides fought for what they considered right. Obviously Sir Kent didn't have her regrets.

"He was getting ready to kill me when you jumped in front of the gun. You saved my life and risked your own. I haven't forgotten."

MATTERS FOR A YOUNG LADY

Elizabeth was nervous as she sponged herself off carefully. The long scar along her ribs that she had gotten from the bullet of Mr. Clark, the smuggling master, was red and puffy but she had survived the wound as she had survived the many other things that had happened to her in the last few years. She had survived the death of her parents. She had survived being pushed out of her home in Carolina. She had survived the battle at sea between His Brittanic Majesty's sloop *Phoebe* and the French lugger *Nymphe*, survived it at the side of her cousin Jeffrey.

She had also survived the shock of finding out that she was a noblewoman with a coat of arms, that the powerful Earl of Severn was her guardian and that Jeffrey's parents, Sir and Lady Kent had invited her to their home of Oakdale Manor in England. Most important was the shock of finding out that she was in love with Jeffrey and he with her. He was the Honorable Jeffrey Kent, Lieutenant, RN, to give him his full title. That was a lot to absorb for a girl not quite fourteen years old.

None the less she was nervous. The Earl had written that he was coming down from London and that he specifically wanted to talk to her. Now he was here with his four-horse carriage, his valet and his coachman. He was her guardian by the law of the realm with complete power over her. That was enough reason to be nervous. She slipped on her best dress and draped a shawl over her shoulders instead of wearing the more comfortable buckskin jacket with moosehair embroidery that she had bought in Halifax. She carefully brushed her hair and threaded a silver ribbon through it. Then she went down for dinner.

Conversation at dinner dealt with neutral subjects as it had to with servants coming in and out. After dinner the men lingered over their port wine while the women withdrew to the parlor. The raised voice of Jeffrey and the sharp tones of the Earl carried through the door. It indicated that the conversation was serious. "They trusted me with the command of my own ship," she heard Jeffrey protest. The sharp tone of the Earl cut him off but she couldn't hear the words. Finally the butler came in and informed Elizabeth that the Earl requested her presence in the library.

His lordship was standing by a bookcase idly turning a globe. "Sit down, please." Elizabeth sat. The chair she was sitting on was really too large for her and she sat on the edge so her legs wouldn't dangle. "I'm taking you to London with me," he announced crisply. "Before I came down from Town I had a talk with Mrs. Chelmford who runs a seminary for young ladies. She has agreed to accept you as a pupil."

"But I know how to read and write and cipher. I served as a clerk as well as a surgeon's mate on the *Phoebe* and I even have a certificate to prove it."

"Mrs. Chelmford will teach you the proper deportment for a young lady and also a second language, probably French. If you have the talent for it you will also learn to play an instrument or to do watercolour. Those are accomplishments that I want you to have. Do you understand?"

"Yes, I understand m'lord. You want to separate me from Jeffrey." Elizabeth's voice was flat. So was her statement.

"How old are you, Elizabeth?"

"I will be fourteen September twenty-first."

"And Jeffrey is not yet sixteen. I do not mate my puppies either. Jeffrey will be allowed to visit you at intervals under supervision as is proper for a young man. He will also be introduced to other young ladies of his class. If he chooses to sow wild oats I want him to do so before he enters any permanent arrangement. If he wishes to continue in his affection for you there is no harm done."

"And I?"

The Earl pulled over a chair for himself and sat down. "Let me make myself perfectly clear. There is room in the family for Elizabeth, Lady d'Raython. I have little use for Elizabeth Troyes, a surgeon's assistant and midwife from the colonies. Such women are of a lower class even if they are courageous and good looking. I haven't forgotten that you saved my brother's life either. A lower class woman who had done that would have been given a sum of money and that would be that. Your courage then and even on the ship with Jeffrey has nothing to do with our discussion."

Elizabeth faced the nobleman squarely. "This is not a discussion, my lord. It is an ultimatum to surrender."

"It is a demand. You are quite right. If it makes you feel any better Jeffrey objected too. This ultimatum, as you phrase it, is something demanded by who we are. You have only a small title and no fortune. That is not enough to open the gates of society to you. That may seem to be a brutal fact to you but it is a fact, believe me. With proper manners and my help you may slip in. Jeffrey alone cannot do that for you. I also value him enough that I do not wish to have him apologise for his wife in the future." Then his voice softened. "I am glad that you have neither resorted to tears nor screams or rage. Many girls would have. It will be easier for Jeffrey and my brother if you can keep up your present behavior. I won't insult you by saying that I am doing this only for your own good. I do care for the family, all of it."

The Earl and the Kents made sure that Elizabeth and Jeffrey had no chance to talk privately either that evening or the next morning but the precaution was unnecessary. Elizabeth had seen that look on Jeffrey's face before when he buried his crewmen after the battle of the *Phoebe* with *Nymphe*. He had seen her when she stood up to Admiral Gambier and Captain Brathwaithe in New York. There was no need for private words between them. The good byes were coldly formal. Only Sophia managed to whisper private words into Elizabeth's ear as she got into the Earl's coach. "Remember that this is your home."

The Earl was curt when they reached the turnpike leading north. "We are driving straight through to London, only stopping to change horses and grab something to eat. You have no maid with you and for a man with a young girl to stop overnight would cause talk. Jeffrey told me that you are used to discomfort so I won't apologise."

The Earl's coach was better sprung than the stage coach and the seats were softer but that didn't help much. The bumps and jolts didn't interrupt her thoughts. School, especially a seminary for young ladies, would be like a jail. The image of the Tower of London rose before her eyes with its grim, gray granite walls and its sentries pacing. The sentry at the school would be called a porter. No matter, he served the same purpose. Other children had studied in the Tower; Lady Jane Grey, the two little princes. They had never come out. She didn't think the Earl would have her killed if she became "inconvenient" but she wasn't sure. She could probably escape from the school, slide out of a window or bribe the porter or a maid. Then she could find a ship headed for

America. Most ships could use a surgeon or even a surgeon's mate. No, that would be cowardice. Jeffrey would be made ashamed for her. She wouldn't run except as a last resort. Maybe it would be good to study more herb lore and anatomy. They would call it botany and nature study in a school. They'd have to be genteel. Dancing? She had never danced although she had stepped lively enough on a deck during the storm. Her mixed thoughts lasted her to Tonbridge. There they snatched a lunch while the coachman changed the tired horses for the Earl's own. They had been left here. They were faster than the hired ones had been but the jolting was rough on her back and buttocks. When they reached London and she stepped stiffly out of the carriage she suddenly realized that the Earl must be stiffer than she was. He must be forty years older and he had driven down from London and back up again. Yet he had come to Oakdale to explain things to her and Jeffrey in person rather than just sending orders down by letter. He cared enough for Jeffrey to put himself to considerable inconvenience. Maybe he even cared for her a bit. It was an interesting thought.

When they went to the school the next morning it was just as she had pictured it, a four storied building of gray granite. The porter wore a blue uniform instead of the scarlet of the guards at the Tower. It didn't matter, he was still a guard. They went in, the coachman carrying her old sea chest from Carolina.

Three weeks later the Earl frowned as he read a letter he had just received from Mrs. Chelmford:

My Lord

Elizabeth is not adjusting well to the school nor the school to her. Most of the girls have made a set against her and that is something that is hard for a girl or a teacher to fight. I have no choice but to ask you to withdraw her from the school. I would suggest that she might do better with a governess. She is obviously quite bright but unwilling to bow to other people's prejudices or assumptions of superiority. Schools are communities where the pupils as much as the teachers make the rules. All the girls are expected to follow them but Elizabeth has been alone too long and made her own decisions to let her bend to others. One might perhaps wish she had been born a boy.

I remain

Very respectfully yours,

Catherine Chelmford
Headmistress

To The Lord William, the Earl of Severn.

Elizabeth knew nothing about Mrs. Chelmford's letter until she was told one day to go to the parlor and found her guardian there. "I am told that you are not adjusting well to the school. Just what seems to be your trouble?"

"I've tried, sir, but it is very hard. They call me the "Colonial Blockhead." I do reasonably well in my studies but when I talk to the other girls it seems I know nothing. I don't know the latest fashions. I haven't seen the latest plays and I don't even know the relationships of the various noble families to each other. And I am clumsy. I can't dance. Three days ago I forgot that I had been hobbled and fell against a side table. I broke two of its legs and a china vase standing on it."

"You were hobbled?"

"Yes. Miss Sisely had tied my legs together so I could only take small, ladylike steps. I forgot and started striding."

"Any damage, to you I mean?"

"Nothing serious. Knocked silly for a couple of minutes and a big bruise. The vase missed my head."

"You don't seem to do well here." The Earl waved Elizabeth's attempt to interrupt aside. "No, the mistake was mine. I placed a young falcon among partridges and clipped her wings to make her like them. They recognized a stranger and attacked. As I said, it was a mistake on my part. However that leaves the question of what to do next. What would you want?"

"I would like to return to Oakdale, m'lord. If that is too displeasing to you, sir, I could return to America."

"You think that you can return to Carolina now that Cornwallis has surrendered and the war will have to be wound up?"

"No sir, I do not think that. The Americans won't let many Tories return, certainly not those who have fought for the Crown. There must be thousands or even tens of thousands of them. They won't be welcome in England either. You already have too many people out of work here. There is another thing that bears on that as well. Barbara Munro told me that her father is improving his estates in Scotland. He is getting rid of his tenants and bringing in sheep. Its less trouble than tenants and more profitable. She says many landholders are doing that. They are also enclosing the Commons where the tenants used to pasture their cattle. I asked her what would become of the crofters and she told me they were being encouraged to emigrate. The Highlanders in our section of Carolina had also been encouraged to emigrate, by burning down their houses. I know that kind of "encouragement."

"And where do you think that all these people will go?"

"Canada probably. When Jeffrey and I sailed to Halifax they spoke of all the farms that had been abandoned by the Arcadians when they were deported after the last war. We were even told that there was lots of good farmland west of Quebec by the big lakes."

The Earl laughed. "They may have hobbled your legs, Elizabeth, but they certainly haven't hobbled your brains. We may speak later about your ideas about Canada. But now to return to your affairs. If you give me a few minutes I will speak to Mrs. Chelmford and have her get someone to pack your trunk. I also want to give some orders to my coachman. I can't leave London right now but I will get you a maid to go with you. You can travel in my chaise to Oakdale. You can stop over in Tonbridge for the night."

"Can't we drive straight through the way we did coming up? I'll get home today. It is still early, only ten o'clock."

Twenty minutes later they left the school behind. Elizabeth stepped into the chaise with her heart singing. She was going home.

Smugglers Shaw

There was considerable surprise at Oakdale Manor when the chaise drew up at the door long after nightfall. Jeffrey just had time to give Elizabeth a very tight hug before swinging into action. He saw to it that the horses were fed, watered and rubbed down and the postillions taken care of while Mrs. Lundridge took care of the maid. Sir Kent poured a glass of wine for Elizabeth. "You look like you need a stimulant. Sophia is ordering up a meal for you. We have already eaten. And we won't bother you with questions until you have eaten and rested."

There weren't many questions in the morning either. Elizabeth's answers were given in so bleak a tone that no one wanted to press her further. She was here and the Earl approved. That was enough for the moment. It was only to Jeffrey that she was able to open up a bit the next evening. "They wanted to shape me like a butter patty, all the girls just alike. They not only laughed at me but at Barbara Munro because she had red hair. And the world they wanted me to belong to was so unreal. Their idea of the deep woods was an oak grove in St. James Park and battles were fought by heroic kings with no troops, no blood and no smells. They worried about their complexions and they were mean to the servants."

"Sounds a little like my time in the midshipmen's berth. I learned to fake it. Only great noblemen or captains were allowed to be eccentric. You saw something of that in New York."

"No, I won't fake it. I'm not a frail, pale-faced miss in a silly hat."

Elizabeth gloried in her re-found freedom. She and Jeffrey cantered along the beach even in wet weather. She rode alone on the silent forest paths in the early mornings. She slept with her bed curtains looped up and her window open. It was winter and the slack season for farmers so she had plenty of free time.

It was only after a week of this that she could settle down enough to be able to listen, really listen, to other people. "It was lonely here," Jeffrey told her. "The Burnthursts don't visit. The farmers don't pay any attention to anything I say because I don't know farming. Morley doesn't trust me any more since I brought in the dragoons. When I enter the "White Boar" conversation stops."

"But it was I who found the smuggler's camp."

"Doesn't matter. You warned everybody that I would bring the dragoons. They call me 'Mr. Lieutenant.' I know what that means. You're a girl and a romantic figure. There's all sorts of tales told about you. That you fought Red Indians as well as aboard ship. That you are able to cure all sorts of diseases by just looking at them. Don't matter if the tales are true. The villagers believe them."

Sophia was worried about Jeffrey too. "He's been pining for you. He even wrote his uncle that he was willing to go back to sea. Sir Crosby and the Reverend Hammond are too old for him and his own acquaintances are all in the navy and away."

One morning in early November Mr. Burnthurst came to Oakdale and asked to speak to Sir Howard privately. After a half an hour Jeffrey was asked to join the gentlemen in the library. Mr. Burnthurst rode off in the rain after another half an hour.

Sir Kent broke custom by speaking of serious things at dinner. "The Burnthursts are in bad trouble. George told me that unless he could get his hands on several hundred pounds immediately he and his family might end up in debtors prison. The mortgagees want to foreclose on his house and land. Once they serve a writ of foreclosure all the others debtors will serve writs on him too. He hasn't been able to pay the arrears on the interest on the mortgages."

"How horrible." Sophia actually turned pale. "What did you do?"

"I don't give out hundred pounds on charity but he gave me an option on Smugglers Shaw. That was part of the Oakdale estate once. The house and the rest of the land will have to be sold as well, of course, to satisfy the mortgagees but he might be able to save the household goods or sell them for money to start over again somewhere else."

"I would let him rot in Kings' Bench Prison," was Jeffrey's sharp comment. "He never cared for anyone else, just himself."

"We can't do that. He is our neighbor and his daughter was engaged to your brother Robert. It isn't done."

"What's Smugglers Shaw?" Elizabeth asked.

"Shaw is an old English word for a scubby piece of woods. It runs from our Upper Hangers to the village of Ivychurch. The village and the woods have a reputation for poaching, illegal wood cutting and charcoal burning. There is a narrow valley that would have shielded smugglers who came from London perfectly. Neither Burnthurst nor his agent Wyant seem to have been that way for years. I don't know how much of that reputation is real or ancient history."

"I could scout it for you."

"You, a girl?"

"I ride up to that clearing often. I think I know the head of that valley and could slip down it carefully. Nobody would think it unusual if I went up that way."

"Take Henry or Jeffrey with you. I really would like to know what is up there. I don't like buying a pig in a poke. I want to know before I make the sale final."

"I have to do that job alone. Two or three horses and we might as well blow a trumpet to announce that we are coming."

Sir Kent shook his head in puzzlement. Elizabeth's idea sounded like something out of the ballads of Robin Hood. He wasn't used to Elizabeth's American way of thinking. It was certainly not something a British girl would come up with. "Take a pistol then. Jeffrey says that you can use one."

"I'd rather not, sir. If I have a pistol I have to show it. If I show it I have to be willing to use it. I'd rather not."

"Well one can't say you don't make life interesting. But be careful. If there is any risk, come back here immediately and we do things openly and in force."

"Thank you, sir. If the weather holds I will take Fancy and ride out tomorrow on a scout."

The morning was gray with just enough of a drizzle to deaded sound. Elizabeth laughed as she turned her horse up the trail. Miss Chelmford and the other teachers at the seminary for young ladies would be horrified at her doing this unladylike ride. She only wished she could have ridden astride instead of this clumsy side-saddle. Her own parents in Carolina would have approved of her doings.

Once she reached the clearing she dismounted and hobbled Fancy. There was plenty of grazing for her, Elizabeth moved carefully down what seemed to be a trail for hauling timber. There were human foot prints and even the marks of the hooves of oxen. She came to a side trail and followed it. She sensed that something was wrong and looked up suddenly. Ketham was standing there holding his musket across his chest. There was a smile on his face. "You're very quiet, miss, but not as quiet as a fox and I hear them."

"Are you going to shoot me to finish off the job Clark didn't?"

"Clark shot at me, you didn't. And you aren't on Oakdale land now either. You're trespassing and best go back."

"It's Oakdale land now. The Burnthursts are selling out. Sir Kent told me to take a look at these woods and I want to see where this path leads."

They went up the rise, Ketham behind her with his musket at the ready. She slipped behind a thick oak, regretting that a skirt prevented her from climbing. There was a village in front of her, a squatter village. She had seen places like this in the woods in America. She counted four, no five, huts. There were a few heads of cattle and her nose caught a smell of pigs. There was a mound where charcoal was being made as well and a few patches of garden.

"Well miss? What are you going to do about us now that you know?"

"I think we should go and tell Sir Kent."

"We? He'll have me hanged real quick."

"No he won't. You'll be allowed to leave as you came. You have my word and my word is good."

They reached Oakdale Manor before noon. Henry's eyes practically popped when he saw Ketham, still armed, following Elizabeth. And it was Ketham who helped her dismount. "Ketham is my guest. Take care of him while I go in and talk to Sir Kent. I think it will be better if there is no smell of beer when I bring him inside the house."

Jeffrey and his father were going over accounts with Sophia when Elizabeth came in. "There is a squatter village in those woods," she said without preliminaries. "We had many like that in Carolina. I didn't enter it but Ketham can give you the details. I brought him back with me, sir."

"Ketham?"

"Yes, sir. I gave him my word that he could leave as he came, without let or hindrance."

"Your word? And he accepted it?" Jeffrey was surprised.

She turned on him. "Yes, my word. You accepted it on the *Phoebe* too. My word was good then and it is good now." She turned to the baronet. "I'll bring him in. He knows what is going on in these woods." She found that she enjoyed surprising all of them. Jeffrey was more practical. He moved over to the gun rack, took out a pistol and loaded it. He felt justified when Ketham came in still carrying his musket.

"Well Ketham, what do you have to say for yourself?"

"Not myself sir. Miss Elizabeth. She wanted me to tell you about the thorp. That's what we call it, Old Thorp, because there has been a settlement there in the old days. The Petmans live there. His woman sells the cook herbs and mushrooms. The Clough brothers burn charcoal. The farrier, he buys from them. So does the smith at Ivychurch. They were driven from their living when Sir Dunning enclosed the commons. Thetford came that way. He runs cattle and collects wild honey. And there is me."

"So the common people around here know all about this place. The Burnthursts and their agent, Wyant?"

"Wyant took the gifts he was brought. He asked no questions that weren't needful. The Burnthursts don't give no leases. Not them. Leases might give people rights under the Charter."

"Elizabeth told you I'm buying the Shaw? Well, I'd give them long term leases if we can come to an agreement about the use of the woodland. However you'd have to stand before a coroner's inquiry for the killing of Clark."

"I'd like my old position back sir, right well."

"No, I can't do that. A gamekeeper is kind of a constable and you haven't been exactly law abiding, have you?"

Here Elizabeth interfered. "You said I needed my own groom, sir, and someone to ride with me." She turned to Ketham. "Would you serve me, honestly and of your own free will? I think your word would be as good as mine."

In answer Ketham laid his musket in front of her and went down on one knee. "I promise obedience and good service in peace or war to you, Miss Elizabeth, as long as life shall last. So witness earth, so witness sky."

Elizabeth had read about something like this in a novel but never thought she would see it in real life. Luckily she remembered the answering formula. "I, Elizabeth Troyes, Lady d'Raython, promise protection and good governance. If I fail may the green earth open and swallow me and the stars in the sky fall and crush me. So witness earth, so witness sky." Jeffrey just sat there and goggled at her. Sophia smiled her approval.

It worked out very well. The three of them rode together, exploring all the woods and the seashore. Ketham showed them how to read animal tracks, set traps for rabbits and hares, how to judge distances and foretell the weather. He also showed both Jeffrey and Elizabeth how to handle a musket and some of the tricks used by smugglers.

The coroner's inquiry turned out to be no problem. The coroner, a fussy little lawyer in a dark broadcloth suit, asked few questions after Henry testified that Clark came out of his office, pistol in hand and that he fired at Ketham before the latter had raised his musket. Elizabeth testified that she was unarmed and that Sir Kent had not drawn his pistol. Nobody mentioned anything about smuggling and the jury came in with a ruling of self-defense.

Elizabeth also found that she was in demand as a medic. Mrs. Whitby introduced her to midwifery. They delivered a pair of twin boys and both mother and the babies lived. The doctor lived two hours away and was expensive so the villagers preferred her when they could. She still avoided handling major surgery. The doctor found the arrangement convenient to himself as well.

Then, shortly after New Year, the Earl's carriage was standing once more in the courtyard of Oakdale Manor.

EARL'S ORDERS

The Earl looked very tired when they joined him in the library. "I am glad to hear that you are both fitting in well here. That's good but I have something for you to do that will take you away from here. I would have invited you to London to talk things over but Town is too full of flapping ears and wagging tongues for comfort. The House of Commons is getting ready to pass a resolution asking the King to make peace with the Americans. That means the fall of Lord North and all his cabinet. The maneuvering for positions in the new cabinet is just like you can imagine." Then he looked at Jeffrey sharply. "How old are you now, Jeffrey?"

"I was sixteen last month, sir."

"No you are not. You are now eighteen as far as the navy is concerned and ready to take your examination for lieutenant. If you pass, and Sir Richard Howe who is taking over the Admiralty in the new government told me you have to pass it honestly, we can drop that silly 'acting' from your rank. I told Howe that you have enough sea time but he wants no more incompetents commissioned." He turned to Elizabeth. "This whole business is you fault. You warned me that there would be a problem with the Loyalists when the war ended. I talked it over with some others and they agree."

She looked at him in surprise. "Me, sir?"

"Yes, you. Naturally Sir Guy Carleton, who is governor of Quebec and future commander-in-chief in America, wants to settle them up there. Some Loyalists will go home and needn't be considered. That still leaves fifty to a hundred thousand refugees to be considered. Doubts have been expressed whether the Canadians, new and old, would be loyal to the Crown. The Quebecois are French and therefore suspect. The attitude of the tribes to new settlers is unknown. Many of the Loyalists and emigrants are Scots clansmen. They would be loyal to a Stuart king but they have little reason to love King George or the House of Brunswick. They might hold to the "Ould Alliance" with the French. The other American Loyalists? Naturally their leaders, people like Thomas Hutchinson and Benjamin Thompson say they will but I don't know if those 'leaders' speak for the common people. Exiles often inflate their influence." He stopped for a moment. "You understand that all this is confidential." They both nodded. "What I want you to do is to talk to the common soldiers and civilians and tell me what they think. You, Jeffrey, lieutenant to be, would be in command of a dispatch vessel, carrying mail to Charleston and New York. Elizabeth, you're Lady d'Raython trying to get your estates back. Jeffrey, you'd be part of the Home Fleet so not subject to anyone in America."

Jeffrey was wildly enthusiastic. He would be out at sea again in command of his own ship. He wouldn't have to smell another pig stye or slap the rump of another oxen. He had little doubt that he could pass the examination and he cared little that he was fibbing on his age. It was done all the time. He would be a real officer, not "acting" or one by courtesy. And Elizabeth would be with him too.

She was much more dubious. She would be plunged into the old problems of the war, the divided loyalties and her own doubts. She knew she had no other choice but to accept the mission outlined by the Earl. If she didn't, she might lose everything, Jeffrey, the Earl's regard and possibly even her new home at Oakdale Manor. She resolutely turned to practical matters. "I'd have to drop the Lady d'Raython first thing. The every day people in American wouldn't tell anything to a noble. The Highlanders wouldn't either. Secondly, I want to take Ketham with me. America isn't a well-groomed and peaceful English meadow and I don't know where I will have to go. Having a a maid might give me status among British officers but a man and a pistol are more useful in the back alleys of New York or among the backwoodsmen of Carolina. We would need money too. Not paper money nor golden guineas. We would need silver shillings and sixpences from here. There is little hard money to be found in America since the first settlement. Anybody flashing gold coins would be suspected of being a pirate. I'd ride astride too. There are few side-saddles to be found outside of Charleston and New Bern and I don't think there are more than ten carriages in all of New York."

"You seem to have all the details at your finger tips."

Elizabeth looked at the Earl strangely. "It was my home, sir."

"But children forget."

"No sir, they don't forget. It's just that their elders tell them to forget. So we don't talk about it. We cover it over like a cat covering its dung."

Jeffrey broke in. "You're home is here now, Elizabeth."

She turned on him sharply, her voice flat. "I have been here only a year. I haven't forgotten the smell of the Carolina woods. The girls in the school turned on me because I wouldn't deny my past. Well, I won't." They left it at that.

Two weeks later Jeffrey received orders from the Admiralty to present himself for the examination for lieutenant. He went by stage coach. Elizabeth didn't go with him. At the Admiralty there were fifteen candidates ranging in age from eighteen to thirty. Each of them was in his best uniform, the breeches white as snow and their swords at their sides and their journals under their arms. The first candidate came out after fifteen minutes, his shoulders slumping. He said nothing as he went out but there was no need to say anything. The second candidate fared no better. The third, a man with weathered cheeks that spoke of recent sea service, had better luck. "They asked me about navigation and sail handling," he told them.

Jeffrey was the fourth man. He knew one of the examiners. Captain Parry had served on the American station. His nickname among the lower deck was "Old Bloody Bones," because of the many and harsh floggings he ordered. The three captains examined Jeffrey's journals and certificates.

"All right, mister. You're two weeks out of Halifax for New York and its been thick fog all the way. How do you know where you are?"

"The deep sea lead, sir. The Newfoundland Banks are only forty to sixty fathoms deep. I'd also look for gannets and maybe even fish for cod. Either would tell me I'm too far over to the west." Jeffrey blessed Captain Nordstein for his answer.

"You've lost your foremast and your captain is disabled. What do you do next, mister?"

"Chop away any wreckage trailing overside. Then furl my squares and hoist staysails to make up for the loss of the jibs. Once I have her under control again I'd try hoisting the mizzen topsail to gain adequate steerage way. Then, if I have the men to spare I'd have them look after the injured." It went on like that for another ten minutes but it seemed an eternity to Jeffrey.

Finally Captain Parry told him: "You'll do, barely. We'll pass you and hope for the best. Send in the next man as you go."

Jeffrey was elated, almost drunk with joy as he returned to the Earl's town house. He sobered up quickly when the Earl sat him down and told him that he wanted to talk with him about Elizabeth.

"You want to keep up your relationship with her?"

"I love her and she loves me, sir."

"We are talking about a possible marriage, not a love affair. There is a difference."

"Yes, sir."

"Elizabeth is an orphan and an exile without two sixpences to rub together and no expectations. Her birth is well enough. Her grandfather was a freeholder in Devon. He served as a captain under Wolfe at Quebec in '57. When he returned home he found that his wife, his son and his brother had all died in an epidemic. He married your grandmother's sister and emigrated to Carolina where his family had holdings since the Restoration. If that were all, your father and I would have broken up the affair with Elizabeth at once."

Jeffrey said nothing but pinned his hopes on that "if that were all."

"Your father says that you are no farmer and never will be one. You're probably going to spend a good bit of your time at sea and that is no place to meet elegible females. Elizabeth knows land and can hold your estate together. She already has the tenants and villagers on her side. Also having no living relatives cuts two ways. There will have to be no big settlements for you to make and no one that can sponge off you." The Earl sipped at his brandy. "This mission will also be a test for Elizabeth. She probably can get her land back. After all her father was prominent on the American side. Carolina was where she grew up and where her parents are buried. She might wish to stay there. If that is so you will return with your information and we will go on from there. I would not blame her if she does so and neither will you."

Jeffrey was too shocked to answer. His uncle not only thought he could leave Elizabeth but that she could leave him. And his father agreed with his uncle. They were setting things up to make it easy for her. He grew angry. "So this is simply a ploy, a charade to separate us!"

"Don't be a fool. If we just wanted to separate you there are easier ways. You're an officer now. Think like one and not a love-struck school boy. We have to know whether we can hold all of Canada or have to withdraw to Nova Scotia. The King of France didn't send guns to the

Americans because he loves rebels and revolutionaries. The Comte de Rochambeau didn't risk hulls and men to enhance George Washington's reputation. France wants a pliant ally and the Americans want Canada. They even made special provision in their Articles of Confederation for Canada to join the thirteen colonies. We don't have enough troops and have to know whether we can rely on Canadian militia if we resettle the Loyalists in Canada. You and Elizabeth are especially suited to help us find out."

"So we are going to be spies."

"No, spies pretend to be something they are not. You are just young people who know how to ask questions quietly. You are not lying."

A week later Jeffrey returned to Oakdale Manor. Something had changed in the time he had spent in London. He was no longer the cocksure boy he had been. He was unsure, unsure of his new status as an officer and unsure of Elizabeth. He had a bag of silver with him, a bag that not only contained crowns, shillings and sixpences but Spanish pieces-of-eight. Those were good all over the world and could be cut into "bits" when smaller change was needed. He also had a pistol for Elizabeth. These things didn't make him feel any surer of himself.

Elizabeth was also unsure. She knew she was useful at Oakdale Manor and now she was going to be useful to the Earl. He was sending her back to America with Jeffrey. Did that mean he didn't think she belonged in England? What would it be like to see Carolina again. She hadn't forgotten Anna in New York either. Meanwhile she rode in the woods with Ketham. Among other things he attached fluttering targets to branches and expected her to hit them with her pistol. "If you have to use that pistol your target won't be standing still and you have only one shot in that thing," he told her when she complained about how difficult it was. Sometimes Jeffrey rode with them and tried his hand at that kind of target shooting as well. Both of them became good at it.

Ketham was useful around the house too. Her shoes and Jeffrey's boots gleamed. Their horses were always groomed and Ketham stood behind their chairs and served their meals. The kitchen was always supplied with fish and game whenever these were requested. He was like a shadow to Elizabeth, always present but never intrusive.

Waiting for orders was hard for both Jeffrey and Elizabeth. Finally, in mid-March they came. They were curt. "You are directed and required to take command of His Majesty's schooner *Phoebe* now lying in Portsmouth harbor." So he was going to get his old ship back but the orders revealed nothing else. Jeffrey presumed he would get further instructions when he got aboard. He wished the Admiralty would have been a little more forthcoming and told him something of the condition of the ship and whether she had a crew or if he would have to recruit one and what was her status in getting her ready for sea.

Elizabeth travelled with Jeffrey and Ketham to Portsmouth but she was not at all sure whether she would sail with him to America. She knew she wouldn't sign the Articles of Enlistment again. She was willing to help the Earl of Severn make peace but she was not going to swear herself again to King George.

The orders awaiting Jeffrey made things clearer and easier. "Orders given by us, Richard Howe, knight of the Honorable Order of the Bath, Admiral of the White, commanding the Channel Fleet to Lieutenant Jeffrey Kent. You are hereby directed and required to carry dispatches to the commanders of His Majesty's Forces at Charleston and New York in America and return. In view of the value of these dispatches you are authorized to avoid combat with units of any enemy you may encounter. You are also authorized to carry Lady d'Raython to any port you might reach." So much for Elizabeth's plan to travel as plain Elizabeth Troyes. British social usage trumped practicality.

Jeffrey was pleased with the changes that had been made on the old *Phoebe*. There was a new foremast up near the bow that changed her into a schooner. Yards for topsails were placed on both masts. That should give her more speed. Armament was unchanged except that the swivels had been removed. Mr. McLeod and Mr. Guerney as well as the two of the original sailors were still aboard. There was a new master's mate, a Mr. Isaacs, to replace Mr. Lawton and a new cook, a Mr. Brown. The quality of the new men and boys had yet to be proven.

"Are we ready for sea, Mr. McLeod?"

"No sir. Six pounder shot was just delivered to the dockyard. We can bring that aboard today and top off the water barrels. And the women are still aboard."

"Women?"

"Yes sir, it's customary to allow wives aboard in home waters since the men are not given shore leave. Some of them may be actually wives."

"Very well. Inform Mr. Guerney that all women must be ashore by dawn tomorrow. We load the cannon balls and the water today and sail with the morning tide. The wind should hold."

Mr. Guerney's daughter was aboard. He introduced her to Elizabeth. She was a slim girl, too slim by Elizabeth's medical eye and looked consumptive. Elizabeth went below with Mr. Guerney and handed him a golden guinea. This is for medecine and things like lemons for your daughter. You were were my friend when I first came aboard. I hope you will let me do this little thing."

"Thank you, miss. We've been worried about her and medecine is so expensive. Are you sailing as surgeon's assistant again?"

"No, I and my servant are passengers. Not part of the crew at all."

Jeffrey sent the *Phoebe* down to the latitude of the Azores and then picked up the trade winds flowing west. Three weeks later they were off the Bahamas heading northwards. What had been a reasonably pleasant voyage so far turned decidedly unpleasant.

After supper Elizabeth heard an anguished "No, no" in a boy's voice followed by a pained yell from right under her cabin. Grabbing her pistol and telling Ketham to follow she went down the ladder that went into the hold. There was a horn lantern burning there where no lantern should be. Mr. Isaacs was adjusting his pants which had blood flecks on them. The moans came from behind them, further into the hold.

"Put your hands on your head right now and stand still," she told him.

"You can't tell me what to do. You're just a passenger."

"This pistol says I can. There is something very wrong here. Ketham, check what that moaning is." Ketham slipped carefully behind her and came back with a ship's boy resting in his arms. The child's trousers had been pulled down and he seemed to be semi-concious. Elizabeth shook with fury but her pistol remained steady. "Very well, mister, just climb that ladder ahead of me and we will talk to the captain in the wardroom. Do it real careful like or this gun will go off. Ketham, you take the boy and come up after us. Lay the boy on the setee in the wardroom. Mr. Brown or I can tend to him there. Then go up on deck and tell Lieutenant Kent he is needed." Both men did as they had been told.

Jeffrey came down fast. "Just what is going on here?"

"That woman of yours has run mad, threatening me with her pistol."

"Not mad, Mr. Isaacs, but very angry. I am charging you with rape." Then she walked over to the boy who was coming to. Turning to Jeffrey she told him: "He seems to have a broken arm, a bruised chin and some injury to his buttocks. Perhaps I can tend to him before you hear testimony, sir."

"Very well. Mr. Isaacs, you can fix your pants. And Ketham, go on deck. You can tell Mr. McLeod his presence is needed. You can also tell him Mr. Guerney has the deck. Don't talk to anyone else, mind you, and come back here." Jeffrey understood the situation at once. Sex between men was not unknown when voyages lasted months and there were no women. After all he had been assaulted as a junior midshipman on the *Amazon*. As far as he was concerned sex was one thing and rape was quite another.

Elizabeth was attending to the boy when Mr. McLeod came in. She told Ketham to secure the lantern before it set the ship afire.

"Lady d'Raython, you have made a serious charge against a warrant officer. I have asked Mr. McLeod down as a second witness."

Elizabeth told what she had heard and seen. Jeffrey then turned to the master's mate. "Mr. Isaacs, you have been charged with sodomy, assault and rendering another member of the crew unfit for duty. What do you have to say for yourself?"

"Wasn't no rape. Dawkins here would have loved it. All the ship's boys do."

There was an incoherent protest from the setee. "You wish to make a statement, Dawkins?"

"He told me he wanted me for something in the hold. Then all of a sudden he grabbed a'hold of me and kissed me. I yelled and tried to fight him but he is strong, he is. He clouted me on the chin and that's all I know until I woke here."

Mr. Isaacs interrupted. "This is no proper court-martial, a boy officer, a crazy girl and a child."

It was Mr. McLeod who answered him. "Mr. Isaacs, this is a special court martial, captain's mast, as any captain can hold. As a warrant officer you can of course demand a general court martial with five flag captains who would almost certainly have you hung. In the meantime Captain Kent can order you clapped in irons until such a court martial can be assembled. That might take quite a time. From what I have heard you better accept what the lieutenant hands you."

"Mr. Isaacs, I find you guilty as charged. I sentence you to be disrated to ordinary seaman and to forfeit your pay. I further sentence you to ten lashes on your bare back under the powers granted me by the Articles of War. I also intend to discharge you at our next port of call as unfit to serve His Majesty in any capacity what so ever." Then he turned to Mr. McLeod. "Please tell Mr. Guerney to have the gratings rigged and the crew turned up to witness punishment."

Elizabeth didn't muster with the crew to witness punishment but she felt guilty none the less. She could have let the matter pass. It was Mr. Guerney who reassured her. "That Isaacs, he is no good. He did something similar on the *Amazon*. Nobody pressed charges but the Captain, he knows all about it. We'll all be glad when Isaacs is on the beach."

THE OLD HOME

Five days later they ran into Charleston harbor. "That's the *Amazon* at anchor by that sandy island," Mr. Guerney exclaimed, "or I'm a Dutchman. Commodore's pennant flying from the mainmast too."

"Mr. McLeod, stand by to fire a salute as we anchor." Make our number and hoist '*Phoebe* to commodore, have dispatches.' And have the boat ready to heave out." Jeffrey was glad he now knew whom to deliver the dispatches to first. The commanding officer of the army and the commandant of the city would come after. He also had the mail bag for the *Amazon's* officers and crew brought on deck. That alone would make him welcome. None the less he had butterflies in his stomach as he stood at attention before Captain Hartman. The captain broke the wax seal and skimmed over the contents.

"Do you know the contents of these dispatches, mister?"

"No, sir, but I know that the House of Commons has passed a resolution asking the king to make peace with America and that there is a new government. The Earl of Rockingham is prime minister and Lord Howe is the new First Lord of the Admiralty." Captain Hartman looked at the figure at attention in front of him. He knew Jeffrey's real age exactly. He also noted the crisp new uniform of his former midshipman. There was wealth and influence here. Influence with the new government too since Jeffrey not only been given a commission when he was under age but also had been given command of a ship. "Will you join me for a glass of claret now, lieutenant, and then come for dinner here. Colonel Stuart, the commander of His Majesty's forces here in the southern colonies, is coming too and you can hand over the letters to him."

A suggestion by a captain to a lieutenant was really a command, Jeffrey knew. In the casual conversation over the wine, Captain Hartman asked about Elizabeth. "Lady d'Raython is on the *Phoebe* now. My uncle thought she could look about getting her estates back now. The return of estates is to be part of the peace terms."

So it was Lady d'Raython and estates and passage on a warship, was it? the captain thought. Defenitly a young man of influence to be cultivated. "Bring her along by all means."

The dinner settled a number of things. Jeffrey was able to tell Captain Hartman about Mr. Isaacs. "I'll send Lawton back to you. There will be plenty of men available if the war is ending."

Colonel Stuart, who was seated to Elizabeth's right, was very interested in what she had to say. "I hope you will stay here for a few days, Lady Elizabeth. I have a meeting laid on with the American Brigadier, General Marion, in four days. Supposedly it's about an exchange of prisoners but if you tell him or his staff about this latest news from London it will be good. And if you tell him, it won't be an official communication either. Quite frankly, I will be glad of an end to this hopeless war. I lost nearly half of my men at that last battle at Eutaw Springs. Won the battle but had to retreat back here anyway. That's been the pattern of this whole southern campaign."

Three days later a sloop came into the harbor flying the signal for urgent dispatches. Half an hour later the *Amazon* hung out the signal for "all captains".

"Gentlemen," Captain Hartman told them all, "the *Albatross* just brought the news that the Admirals Rodney and Hood have smashed the French fleet. The *Ville de Paris* of 101 guns with Admiral de Grasse aboard and four other ships of the line have been captured and the rest of the fleet scattered. So we and the other garrisons no longer have to fear sharing the fate of Lord Cornwallis."

Jeffrey was exited when he came back from the flagship. The Royal Navy had once again proven its value and the peace would no longer be an acknowledgement of defeat. Elizabeth had entirely different feelings. With both the British army and French navy defeated there might be the kind of free America her father had dreamed of, an America where there might be room for fourteen year old Elizabeth. In any case that meeting of which she was going to be a part of was going to be important. If Washington and the American Congress hadn't heard the news yet there were going to be messengers galloping northwards.

So it was with very mixed feelings that she rode out with Colonel Stuart to meet the American emissaries. The smell of the woods and the landscape was familiar but to be introduced as Lady d'Raython was not. The American brigadier listened to her with obvious interest as he had when Col. Stuart told him of the French defeat. He didn't show what he thought. "Thank you very much for coming and telling me the news. Now the Colonel and I have things to discuss. I'm sure Captain Leslie will entertain you outside." He indicated a figure in a new brown uniform. Elizabeth had recognized Captain Leslie at once. It was her uncle whom she had last seen at the riverbank when he had put her on the *Phoebe* on the way to Boston. That was a year and a half ago.

"Elizabeth, Lady d'Raython! Captain Abner told us you had taken up with a Britisher."

"The title is from my grandmother and the Britisher is my cousin," she returned hotly.

"What do you want here? You can't have the house back. Anne and I are living there now."

"I thought a Mr. Smith bought it."

"Never was a Mr. Smith. Rev. Gillivray thought it wouldn't look fitting if I bid on my ward's property. So he made up Mr. Smith. When we heard you turned Tory the Committee of Safety condemned it and turned it over to me, all square and above board. You couldn't have run the farm, no way, in any case. And I gave you part of the money."

Elizabeth's heart sank. So sending her to Boston was simply a way her uncle, no, he was Captain Leslie, used to get his hands on her land. Carefully she explained about the peace treaty which was to return all property that had been seized.

Some of the other American officers had listened in.

"Ain't no way them back-stabbing Tories are going to come back here. They rode with 'Bloody Tarleton' when he killed my brother on the Waxhaxie. We'll give them 'Tarleton's Quarter' and see how they like it. Don't care what that passel of lawyers up at Philadelphia sign. We're free men and do what is right." There were sounds of agreement all around. "And we don't need no English miss here to tell us what that damned king in London agreed to."

Out of the corner of her eyes Elizabeth saw Ketham move behind her with his musket very much in evidence. He's right, she thought, these are my enemies. That is what seven years of war has done. I used to consider them my neighbors. "If you gentlemen will excuse me I will wait over by that tree until Colonel Stuart is done with his business." Her beautiful dream was drying up fast. There was no room here for a girl named Elizabeth. It had been such a short meeting, only a few sentences exchanged. Now she was no longer an American. She was Lady d'Raython living at Oakdale Manor in England. Her uncle was William, Earl of Severn and her cousin was Lieutenant Jeffrey Kent of the Royal Navy.

Ketham was covering her with his musket as she walked over to the large oak. He was right, she thought. They would shoot Lady d'Raython in the back without compunction. "Shouldn't have called them gentlemen, miss. They're just a bunch of vicious, land grabbing sharks. Should have spit in their faces the way they talked to you but I figured you didn't want to start a fight here." It was also Ketham who was able to penetrate her state of mental fog and shock. "I will show you the Marsh, Romney Marsh. You will love that too. And Oakdale and Ivychurch need you. You've done good there already."

Jeffrey didn't allow her any time to rest and recover. "Come on, we need to go out and walk around. Rumors about the peace are swirling around, wild rumors. They scare the Loyalists, soldiers and civilians alike. They think they will be abandoned by the British to the Rebels."

Elizabeth forced herself to think. She could understand panic. She had felt panic herself in New York when she heard Captain Brathwaithe condone the seizure of her trunk and again this morning when she was told so forcefully that she could never return to her birthplace. And panic is very contagious. They had started this panic with their news. Now they would have to try to stop it with facts. "If we go out for dinner at Ashley House people will see us and ask us questions. We can tell them about Canada." She didn't feel sure about anything herself and thrust her pistol into her sash. Panic will make people do strange things. Jeffrey was also armed and Ketham carried his musket. People did come over to them and asked about the peace treaty. They felt free to repeat what the Earl had told them and to talk about Canada. They only spoke to a few people but they hoped the message would spread.

It was Ketham who brought further scary news. "Old Sarah, the Black cook at the Ashley House, tried to buy my gun. I asked her what she wanted it for and she told me that the Blacks of this town weren't going to allow the British to hand them back to their former masters as property. They would hide in the swamps and form their own communities as the Maroons had done in Jamaica and shoot anyone who came after them."

Jeffrey told that to Captain Hartman when he went aboard *Amazon* to pick up dispatches for New York. "Don't worry, Mr. Kent," Captain

Hartman told him. "If we evacuate Charleston we will take everyone with us who wants to go; White, Black and even Red Indians. But your news has put the cat among the pigeons. There was no way of keeping the news secret. I'm not sure that Stuart can rally the militia if the Americans decide to assault the town. I'm putting all the ships on alert and I think it is better if you sail today."

The *Phoebe* slid out of the harbor two hours later. Elizabeth stood by the rail staring at the shore. Ketham stood behind her in case she tried to do something foolish. Jeffrey was busy handling the ship.

Much later Elizabeth was able to tell him what had happened at that meeting. She told it as if it had been something that had happened to someone else. She was able to communicate the bitter hatred in the voices of the Americans and the perfidity of the man she had called her uncle. In her mind she tried to think of him now as Captain Leslie of the North Carolina militia but she remembered that scene at the riverbank only two years ago. "We can tell the Earl that all who took the side of the Crown will be loyal, even those who tried to be neutral. They have no choice. They will have to be loyal to the King. For them, like for me, Carolina is no longer home."

For a while there was no answer from Jeffrey except to put his arm around her shoulders. Then he said slowly, "I'm glad Ketham was there with you since I couldn't be. You need someone behind you. He's right too. You will learn to love England."

Elizabeth had sworn to herself a year ago in New York never to cry again. She didn't cry now. The hurt was too deep. And now they were headed for New York. She would try to find Anna. And she would no longer be Elizabeth Troyes, a homeless orphan. She had relatives now, a place to live and someone who loved her.

The first person Jeffrey met when he went aboard Admiral Graves' flagship was Midshipman James Smythe. "By all that is holy, it is Lieutenant Kent turning up like the proverbial penny."

"I have dispatches for Admiral Graves. Good news."

"We can use good news. Since that fiasco at Hampton Roads all we have done here is to polish chairs with our bottoms." He took Jeffrey to the Admiral's cabin. "Lieutenant Kent, sir, of *HMS Phoebe*, schooner. He has dispatches from London and Charleston."

Jeffrey saluted. "Admirals Rodney and Hood have defeated the French fleet. Admiral Grasse and his flagship, the *Ville de Paris* as well as four other ships-of-the-line taken. Admiral Rodney calls it the Battle of the

Saints after the small islands off Haiti. Also there is a new government in London. Lord Rockingham is the new prime minister."

"So you have read the dispatches, have you?" The admiral's voice sounded peevish.

"No, sir. But the news was all over Charleston. My uncle, the Earl of Severn, told me about the new government. He also told me that Lord Keppel was offered the Admiralty but he is ill and it will probably be Viscount Richard Howe, sir."

"Very well. Wait outside until I have perused the official dispatches. I may have orders for you. Smythe, keep him company and don't spread this around."

"Aye, aye, sir." The two went on deck. Smythe looked at Jeffrey. "You're a full lieutenant now, not just 'acting?'"

"Yes, passed the examination, got a royal commission and the old *Phoebe* back but she is a schooner now."

"Congratulations sir." A grin went over the midshipman's face. "I always said having an earl for an uncle is useful. You'll make a good officer too, if I may say so, sir. By the way, what happened to that stray cousin you picked up here? She was a pretty girl, I remember."

"You mean Lady d'Raython? My uncle found that she has a French title through her grandmother. She is on the *Phoebe*, officially and recognized." Jeffrey enjoyed Smythe's look of surprise.

Before the midshipman could say anything the word was passed that they were both wanted in the cabin. "Mr. Smythe, make a copy of that dispatch and take it up to the city to that printer fellow of the *New York Gazette*. Let him make it a bulletin. It will buck up the city. The lieutenant will wait for you and you can use his boat. Saves us trouble." Then he turned to Jeffrey. "I presume you have dispatches for Sir Carleton too."

"Yes sir."

"Very well. Deliver those. Dock at the victualling yard and top off your supplies and water. You'll escort the convoy that is making up for England. *Greyhound 28*. Commander Keith will be glad of another escort. Too damn many privateers about and the war isn't officially over and won't be for months. There will be civilians and invalids on the transports but I won't clutter up warships with passengers. Damn nuisances if you have to clear for action." There was no indecisivity in Admiral Graves manner now.

"He is a good man but he won't take risks like attacking a superior fleet. He might have won at Yorktown but he probably would have lost and then he would get all the blame." Suddenly the midshipman realized that Jeffrey was his superior officer. "Begging your pardon, sir. I was presuming." They pulled to the *Phoebe* where Mr. Smythe made a proper bow to Elizabeth. She smiled, almost. She remembered that this well-turned-out midshipman had advised his fellow midshipman Jeffrey to dump her since she couldn't help his naval career. Well, now Jeffrey was his superior officer and she was Lady d'Raython of Oakdale Manor.

"We are docking in the city, Captain?" she asked formally to rub it in a bit. Then her voice became normal. "I want to see if I can find Anna while you deliver your dispatches." She turned to the midshipman. "We owe you a dinner. If the admiral can spare you I would love to have you join us for a meal. I remember that there were some good inns near the river the last time we were here."

"I would be honored, my lady."

The city seemed even more slovenly to Elizabeth than it had been a year ago. The makeshift huts were still there near the pier but she noted that now they were selling furnishings rather than buying them. She stopped for a moment, looking for a hackney cab, then remembering that there were no such coaches in this city. Ketham stayed right behind her. He had exchanged his musket for a sailor's pistol and cutlass. They walked over to the hospital and asked for Dr. Schmidt. An orderly took her up to the third floor and opened the door. There were the doctor and Anna.

With a cry both girls rushed forward and fell into each others arms, laughing and crying at the same time. "Since you know my wife," the doctor said, "I will leave you two to talk. He walked out, shooing Ketham ahead of him.

"Wife? You married him? He must be forty years older than you are."

"Yes, I married him. He is very kind to me and there is so little kindness left in the world. And you? Are you still with the Lieutenant?"

"Jeffrey? He's fine and he is back in command of the *Phoebe*. He brought me here." Then Elizabeth launched into the tale of the past year. She told how she had been accepted by Jeffrey's family, the discovery of her title, the attempt to turn her into a proper English miss. Anna was a good listener as she had always been. Then she cut to the basics.

"Are you going to marry the Lieutenant?" Elizabeth noted that Anna still didn't use Jeffrey's name.

"I hope so. I love him and he loves me, though I come after the Royal Navy of course. But it's complicated. He is an heir now and I have nothing and we are both minors. My guardian is the Earl of Severn, though sometimes I feel he is my jailer rather than my guardian. To every one else I am just slightly better than the alternatives offered. I will always be someone with a tag attached, never quite complete without that tag. Then she also told Anna what had happened to her in Carolina. "There my tag read 'Tory' and 'Traitor', very much in capital letters. In England my tag isn't even 'The American', it's just 'that colonial'. That's almost as bad as being a redhead or having only one arm."

They talked until Elizabeth realized that it was time for that dinner with Midshipman James Smythe, Esq. He had a tag too.

The dinner was good; oysters, fish but only one meat course. James Smythe explained. "Except for fish and a few vegetables from Long Island we are totally dependent on convoys from home. The wine and brandy comes from French prizes. We send out privateers too. We raid Westchester County and the Jerseys for wood, hay and whatever the Hessian Jagers and the Light Infantry can loot. The Loyalists and the Rebels have their own war with whaleboats on Long Island Sound raiding the shores. The navy is not involved." The he spoke of the general conditions in the city. "It was a bit of a *sauve qui peut,* every man for himself, after Cornwallis' surrender. Every one knew the war was lost. The panic subsided a bit after Carleton came and posted that proclamation about resettlement in Canada. Meantime he is sending away dependents, invalids and surplus officers." Suddenly he turned to Jeffrey. "Would you have room for a surplus midshipman, sir?"

Jeffrey considered. He liked James Smythe and he had helped them last year but Jeffrey didn't know whether he could trust him as a sea-going officer. Luckily he found an easy way out. "I only command a schooner. The establishment doesn't allow another officer. She isn't rated as a sloop-of-war. Even Elizabeth isn't rated as a member of the crew. She is a passenger. I'm sorry."

"Don't know what I will do after the war ends. Being an aide to an admiral isn't much of a recomendation for anything."

Elizabeth saw that this was true. James Smythe, aide to Admiral Graves, was an important person here. When the war ended he would be just another sixteen year old boy looking for something worthwhile to do.

The next morning Elizabeth went back to see Anna. They went to the docks where they had first met to talk. Elizabeth told Anna about what the Earl had asked her to find out. "The Doctor and I will stay right here in New York. So will a lot of other Hessians and even some of the British soldiers. The Americans don't hate us like they do the Tories. As a matter of fact they have sent agents into the camps offering free land and the free practice of crafts. That's more than most of the men could expect if they went back to Germany or England. Johannes says there will be lots of room for doctors to practice right here in New York. The Americans don't look down on doctors the way European nobles do."

"And the Loyalists?"

"No, the hatred is too strong, on both sides. And the Rebels have been expelling more people recently. They are being accused of not being patriotic enough, of not accepting the Continental paper currency at full value. Printers in New York have been turning out counterfeit 'Continental' dollars almost free for the asking. Those expulsions keep the pot boiling."

A more disturbing bit of information came from Sarah Tantequidgeon when the two girls visited her stand to buy sassafras leaves and other herbs. "The fighting will stop here?" the old woman asked.

"It's supposed to in a while," Elizabeth told her.

"The tribes won't stop fighting. The 'Burner of Towns', the man you call Washington, wants to drive all of us off our land, the land of our ancestors, and give it to his soldiers. Little Turtle is gathering the Delawares, Shawnees, Wyandots and all the other tribes together to fight. The Redcoats are giving them many guns."

Elizabeth knew what an Indian war meant. It meant cabins burned and settlers slaughtered. She had also heard in Carolina about the American veterans being promised land in Kentucky and the Ohio country. Canada was beginning to look better and better as a place for the Loyalists to settle.

Both Elizabeth and Jeffrey found that a good place to get information was the markets. So they went and made purchases while getting people to talk. Jeffrey bought two dozen bottles of old French brandy that had been taken out of a prize. Elizabeth bought a superbly crafted mahogany desk cheaply because the owner didn't think it would be useful in Canada. Another Loyalist sold her a fine Chinese porcelain tea set and a good spy glass.

Soon enough the *Phoebe* received orders to drop down to Staten Island where the convoy was assembling. Commander Keith was a hard bitten sailor with a no nonsense air. "Your ship is ready for sea, mister?"

"Yes sir, crew and supplies aboard. We're armed with six pounders but the *Phoebe* is not a particularly fast sailer.

"Been on convoy duty before?"

"No, sir."

"You'll learn now. We're escorting ten sail, half of them transports, half merchantmen. They'll scatter like sheep if you let them. You will not let them, understand. Have someone with a good glass watch *Greyhound*. I'll be in the rear. Don't be afraid to fire a gun to get those no-sailors to pay attention to signals. Here are your written orders, including those if we get separated. I expect them to be obeyed."

"Aye, aye, sir."

Convoy duty was hard, boring work, Jeffrey found. The flag signals were often ignored even if reenforced by the firing of a gun. Yet the risk of a single ship being snapped up by a privateer was a very real one. So the *Phoebe* and the *Greyhound* skittered back and forth, taking in sail, spreading sail. Luckily the weather stayed good and the whole convoy arrived safely in England.

While they were at sea Elizabeth tried to get the information they had obtained into some kind of order. As she did so her anger rose in the back of her throat like vomit. She had been driven back and forth like a stray pig. The Reverend Gillivray had simply assigned her to Captain Leslie of the militia, as he was now. That man had tried to ship her off to Boston while he seized her house and farm. Then she had to say 'aye, aye, sir,' to her cousin because she had become part of the crew of His Brittanic Majesty's ship *Phoebe*. And now she had to say 'yes, sir' to William, Earl of Severn, and she was only a guest at Oakdale Manor. Anna had done better. She had a husband and a plan for her future.

Elizabeth's only relief was to walk the deck with Ketham. He told her of his home on Romney Marsh and of the fairies and ghosts that were also supposed to live there. Those stories were like the ones her parents had told her when she was a little girl and took her mind off the present.

After a four week trip Jeffrey was able to deliver his dispatches to the Admiralty and was told to await further orders. As the captain of a ship he was not allowed to sleep anywhere except on board. Elizabeth supervised the unloading of their personal baggage and went to the Earl's town house. It was she who gave the debriefing. Not only did her uncle listen carefully but so did the other men present. There was a Mr. Sars from the War Office, a Mr. Sewell from the Colonial Office and Benjamin Thompson, the American who until the fall of Lord North's cabinet had been head of the Northern Department, a scientist considered the equal of Benjamin Franklin and the head of the British spy service. All the men paid close attention to her account of the violent ill feeling between the American rebels and the Loyalists. She also told them of New York and the recruitment of the Hessians and British enlisted men by the Americans. When she came to the story of Sarah Tantequidgeon she suddenly realized the the Earl and Sir Kent had an interest in the Hudson Bay Company which owned northern Canada. The men in this room might be the very ones who had ordered guns to be given to Little Turtle and his tribesmen. Elizabeth was glad she was only reporting and didn't have to take responsibility for any action.

THE NEW HOME

A week later Jeffrey received his orders. He was to take the *Phoebe* downstream to the Chatham navy yard to be laid up. Her crew would be discharged and her surplus supplies and guns sold. He was entitled to take the cabin furniture with him as the captain's personal property. Not only was the navy being shrunk now that the war was ending but old ships originally built as merchant ships were being replaced by a class of new, handy cutters suited for custom work as well as navy use.

"My naval career seems to be ending before it has well begun," Jeffrey complained. "The Admiralty waiting room and the coffee houses are full of officers seeking berths. People like Mr. Guerney are going home with no prospects. He has no experience in the merchant marine and he is over fifty. I took his address in Bristol but there is really nothing for him to do. There is no half-pay except for commissioned officers."

"Don't be silly," the Earl told him "The French will be back in the ring as soon as they can rebuild. And you are needed at Oakdale. I presume you don't want to be one of those absentee landlords who care neither for the land nor their people. Your father isn't getting any younger and he needs you. He doesn't even have a bailiff."

Elizabeth's heart sank. If Jeffrey was living permanently at Oakdale she couldn't. She would be classified as a mistress or one of those scheming women trying to entrap an heir. The Earl must have seen some of her thought on her face. "You haven't been fool enough to get yourself pregnant, have you?"

"No." Elizabeth's answer was short.

"Good, then we can regularise your status as well. Officially Jeffrey is now eighteen. If he gets engaged at nineteen nobody will consider it remarkable. Meantime you can help us with another problem. We have had to take over the Burnthurst's estates. They have been disgracefully mismanaged and the Burnthursts have sold off all of the good furniture. With good management we think the land can be made self-supporting. It's mostly woods with three tenant farms and a few fishermen's huts along the shore. We also don't want just anyone holding land next to Oakdale. So we made the land over to you. It'll look better too if the bride brings something more to the marriage than the clothes she stands up in." Before she even had a chance to think of how to thank him he was going into practical details. "Here are the maps and the leases for you to look at. I have rented the outbuildings out to Lt. Waller and the dragoons for the time being. That will keep order and a small cash reserve. I will add to that. Mrs. Goodwin has been taking care of the house and her husband is the gardener. Since the Burnthursts took the furniture with them I have sent some things from my country estate in Wiltshire. Your man can supervise the woods and you can draw on the village or perhaps that man Jeffrey has been talking about for additional help. That will be up to you."

It was only after dinner that Elizabeth was able to get her thoughts together. She had land again and a farm to manage. The Kents thought she was doing them a favor. Well, maybe she was. After all the Burnthurst estate would be part of Oakdale if she married Jeffrey. He had suggested that she might want to change the name of her place but she had other things to think of. She didn't have time to come up with a new name.

But it was Ketham who had the last word. He laughed with a sound like a seal barking when he heard about her being the new owner of Burnhurst Hall. "You won't have to do anything to support the estate, miss. That cove by the beach is considered the best place to land smuggled cargo in the whole district and the Burnthursts provided a place to store the cargo until it could be transported to London. You can live on that if you are not too greedy as the Burnthursts were."

The former owners had left the equipment of the kitchen and the furniture in the servants' rooms, probably thinking it wouldn't bring in much money at auction. The ground floor and the upstairs family rooms were echoingly empty when Mrs. Goodwin showed Sophia and Elizabeth around. The arrival of two wagon loads of furniture from the Earl helped. However Elizabeth felt that the most important thing he sent was a copy of the portrait of her mother. With that hanging above the parlor mantelpiece she felt the place was truly hers.

Ketham discovered the entrance to the wine cellar. It was full of smuggled French brandy and claret. There were also goods that must have been lifted from an East Indiaman. There was a chest of tea, some bales of damask. Sitting on a box of lace was a French doll, looking just as lonely as Elizabeth felt. She took it up to her bedroom which had been furnished with material from Oakdale Manor. She hung her Pennsylvania rifle above a massive side table of black oak, where other families would have probably placed the swords of their ancestors. The desk she had brought from America she defiantly placed in the otherwise empty library together with a map of the estate given her by the Earl. A trip to Tunbridge Wells allowed her to trade a number of seasoned oak logs from her estate for Staffordshire place settings and some silver cutlery. She felt good that the product of the Burnthurst woods were paying for something. She had no hesitation in using the materials that the smugglers had left in the wine cellar and couldn't recover because the dragoons occupied the outbuildings while the place was empty.

On the strength of all this she invited the Kents, including Jeffrey, to dinner. Her tenants had furnished hams and vegetables, Ketham added a hare and a brace of ducks and Sir Kent had praised the wine. She felt that she was really living at Burnthurst Hall now and preparing a home for Jeffrey as well. His parents would be occupying Oakdale Manor.

Elizabeth was riding through the woods with Ketham. Some of the trees here were big enough for use in shipbuilding. She thought of them as a cash crop. Perhaps it would be possible to put a slipway and a small ship building yard down in the cove. It was something to think about.

Ketham sniffed the air. "The wind is shifting southwesterly. It will be a dark night, no moon and the tide will be making after dark."

Elizabeth knew what he was talking about. A moonless night, the wind straight from France and the flood tide coming in after dark were almost ideal conditions for smugglers wishing to land goods. The Burnthursts had profited from the Trade, as it was called. Her tenants and probably some of the Oakdale villagers were probably gathering to add to their income by helping to unload and transport the contraband. Everyone profited from the lower prices of goods that had not paid taxes. Yet Jeffrey and his father were against smuggling. The dragoons were no longer living at Burnthurst Hall so the decision of what to do was hers.

"I think we will get some fresh air this evening after supper. We are likely to have visitors. They should be told of the change of ownership here and that they are no longer welcome."

"You sure you want to do this, miss? After all you were hurt the last time you went against the 'Gentlemen'. Master Jeffrey need never hear about this and the 'Gentlemen' do help some poor people. They're hard men too and don't like interference."

Thinking about it had convinced Elizabeth. The whole American Revolution had started because John Hancock and some of his friends had objected to paying a tax on tea. They had marked their disapproval by dumping the tea into Boston harbor and throwing stones through the windows of the custom collectors. The British government had retaliated by closing the port of Boston until the tea was paid for. The "Patriots" had reacted by arming their followers. Soon bullets were flying, houses were burning and people who didn't agree with them were being driven out of their homes. Now smugglers were going to land goods that hadn't paid custom duties. They were going to be landed in her cove. Yet she didn't want to hurt her neighbors by calling in the dragoons.

That evening she took out her gray cloak and took down the Pennsylvania rifle. It was accurate to half a mile. Ketham's musket didn't carry that far but he was a better shot. They took cover behind the bushes on some low dunes. Right enough. An hour after dark a black shape glided into the cove. The white bow wave was visible and soon two lanterns were lit, placed low near the water, bow and stern. Her rifle cracked and the stern lantern went out amid a tickle of glass. Ketham's musket roared and the bow lantern dropped into the bay. There were some loud curses and the shape of the ship changed to shouted orders. Two days later Mr. Morley told her that the Revenue Cutter *Curlew* had intercepted the *Belle Marie* out of Guernsey but had to let her go since she was obviously not headed for the English coast. That was satisfactory to Elizabeth. The message had been sent and received and nobody had gotten hurt.

Other things were satisfactory too. The harvest had been good but she would have to talk to her tenants about mulching and winter crops. Most important her engagement would be announced in November and the marriage to Jeffrey would take place in spring.